THE MATSYA CURSE

Shweta Taneja is a bestselling author based in Bangalore. She's been a Charles Wallace India Writing Fellow, a roadie for an amateur band, a volunteer for a tree festival, and a cashier at a play. Her ambition is to writes stories that challenge preconceived notions and prejudices. To attain it, she regularly drinks Makaibari tea, hogs on popular occult books and shows, and asks all sorts of unseemly questions to ghosts, half-dead plants and recently, drongos.

The Matsya Curse is the second of the Anantya Tantrist mysteries. The first one, *Cult of Chaos* (2014), has found a cult following owing to its name. Her other novels include *How to Steal a Ghost @Manipal* (2016), and *The Ghost Hunters of Kurseong* (2013). She has also written two graphic novels: *The Skull Rosary* (2013) which was shortlisted for Best Writer Award at Comic Con India and *Krishna: Defender of Dharma* (2012) which is part of CBSE's must-read list for a reason she can't fathom.

If you'd like to hear her ramble, become a patron or tell her you've just met a ghost, visit her website www.shwetawrites.com or find her on most social networks with her handle @shwetawrites

Praise for *Cult of Chaos*

'[*Cult of Chaos*] is racy, rousing, rambunctious and rakshas-ful. Read immediately.'

– Samit Basu

'An author with an impressive imagination and terrific storytelling skills.'

– Ashwin Sanghi

'[*Cult of Chaos*] is a chick-lit take on the horrors of the megacity.'

– Zac O'Yeah

'Anantya is one feisty character.'

– *Femina*

'*Cult of Chaos* is a crime-busting story unlike any other.'

– *Asian Age*

'The terrible, scary and horrific side of society is explored ...'

– *Economic Times*

'Supernatural thrills, horror tropes and enigmatic women in old havelis.'

– *Mint*

'Taneja sure knows how to get the readers hooked and hang in anticipation.'

– *Mail Today*

'Anantya Tantrist is the new gumshoe in town.'

– *The Hindu*

'Her protagonist is so well developed that she can have Twitter discussions with her.'

– *The New Indian Express*

'... the country's first tantrik detective novel, which also talks about the key issue of women's safety.'

– *Business Standard*

'... engages and piques your interest at every level ...'

– *Deccan Chronicle*

'Edgy thriller.'

– *Mid-Day*

THE MATSYA CURSE

An Anantya Tantrist Mystery

SHWETA TANEJA

HarperCollins *Publishers* India

First published in India in 2017 by
HarperCollins *Publishers* India

Building 10, Tower A, 4th Floor, DLF Cyber City, Phase II,
Gurugram Haryana – 122002, India
www.harpercollins.co.in

P-ISBN: 978-93-5264-502-2
E-ISBN: 978-93-5264-503-9

2 4 6 8 10 9 7 5 3 1

Typeset in 10.5/13 Adobe Caslon Pro
by Saanvi Graphics Noida

Printed and bound at
MicroPrints India, New Delhi

To
Kali who is an ocean of creativity and
Ashwani who is an ocean of patience

Prologue

Banaras, New Moon Night

USUALLY SHUSH yearned for the screams that began the Seed of the Moon ritual. And it was the perfect night for it. The sky was ravenous – thirsty for the squeals of the sacrifices. The sacrificial fire pit, a frenzy of reds and yellows, danced hungry, eager to devour the holy offerings: the five young women who sat across from it. Even the women themselves were perfect, their eyes sparkling in the flames, soft sighs occasionally escaping them to melt into the warm breeze.

Punctuating their moans and the crackling of the fire, was the low chanting of the Bhairava's mantras. Shush eyed his apprentice, feeling a swell of pride. The apprentice stood across from him as part of the ritual circle, his face in the shadows of his cowl, his voice powerful and confident. Someday, thought Shush, he will become as great as Matsyendranath, if not greater. Even now, though he was a mere mortal, his power was palpable. He was so proud of what his apprentice had achieved. The bold and confident way he had walked the path of equality. It was perfect.

Or would be if it hadn't been for *him*. Char, his guru, his enemy, his other. Why did he have to come yesterday to warn him? Couldn't he have stayed away for a few more nights and let him finish his business in peace? Shush knew he didn't agree with his ways, *their* ways, but he had accepted that there was nothing he could do about it. There was nothing anyone could do to stop their plans. Then why did he have to come and try to warn him about this and leave without saying goodbye to the Bhairava? Didn't he realize that the Bhairava's work was their only chance at achieving real equality? In a world where some died without reason and others lived on forever, without reason, immortality for all was the only equalizer.

Their lives had been spent searching for that one thing, that one solution that could give the human race eternal life. And now that they'd found a way around the curse of death, of mortality, he was running with his tail between his legs. Too scared to use the power for the greater good. Yes. That's what he was. *Scared*. Char was nothing but a coward. Shush dug his fingernails into his arm. His vision clouded over and for a moment, the fire in front of his eyes became a thing of darkness rising up to a blacker sky.

Bhairava seemed to be aware of Char's absence. Nothing escaped his notice. Char didn't realize that even the defiance he showed the Bhairava was because a long time ago, Bhairava had been their pupil. It was Bhairava's clan that had brought them back to life from the deathless existence that they managed to get in, the black tantrism-bought space where they had been neither dead nor fully alive, waiting for centuries. And he could very well take it away. Only his generosity kept both him and Char alive. But instead of celebrating the fact that their quest of immortality was within their grasp, Char was getting palpitations about the ethics of it all. Stupid, stupid coward Char.

'Come. It's time,' said the Bhairava, his soft voice soothing Shush. The Bhairava flicked his staff and the praniks got up, surrounding the yantra. Shush was proud of his pupil and the things he'd been able to achieve, the fearless way in which he'd taken the Bhairavana clan forward. He was the true tantrik. The tantrik who wouldn't stop at anything in his exploration of the tantrik science.

The Bhairava stood across from the praniks, his legs apart, his hands spread, his face grim. His bare head moving side to side and his shikha – the long, thin ponytail – swinging, rattling the rudraksh beads woven into it.

'Oh Agni, raging goddess of fire,
drink the radiant wine of true blood,
gorge on the charred flesh and bone,
devour it all with the cemetery wood,
for all that touches your womb,
the leftovers and the crumbs,
become pure and immortal as thou art.'

The fire danced invigorated, reflecting in the eyes of the five women as they were pushed into the circle, stepping over the line carved into the ground sweetened with fresh blood. Under the Vashita spell, they kept walking without hesitation straight into the flames. Some cringed, but none of them stopped. The first one walked on the burning corpse wood, stacked in the form of steps to lead them to the top of the pyre. She walked on, followed by the others, the charred smell of burning flesh spreading into the sky. One by one they climbed, and perched quietly, their eyes still blank as Agni drank their flesh and bones. The Bhairava's power was palpable now, narrowing Shush's world to the sacrifice in front of him. With a flick of the Bhairava's wrist, the flames roared.

That was when the screams began. They rose up in unison, dancing together in the night, weaving around each other, spreading a chorus of yells and cries of pain and fear. Until the fire goddess gobbled them whole.

'Devour them! Devour them!' he screamed, in unison with the others, tears running down his face, a thrill rising up his spine. He shook in the throes of passion. The fire goddess crackled and whipped and lashed over skin, blood and bone. 'Blood for blood, life for life. Life for immortality! Devour them! Devour them! O Agni! Goddess of fire!'

As the screams died, the stench took over. It was not the smell of meat, or bones, but of ash. The Bhairava stood still, only his eyes were visible in the dark, reflecting the fire. Agni had accepted his offerings and the remains smouldered – the corpse wood, the five female bodies, their skin, their hair, their bones, all unified in black charred remains. Bhairava entered the tantra, his feet sinking in the pile of ash and crouched down, whispering to the remains, calling out to the moon that hid within it.

The smouldering pile of ash began to stir like a dark storm around his feet. When it settled, he reached for it and raised it high in his hand, giving a triumphant bark. A tiny porous ball, white and shining, both hard like a diamond and soft like soap bubbles. Fountain of immortality. Elixir of life. Raaka. The seed of the moon.

Shush knew it was time. He hurried to the pen, followed by the praniks. Inside the pen, the nishadas cowered. They were young, the black scales of their bodies not yet fully formed, their cat-like eyes a deep mustard with fear, shining sapphires in the dark. Their black breasts heaved and their blue-tinged lips trembled.

'Come!' he tried to say softly, but his voice came out sharp, breathless with his excitement. Agni, the fire goddess, roused the life in him, making him *feel*. He asked his praniks to take hold of the nishadas and bring them to the yantra.

Bhairava filled the Raaka in a syringe. It shone inside, like a droplet made of light. As if on cue, the praniks took the nishada girls into the circle. They lay there, naked, on the remains of the corpse wood and the freshly sacrificed women, their legs spread. The Bhairava bent over one of them, his hand snaking up between her thighs to inject the seed of the moon into her womb. Her nether lips turned blue, then glowed. He repeated this with the others and when it was done, the ten nishadas screamed in unison as the power of the seed began to spread, eating, rebuilding. Their screams died within seconds and then they were still. Raaka had been seeded.

'Shush,' said Bhairava. 'The wombs are yours now. Leave for Delhi at dawn.'

Shush nodded, excited and proud. The thought of his guru, Char, swept away in the dark night, like ash.

1

Gloop.

SOMETHING SLIMY dripped onto my ear. My hand reached out, trying to wipe it off, instead touching a leathery thing. Eyes now open, I turned around and saw it, a large mouth, wrinkly and green with yellowed, broken teeth. A blue-black tongue hung out the side. Behind it were bulging yellow eyes. A vinaat: a supernatural being from the Sundarbans whose skin had magical properties.

'Hello, beeautifool,' the dripping mouth crooned. A blast of stale air and spit.

'Who—' I looked down to see my naked glorious self, trying to ignore the leathery thing beside me. My bed was a mess and a grey light filtered into the courtyard of my haveli, down through the broken ceiling.

Then it all came rushing back to me: noon; Bedardi; challenge. Heavy-duty shots of the vile Rajasthani boola. Challenged while drunk. The rest was a blur, except for the memory of cuddling with something leathery. For a second, we both eyed each other.

'Don't you remember me?' the leather bag said, his droopy lips flapping some more spit. 'We were grooving together just a few hours ago. You snore, you know? I could barely sleep.'

'Swat off,' I mumbled, reaching for my satchel, grabbing a beedi and lighting it. I took a puff, making a face. My teacher, Dhuma, had made special beedis for me, to make sure I smoked up gloogoo, a gooey vat of vileness that was the only thing protecting my mind from the charming invasion of Shamshana Kalika. A few months ago, I had pissed off the charnel ground goddess by calling her on this plane and saving my city. To make sure I had my mind protected from her vast consciousness, I had to have gloogoo. And my dear teacher, always up for a laugh, had filled my beedis with it. Hundreds of beedis later, I still wasn't used to the gummy vileness. Ugh.

'I am hoongry,' cried the beast. 'What're you going to feed me?'

'Do I look like your fucking mother?'

'Not really. She's not a tantrik and she doesn't like cities,' said the creature, wrinkling its broad forehead. He was up, wriggling into a pair of jeans. 'Silly dress this is,' he said, 'like getting into a pipe.'

'I take it you're new to the city?' I said, munching on a piece of biscuit.

The vinaat's green skin glistened, like a rain-drenched sop. His eyes lit up like bulbs. At least come morning I could understand how I could have picked this one under the influence of what can only be termed as the vilest semi-liquid with alcohol-like properties. I burped, tasting the biting edge of the Rajasthani boola and cringed, promising myself never to do it again as I took another drag, puffing the smoke out in a spiral pattern the way I'd just learnt to do.

'But last night you said, you … you have a nice place here. I am pretty small and—'

'I don't know what I said to you a few hours ago, sunshine,' I said, stretching my left hand into my satchel, 'but the honeymoon is over. There's a whole city out there teeming with opportunities. I bet you'll find grub and a place to stay. And here' – I slapped a little vial on his rough palm – 'you'll need this while you figure the place out.'

He looked at the maya potion in his hand and nodded. 'Would I need this all the time?'

'Ooh yeah. Can't destroy the innocent humans' conviction that they're the only intelligent beings in the universe.'

'Really? They are?'

'Wear your clothes, will you. And you know what kind of a human you are?'

'Yes, yes! Just got a two-legged's skin-piece from the immigration department with my papers. You want to see?'

'Nope. Keep the skin with you, always. In case you forget what you look like as a human. Now get out.' I got up, wriggling into a ganji and an oversized sweater and flopping onto the sofa. The vinaat started to gather his things. From the corner of my eye, I looked at his buns, appreciative. Not a bad choice given the circumstances.

Zaazee was coiled up in his usual spot on the couch, staring at the television. A hunchback stood on a podium, his left side paralysed, talking to a cheering audience.

'Manu Manava gots hiss own Ministry? Hospice in Qutab Institutional Areas. CATs going mads?' he asked. I scoffed.

'When weren't they? The stupid Central Association of Tantriks have named it Ministry of Miracles and Health. And the Indian government thinks it a perfect opportunity for a photo op.' I rolled my eyes, squatting myself in front of the telly. 'Like, *really*?'

'And Swami Narahara allowings it?'

'Rishi, now. Remember how he got his promotion for taking credit for saving Delhi when it was being attacked by the god of Chaos?' I snorted. 'My nasty half-brother does what Daddy dear instructs him. I bet he got a favour in exchange for not protesting about this. Manu Manava's not a Kaula, so let's hope he can do something more than that rattlesnake. I wouldn't hold my breath though.' I swallowed the dour-smelling ayurvedic lotion Dhuma had prepared for me, swirling it in my mouth and spitting. On the telly, Manu Manava touched a man sitting in a wheelchair. He stood up and started to walk in front of the audience, who went nuts clapping and chanting his name. *Miracle baba! Miracle baba!*

'Sss does seem more popular and better showmans than Narahara,' he whispered, uncurling and slithering onto my lap. I smoothed my hand over his glossy scales. 'Your male friends called.'

'Shukra?'

'Nos. The CBI fellowsss.'

'Madhu? *When*?' I cried, jumping up and swatting him so fast he rolled off the couch.

'Why didn't you wake me?' I screeched, reaching for my phone, which stood balanced precariously on the broken table beside the sofa. Three missed calls. *Shakti's shit.*

'Five minutes agos. You seemed tea cozies, sleepings with leathersss.'

'You rotten wriggler,' I said punching in Madhu's number. 'Yeah, Anantya here. No, I was busy. Umm, a case. Yeah. Uhun. Uhun. *Shakti's shit.* I'll be there.'

'New case, eh?'

'Let's hope so,' I answered running towards my bed, hoping for an end to the winter rut with a new case. I scrambled into underwear, a tank and a salwar, exchanged the oversized sweater for a military jacket and satchel. Septifocals on my head, check. Scabbard around the waist with boneblade, check. Treta rings and yugma locket with its twin snakehead vials, check.

I was ready.

'Do shut its up on the ways,' said Zaazee his eyes glued to the telly.

'Wha—' I started, turning just in time to see the mayan, who had become a middle aged human post his maya potion swig, climbing up the rickety stairs in the corner. 'No! Not there!' I cried, but it was too late.

Creak, creak.

'Haye! Haye! Sharam hain hi nahin! Sabak sikhatain hain tumhe hum.'

The mayan tumbled back, sneaking a look at me as the furious ghostly Nawab Sahib stormed at him like a preta. '*Bandar ka ghulam! Gaddhe ki aulad!*'

'Aiiiya! You come, you come. My mother taught me martical farts!' screamed the vinaat, slapping his wrists and backslapping his foot into the airy groin of Nawab. Nawab, more surprised than affronted stopped, staring at the beast before him.

'It's martial arts.' I walked up to him. 'What's your name again?'

'Baal,' he said, his chest puffing up.

'Baal, that's a ghost. You can't hit it with your hands.'

He looked at Nawab Sahib, who radiated righteous anger.

'I can't?' He stopped, his hands limp, his face bunching up and his tongue coming out, licking his face. 'What about legs?'

I shook my head. He had so much to learn.

Chancing an opportunity, the Nawab opened his mouth. '*Jallad ki aulad! Khansee ki paidaish!*'

'Not now, Nawab. He's leaving.' I steered Baal away from him, towards the exit behind, firmly shutting the door.

'*Aise zaleel janvaron ko hamare beech main bhej rahi ho!*' cried the Nawab from behind as I firmly shut the door.

The Meridian hotel stood like a giant metallic sentry, rising out of the January smog. I turned at a roundabout to get there, almost crashing Chhotu, my fifteen-year-old mobike, into an oncoming ambassador, which no doubt had a lunatic behind the wheel. Accelerating, I flew my bike into the hotel's landscaped grounds, announcing myself with a belch and speeding up to avoid the security guy who ran after me, hollering. I screamed back that I was with the police and that I was going to the suite. He stopped chasing.

The glitzy lobby grew still, the staff looking at me like a herd of stunned deer, as I ran towards the elevator, getting in and pressing thirteen. The floor corridor was filled with a gathering of policemen, onlookers and hotel staff. All a little too silent.

When the scream came, my ears barely heard it. It was at the edge of human hearing. I saw it in the reaction of others, humans like me and felt it tear my gut. Everyone grew stiff, edgy, looking at each other. It was not the kind of scream that came from a creature about to die. Not even the one that made your blood boil. It was a thin whisper of a screech. I dropped my septifocals and whispered the Drishti mantra. The world changed colour, washing up in shades of the rainbow. My pace slowed down until I was inching forward. Nothing supernatural here. Everyone was human, on all levels.

'What took you this long!' cried Madhu Tripathi, his barrel chest moving towards me like a bulldozer. 'It's pretty bad … and *weird*.' He wiped his bald forehead, beckoning.

Madhu headed the Special Crimes Division at the Central Bureau of Investigation. It was on his desk that all paranormal and unexplained cases landed. He called me for consultation on things that were a bit beyond him. 'Weird' was part of his everyday job, though he had never used the word before. It would take something super weird to make him sweat.

I simply nodded, following him as we squeezed our way between the two policemen at the suite's doorway.

'Is this the healer?' asked a sharp voice. It belonged to a primly dressed, broad-shouldered man in his twenties. He had a bouffant-like hairstyle, sharpened by his jutting chin. All together, it made him stand like a rather puffy squirrel. 'I hope you've got her checked from Central Association of Tantriks. I don't want any charlatans working their voodoo on this case. First that ape, now this. Do you work with any normal hu—'

'This is Anantya Tantrist,' said Madhu, cutting off his steam, 'she's helped me on a lot of my cases, as has Shukracharya, who is just rather big for his age. And Anantya, this is my colleague Wizam. Can we go now and try and save that woman?'

'Sure, as soon as she learns whose jurisdiction this is. Miss Anantya, I must pronounce that I'm the one handling this case and will hold you responsible for what happens to that thing … that person in there.'

'Good,' I said smiling sweetly, 'don't piss me off before I start. Its bad juju for my healing talents.'

Before he could react, I walked past him, straight to the room from where the scream came.

'Has she signed the no-disclosure form?' Wizam asked behind me. 'It's a very sensitive case and we don't want anyone to leak information to the press in hope of extra mileage. As you know, it's a high-profile prostitution case which involves a few well-known names. Delhi's elite. Very, very important, you understand? It was all thanks to my lead that we even found out about this suite.'

'I'll tell her the rest, Wizam. You know how it goes from here. Non-human crimes are my desk.'

'But, a human was involved too! I'm already interrogating him. It's still my case!'

'You have issues, you take it up with the Nandan. *Later*,' growled Madhu.

The squirrel quietened, continuing to follow us as Madhu pointed me to a corridor, hurrying after me.

'He busted this place about an hour ago,' Madhu said, 'as part of a lead of a prostitution case he's handling, which as you heard, involves quite a few influential people. The bust did give him three young women and an old man in his seventies, who we've since identified as Brij Srivastav, a textile wholesale businessman. There was no one else around. Mr Srivastav was found in this room, along with … you'll see … naked and delirious, sitting in a corner. All he kept saying again and again: "I will die … I don't … will die if I don't have sex." Since then, we've found that the man was diagnosed with blood cancer, fifth stage. Wizam sent him off to the hospital, before I could even question him. As I said, he was found in the bed, naked, along with *this* …'

'… hasn't stopped …'

The four-poster bed, covered with tuille curtains hid the scream, but you could feel it in your bones. In the middle of it lay a woman, a nishada – a tribal sup from Madhya Pradesh – writhing like a headless snake, her body covered in black scales gleaming in the patch of bright light from the tall window on one side. Two policemen stood on that side, holding her down as she flapped like a fish out of water. On the other side, crouched Shukra, who even sitting, filled up the whole room with his sheer size. Shukra was a forensics expert and one of my close friends who had, in a recent case, beefed up because of a danava and become twice his size.

'We've tried everything, Anantya!' cried Shukra as soon as he saw me, pushing up the tiny spectacles on his broad face. '*Everything*. But she keeps bleeding.'

'Lizard's shit,' I whispered, bending close to her, not forcing her. I gently pressed my hand on her clammy hair. A spasm rocked her body, her black scales flapping so that light reflected on them, shimmering with red as if she was on fire.

Her dress was up. Black, congealed blood flowed out of her vagina, spreading out on the soft white bed. Her blood was black and thick, like tar, spreading out from her. Her stomach heaved and sank back, quick successions and then less and slow. I gulped, supressing a shudder. Had she been pregnant? Could she?

'Hold her head,' I instructed. Shukra gently put his massive hands on each side. I chose one of the vials from the two intertwined vials in my snake-shaped yugma locket and carefully put a drop of rakpiss, rakshasa urine, into her mouth, a magic healer that worked on most wounds. She swallowed, head thrusting back violently as her lips dribbled blue foam. The moan came back again, a long, gut-wrenching one. The girl writhed in her last throes of life and screamed, filling the room with terror. By the shine of her scales she must have been barely into her teens. 'So young.'

'Is it going to explode?' squeaked Wizam.

'Hold her legs, Shuk,' I said, glaring at Wizam. Shukra delicately touched her trembling legs. She wore what was a dress in mustard, but now was just tatters of cloth. It barely covered her breasts and rode up her legs. Bending down between her legs, I put a drop of rakpiss, hoping it would stop the blood's flow.

Jaadugar tu jaadugar …

I ignored my phone which was soon drowned out as she screamed, shuddering as if the ring was vibrating in her head. I shot Shukra a helpless look and an icy one at Wizam, who stared at me furiously

… tu hai badaa dilbar …

'Hurts …' she whispered, starting to moan, heaving. The blood didn't stop. It kept gushing out, soaking the bed, dripping from the side. 'Hurts … hurts … the moon hurts …'

I slashed my wrist, focused on the Ajna chakra of my body and held it close to the bleeding, muttering the Ayur mantra, the only healing mantra I knew.

'Jhod jaad samaya nikaal'

Her black blood drank my red and made everything dark. The pouring slowed then. Not enough though. Her lips were almost purple-black and now instead of screaming she just whimpered, her body still shuddering.

'Blind mother's—' I muttered to myself, grabbing a glass of water that Wizam was drinking from, I splashed it against the source of her bleeding and muttered the Shayaya mantra.

'Ghani bhavati!'

'The moon … it's eating me,' whispered the girl. Instead of freezing, the black blood slowed, beginning to bubble, like it had reached its boiling point. 'Sisters …' Her back arched and her legs swung up, as if pulled by an invisible thread. Her face, just a few inches away from me, she grabbed my shoulders, a weak grasp as she looked into my eyes. She stared into me, her catlike eyes still full of pain. She whispered, 'Help us, yog— '

She cringed and fell back, and suddenly she was still. Her face began to soften and soften like butter and as suddenly as that, it melted away.

'Stop!' I said, uselessly, helplessly, seeing her body loosen its hardness and drip away, liquidating. Desperate, I screamed the Jodh mantra to try and fix it, cutting my finger too deep in the process.

'Jhod jaad samaya nikaal'

The seconds passed slowly as we witnessed her scaly body turn into a tar puddle.

'Bali's swearing soul!' exclaimed Madhu.

'Bald bull's ass,' I muttered. My hands were completely gloved in the black, sticky substance. 'What in Patala's name happened to her?'

'How should I know? You're the tantrik!' exclaimed Shukra. It was silly to have asked Shukra that, considering that a few months ago, he thought there were no such things as sups. That magic, tantrism was just hogwash. But what could one do? A girl had just melted in front of me like ice-cream in June.

'What happened here!' screamed Wizam. 'I warned you, Madhu, that if you—'

'Was the old man with cancer having sex with this girl?' I asked, butting in.

'Yes, we suspect that,' answered Madhu. 'What kind of—'

'She's a nishada, a tribal creature from the jungles of Madhya Pradesh. She was in her teens, fucking under-aged. Slap the POSCO. That's after I speak to the creep and squeeze the truth out of him.'

'That's none of your concern, miss,' answered Wizam. 'Mr Srivastav will be questioned by our team. You had to save this creature for our questioning, but unfortunately, you couldn't manage that, so I guess he is our only lead now.' He stuck out his chin. Madhu placed a warning hand over my arm as I took a step in his direction.

'What about the other girls you found? The humans?' I asked through clenched teeth.

'They don't know anything about this creature,' said Wizam. 'They were trafficked to Delhi from different villages and were locked up in a room together. All they know is the name of their hometowns. We're looking into it.'

'Wizam, why don't you head to the hospital and question Mr Srivastav. There's no human left for you here,' said Madhu. Wizam's lips moved silently, before he nodded and left with his entourage.

'Madhu, hate as I do, we should go to the RC and register a formal complaint,' I began.

'RC?'

'Non-Tantrik Rights Commission. Remember I told you the Central Association of Tantriks had put a commission up to protect the rights of non-tantriks like humans and mayans? They sit at the Non-Tantrik Department and take on cases of abuse of mayans and humans by tantriks. Since nishadas are endangered mayans and this is a crime, we need to report it to them. The person who runs it is a friend of mine, a mayan by the name of Talab. He and his team are far more efficient when it comes to solving crime than the CATs, and might be able to help us understand how this girl ended up in this hotel room.'

'Madhu,' said Shukra, 'I will examine the remains and let you know what I find.'

Madhu nodded and Shukra used his index finger, carefully scooping up each side of the once-white bedsheet to fold it. Something red gleamed in it.

'Hold the linga, what's that?' I said, jumping up on the blackened cushion.

'Anantya! Don't touch it!' hollered Shukra, but I didn't wait. I pushed my hand into the fast-thickening goo and took out a thin, pencil like thing, black in colour, hanging on a thin metallic chain. It was an enamelled piece of beautifully carved black wood.

'Is that a paint brush?' Madhu said, frowning.

'Looks like it. Worn like a necklace?' I said aloud, looking at its metallic chain. 'Let me check it for curses. I wouldn't want anyone else to go through whatever that nishada did, if it's communicable,' I said, placing the brush into my satchel. My phone rang again. I picked it up, chewing on a strand of my hair and distractedly murmured a hello.

'Oh, Shukra,' said Madhu behind me, 'CBI is currently consulting a forensics scientist who is visiting the Jawaharlal Nehru University from the USA. He's quite renowned. Published a few papers on a new blood type he discovered—'

'Dr Bodhgaya? Oh! He's here, isn't he?'

'Where were you?' whispered a panicked voice from the other end. I cocked the phone off my ear and checked the number on my T9 phone. 'Ashwa?'

'You have to go there, now,' he said, breathing hard. 'I … I have made a … just *go*.'

'Where? I—'

'It's a mess. Just … Just go to Guru B's place. He … save him will you?'

'But what has … hello? *Hello?*' I stared at the phone, wanting to bang it on Ashwa's head.

'… Will introduce you over email,' Madhu was saying. 'He's at JNU for a few months staying at the Biotech department.'

Fixing my date with Madhu, I ran to my mobike, wondering what it was that Ashwa had done to sound so unlike himself.

2

CHHOTU, MY fifteen-year-old mobike, wove a lazy S along the uphill road, trying to clear the way by throwing a tired purple beam onto a few feet ahead of us. The smog smothered everything else.

I scrambled up the ten-foot wall and dropped in to the compound. *This better be interesting enough for me to have come all the way here.* If I found Guru B, sitting in his lounge chair, hoping I'd brought him peacock meat, I would be very, very angry. I dusted my culottes and cupped my scraped knee.

Ashwa and I were old drinking buddies at Bedardi Bar. Though I spent many evenings with him there, I didn't know much about him. We liked our silent contemplations. He always wore a black cloak over his head, even indoors, his eyes bright through its gaping hole in the dingy bar and his voice husky and calm.

Earlier in the hour, he'd sounded very unlike himself – almost troubled. He was the one who had introduced me to Guru B, an old tantrik with a soft corner for documentation.

Guru B ran an underground library of tantrik archives. Old books, documents, speeches trapped in stones, and other things of tantrism and arts that would have been dust if he hadn't been around caring for and preserving them. I respected him, respected the vast knowledge he had collected. Guru B had been collecting books, artefacts, and histories for three hundred years if not more. I didn't know much else about him either, except that he was knowledgeable and looked about seventy-five (way younger that he would be).

The fog thickened around me as I walked ahead, clutching my boneblade. It was eerily silent, not unusual for the middle of the night, except there weren't even owl screeches to be heard.

Since I knew the path well, having come to Guru B for various consultations on cases, I led by instinct, my mind still distracted by the nishada teen. Where had she come from? What led to her capture? A prostitution ring? Was this some kind of a new fetish that Delhi's rich had invented to keep themselves from getting bored? Was she trafficked for that? But why did the businessman say he would die without sex with her? From what I knew, no one died of plain old horniness. And what had made her melt? What had made her scream in pain?

Without me noticing it immediately, the air became heavier, bringing with it a sweet, rotten, diseased smell. I sniffed, instinctively taking out my boneblade and pulling down the septifocals over my eyes as I muttered the Drishti mantra.

'Dekh saaf, khol sab raaz.'

The world flashed in a ghostly array of lights, immediately absorbed by the thick mist, dying down a second later. I blinked, as my kidneys fell to the ground. I slipped down, clutching my abdomen. It felt like sudden menstrual cramps. I cried out in pain, on all fours.

'Shakti's tits!' I cried, the mist sizzling before my eyes in a reddish hue. It had to be a shift, as if all life from around us had been drunk in one go, all shakti gone, carried away in the fog. My core contracted and I took a deep breath. My stomach roiled, as if I had eaten bad curry and was about to throw up. Shakti. Someone had used it all, a lot of it, very near us, so that even a simple mantra for sight didn't work. And the closer I got to the library, the worse it became.

'Sharmila's shit-filled ass,' I said, groggily inching forward. The fog had become so thick that I almost had to swim through it and so at first missed the stepped pyramid, the Garhgaj, which held the dead body of Muhammad Quli Khan. That was the entrance to Guru B's library. I took out my boneblade to slash my index finger because the opening to Guru's library always demanded blood sacrifice, but it wasn't needed. On the other side of the tomb, a jagged black hole sucked the fog around it, like a dark whirlpool. Readying my boneblade, I carefully peeped into the hole, a tunnel dug by forceful use of shakti. The stairwell to Guru's library, lay exposed and broken to bits. I jumped in, creeping down the broken stairs, boneblade in my left hand.

Everything screamed of an intruder. Lights didn't switch on when I entered the vestibule, the usual freezing air-conditioning was off. The robotic voice didn't prompt me to put our things into a compartment. It was all silent, dead and dark. I curbed my instinct of using a mantra to test out the inside. Rather I remembered the layout from my earlier visits and walked in. The vestibule opened up to a long corridor, which instead of its usually pristine white-lit walls lay in complete dark. The white corridor lay in shadows, quiet and heavy with secrets, much like the tomb it was built under. A thin wailing travelled through somewhere inside.

I crouched, taking out the mandalas from my satchel and holding them in front of me with my right hand. In my left was the boneblade. I felt like I was being watched. No, not watched, but stared at, as though every step I took was into a well-laid trap. I couldn't shake the feeling.

Inching into the library, my senses powered up. The stench of rot filled the room. Though I couldn't see them, I knew that the books on my left stood like silent spectators. I felt rather than saw the dark corridor open up to a bigger space, where I had last met Guru B when he had told me about the Cult of Chaos. In the darkness I pictured him, sitting on his favourite lounge chair, his long white beard flowing till his navel, his brown skin shiny as he sat in a white robe and gobbled down the peacock meat I had brought him.

'Camel's buttocks!' I tripped over something round, falling and losing the grip over my mandala. Reaching out, my hand touched something else – hard, thin and cold. The other hand found something hairy, attached to a skin-like grimy—

Then I remembered where I had first smelled that particular smell. The rottenness of it, mixed with a sweetness. The smell was moist, slushy with decay and foulness that comes when a dead rat is lying for a few days, in a rank corner of the attic, without anyone knowing about it. It reminded me of the first human dead body I had seen when I was but a child in Kaula Ashram in Banaras. An ashram swami brutally chopped up and thrown into the river. By the red tantrics I was told. It was a decomposed body about three days old but barely any face left in its bloated form. Fishes had taken claim to it all. I remembered the bones the most, jutting out from various parts, shining white like fresh snow, still pristine, still beautiful. The smell of death, of a decomposing corpse. Of a decayed, destroyed body. Sitting up, I tipped the vial of my yugma locket and let a drop of rakta fall over the boneblade. Rakta was the blood of a chandaali, much denser than a human's and much more powerful. Maybe it would allow me to do some magic in this dark, shakti-less place. I whispered the Dhumra mantra.

The boneblade gleamed purple, casting dark shadows. As my eyes adjusted to the glow, the chairs and the long table formed out of the shadows. They were scattered on the ground in front of me. A pair of eyes, opened and shining in the purple light. Head and hair jutting out from the haphazard shape. Arms and hands with flesh missing to the bone, legs falling onto the ground with jagged edges of bone jutting out of the eaten flesh. Torsos emptied and heads with their cheeks cut off in a chunk. Naked corpses, dead flesh, which I had mistaken for broken furniture. There was one thing missing. Blood. There was none.

Turning around, I spread the purple light emitting from the boneblade in all directions. *Crunch*. I turned around, looking at the pile of rotting flesh. A foot above it was a chunk of flesh from the face, one eye hanging from the cheek and side. *Crunch*.

Taking a chance with the low shakti, I put on the septifocals, speaking the drishti mantra again. The room turned red as I staggered, the simple spell making my head swim. The pile of corpses wasn't alone. The empty space between the bits of flesh and who-knows-what-else was filled up by two pretas: oblong faces, thin lips and long necks attached to huge hungry bellies. I stood still, crouched on all fours. Pretas were creatures from another plane and loved to feed on corpses. Why had someone summoned them here? They sat, focused on their food, hungrily slurping brain.

In their hunger they hadn't noticed me, which was good. I didn't have my powers in this place and handling them would be a task, even though they were just two. Itching my boneblade, I wondered if I could take a chance at another spell and capture one of them for questioning. Where was Guru B? I looked around, still. The lounge chair sat empty, though the floor was filled with the litter of body parts. My boneblade flickered, more shadows than light, the shakti in the mantra drying up fast. That's when I saw it.

Guru B's robe, a blotch of grey under the corpses.

I crawled slowly towards the pile. Bad idea. I pulled the robe, hoping to pull out Guru B by grabbing his robe. The corpses on top fell all around, with a dull clatter. It wasn't the noise, but the disturbances in the smell that attracted the pretas' attention. They flew upwards, screeching grey blobs. They hung there near the ceiling as I pulled Guru B's robe. Only it wasn't a robe. It was skin. Guru B's skin. His face and body and legs and hands, deflated, like a balloon without air. His white beard was spread out, an abandoned nest on the dirtied floor. Bloodied.

The screeching grew louder. I looked up to see a swarm of pretas hovering at the other corner of the long, low-ceiled room. They rushed towards me, making a *seee-seee* noise through their sharp teeth.

'Balls of bulls!' I cried, making a run for it. The pretas attacked together, digging their tiny sharp teeth into my back and shoulders, claws sinking into my back. My boneblade light flickered and died.

'Eugh!' I wriggled in the darkness, wincing as the bites went in deep. They were scavengers, but this lot seemed keen on live prey.

'Get off!' Rolling out of their clutches, I reached for the edge of the pile, grabbing my mandala, a pack of geometric shapes created with bones. My well-trained hands automatically selected the shape of a circle inside a square. I held it in both my hands and tried to say the Nodha mantra. The words didn't come out. My lips felt sealed, tight against each other. They were upon me again, gnawing my arms and chest and back and shoulders and face. I slumped to the ground, fast falling into a daze. A minute passed or maybe two, as the swarm fed on me. I picked up Guru's skin and stood up, the pretas around me like flies. It felt like an empty sack of cloth, a costume hanging by my hands. Flat, deflated and two-dimensional. There was a ringing in my ears. I waved the boneblade to stop it, reeled, sending dizzying sparkles of lilac on the ground. Guru B's dead skin fell to the floor. I swayed, putting my hands on my forehead. I poured rakta on the mandala and tried to speak the Nodha mantra again.

'*Bhuta pishacha darke bhag*!'

With the whisper, came a soft whoosh. The pretas drifted away. They could've come back since my spell wasn't strong enough, but for some reason, they lost interest and wandered off, as suddenly as they'd come. I stood still, breathless and tired. I wondered where they'd come from. The same place as these corpses, most likely.

'Ahum.' It was a gargle, like the clearing of a throat. I raised the boneblade with its flickering purple light, bringing it up. A body clung to the low ceiling of the room. A creature, wearing a human skull on his head, his long beard and dreadlocks falling below. He waited, his hands and legs spread across, a gecko, patiently waiting.

'Who are you?' I said, clear, confident into the darkness. 'What have you done with Guru?' There was no answer. He somersaulted on the floor, a silhouette in the flickering light, and stopped before me. He rose to his feet then. I readied my boneblade, slashed my finger, and took a deep breath, hoping a mantra would form.

'Is anyone here?' A thin, high-pitched voice, that of a child. From behind. Distracted, I turned to see a light rocking up and down, blinding me for a second.

'Stop!' I said, raising my hand.

'Ai! Who's there!' Light wavered on my face, as the creature somersaulted. A boy.

'Get away!' I shouted rolling and hurling myself towards him. Before I could reach him, the dreadlock mystery man swung, grabbing Guru B's skin from my clutches, and was behind the boy, holding his neck with his right hand, grinning a toothy grin.

'No, wait!'

'Ugg,' said the boy, raising his hands to free his neck. The torch fell and rolled across the floor, its beam running a spotlight over the macabre surroundings. I stopped, facing the boy and the intruder, still and waiting for a chance. The intruder looked at me for a second, a smile curving his lips. Only his lips and eyes were visible from the white beard, which caught the torchlight. He pushed the boy straight into me, letting him stagger and fall while he headed for the corridor and ran away, Guru's body flapping on his shoulder like a tattered carpet. I jerked away my left hand with the boneblade and held the boy with my right.

'Stay here!' I shouted to the boy, scrambling after the creature who was already on the stairs, taking them three at a time. I clamoured up behind him panting, wondering how that old creature was so fit. He had vanished.

I stopped, hands on my knees.

'So do we take these or not?'

I turned to find the boy standing behind me. Not as young as I'd taken him to be. He was a teenager, small for his age, thin and lanky, with a bowl-style haircut and sharp features.

'Take what?'

'The unknown dead?' he asked. 'Me and Para came to the cemetery to collect them but found nothing but these body parts. We came all the way here, it was quite a long walk and then Para got lost and I kept on following the trail and then finally I reached that dungeon where I saw the dead bodies we were supposed to take but before I could, that thing attacked me and now I'm not sure. Are we supposed to take these or not? We have to go elsewhere too, you know.'

'Hold your pumpkin, why are you and this *Para* collecting these corpses?' I asked, heading back inside to the pile of flesh. I took my septifocals and spoke the Drishti mantra again to check for pretas. There were none. I walked around, looking at the lounge chair on which I'd seen Guru B sitting many times. It was freezing cold, but my hand came across kernels strewn on the chair. Food crumbs. An abandoned plate of half-eaten meat lay in a corner. Could be peacock meat. Someone had brought it to him. Someone had *fed* it to him. Someone who was a friend, who knew Guru liked peacock meat. Something glittered in the left over plate. I picked it up with a pincer. It was gooey and glittered.

'That's our job. We're corpse collectors. May Maut grant you death.'

'Maut?'

'That's our goddess.'

'Death goddess? Well, that's sure to bring you more business. Take me to the cemetery you're supposed to be at,' I said, carefully folding the little gooey blob into a piece of paper and putting it in my satchel. I got up and dusted myself off.

'But first I have to take all these corpses back, else Para, he's a bit of a grump fart, he will shout, he has a really bad temper and I don't want him to shout and scream at me because then I can't eat anything for the whole day.'

'Fine, let's collect the dead.' There was no use letting this remain open and warn the guards who would come within an hour.

We quickly brought out all the corpses from the dungeon, putting them into a wheel barrow the boy had brought with him. His name was Marty and he was stronger than he looked.

'The friend you came here for – he dead too? Do we need to collect him as well?' asked the boy as we walked out together.

'Not sure,' I answered.

'Whatever suits your boobs,' shrugged the boy, sauntering off, pushing the cart and singing some out of tune song.

'Who taught you to talk like that?' I shouted, following him. The mist gathered, colder and denser, gathering forces against the sun which would soon rise. We got out of the Qutab Minar complex, walking along the fort wall beyond the thin, meandering roads of Mehrauli village and heading to the forest ruins behind it. Marty pointed to a small entryway – a broken wooden gate to a cemetery. We walked inside, the half-moon showing us the way under expansive banyan trees.

'See? He's left,' said the boy, stopping the cart. 'All your fault, miss.'

'How is that—'

'B—burn them. Burn them all before it's too late!' The cry came from the tree. Under it, sat a man, his back against the trunk. His sweater was bloodied.

'What happened to him?' I asked, approaching the man. Blood leaked from his thighs and shoulders like he had been attacked. I popped open my rakpiss vial and put a couple of drops on his wounds. I gave him a sip of it and lay him back. Thankfully, the wounds weren't too deep. 'Why didn't you help him?'

'My business is the dead,' scoffed Marty. 'May Maut grant you death.' With that he walked off, dragging the cart full of broken corpses. I sat next to the injured man, made him sip rakpiss and then lit myself a beedi.

'Want to tell me what happened here tonight?' I asked after he had recovered a bit.

'Three, dead … hum … they rose from their graves.'

'How?'

'All … hum … I heard was someone call them … by their names.'

'All fresh?' I stared at his face, twisted with pain and maybe fear. He nodded.

'I have been the caretaker for forty-three years now. Never, I have never … hum. The oldest was buried three days ago. In the middle of the night, I came out of my room and saw them rise, crawling out of their graves as if itching to be free … hum … I … I lit up a fire torch and tried to stop them, but something … hum …' He got up, hobbling to where a burnt-out torch lay. It hadn't even started to burn before it had sizzled off. I followed, taking a long drag. I'd need it.

'A dark shadow … hum … that's all I saw … a big dark shadow came in through the fog. It was a solid shadow walking in the cemetery, like it walked not only here, but in the other world too. It called to them, all three, by name … hum. Then it spread three tentacles and the three dead rose. Hum. Like puppets on a string. Like they had eaten some of the shadow and were alive with dark things.'

'Food for the pretas,' I whispered, crushing my spent beedi with my chappal. 'Wonder who this tantrik was.'

'… Hum …'

'And so you called the Maut guys here?'

'What … hum … Maut?'

'The one Marty was with? That boy who came with me.'

'I don't know him. He just came here and told me he would bring back the corpses. Then he said hum … may Maut—'

'Grant you death?' I snorted. Leaving the caretaker to rest, I left for my mobike, wondering who the hell Marty was and why'd he gone off with the corpses. Was he the tantrik? The wizard who could make the dead walk and the pretas do his deed, had to be a powerful one. Marty somehow didn't fit in. And for what? For Guru B's body? Why? I dialled Ashwa's number. Bloody thing was switched off. I left a message with Maaki, the bar owner at Bedardi to tell me when his highness showed up, and left for home deciding to work on the paintbrush.

3

THE OFFICE of the Non-Tantrik Department was easy to miss even though it lay bang on a main road on the outer circle of Rajiv Chowk. The reason? It worked from a forgotten floor of a corner building. From outside the place looked unfinished – just another multi-storeyed building gathering dust because its ownership couldn't be decided in the legal courts. To add to it, there were mysterious suicide stories around the building about a couple of women who had jumped off the ninth and eleventh floors to kill themselves.

Madhu got off from Chhotu as I parked it in the afternoon sun, rubbing my hands for warmth. A guard snoozed outside in the courtyard, looking deceptively like someone who might fall with one little shove.

'Don't go by his looks,' I whispered to Madhu as we walked towards him. 'He's a warrior from the Kroor clan from the Himalayas.' Though he didn't look it, he was enough to deal with the biggest of daityas to critin, tiny sups who could kill you slowly by chewing your brains and cuddling on it while you slept.

'Laado!' he said sniffing like he had a cold, his eyes still closed, his body in the sleeping position. With one move, he was up and standing next to Madhu. 'You look like a healthy gyag with milk in her fat juicy boobs.' He cupped his flat chest and jiggled a little, his sinewy arms rotating in circles on his chest. It was a compliment. Anything to do with gyag was a compliment in the Kroor tribe. It meant he was open to mating with me, which was the biggest compliment he knew for a woman.

'You are a healthy bull as usual, Siyara,' I said trying to jab him with my elbow.

He then moved behind Madhu, sniffing. 'New catch, this?'

'No. I'm here for a case, Siyara. This is Madhu Tripathi from the CBI.'

'Nice to meet—' began Madhu, extending his hand.

Siyara sniffed and spat. 'Asura father, manava mother, with a hint of the bloodline of daitya and a tendency to mate with males of other species, mostly manavas.'

'How did you—'

I looked at Madhu sheepishly. I had warned him. Kroors had a natural ability to sniff out a creature's composition, taste, and who knew what else? It had never failed to fascinate me.

'Talab has left in case you came to meet him.'

'Where?' I asked lighting the beedi and offering one to Madhu, who declined with a frown.

'Left. Someone else runs the RC now. A tantrik.'

'A tantrik? Runs the Non-Tantrik Rights Commission?'

'Bulls do fly, Laado, bulls do fly.'

'Aghori-eating idiots!' I spat, taking two beedi drags before snubbing it. Asking a tantrik to head the Non-Tantrik Rights Commission was like asking a lion to head a commission for the welfare and protection of deer. It was in the nature of all tantriks to abuse supernatural creatures or sups. Just like the Nishada girl. From what I knew of the law, a non-tantrik could not be legally appointed to head RC. But then the law-makers were tantriks themselves, the Central Association of Tantriks. Of course they could amend the law to suit them. Bloody leeches to the ecosystem, all of them.

We took two steps at a time to the eighth floor. The corridor was dusty, though there were all kinds of footprints there. The rooms lay bare and unfinished, bare bricks peeking out. The rooms had no glasses on the windows letting in a draft. I went to a corner room, just columns and cemented walls with tall windows, and walked to the very edge, to a window without a pane.

'Come,' I asked Madhu, who stood behind me, a bit dazed. He wandered to the edge, gulped. Below, lay ninety feet of nothingness and then bam – the hard ground.

'Anantya, make this fast. I am a bit uneasy with heights,' he said.

'I know, which is why I didn't tell you about this,' I said, taking a deep breath before jumping into the air, pulling him along. He opened his mouth to scream but no sound came out. His flapped his hands in desperate panic, trying to find something to steady him. For a split second, in which Madhu's eyes popped out, we were suspended in air before our feet felt a sudden hardness of ground.

'Of all the fucking Patala's pimps!' I swore, getting up, rubbing my scraped knees. Besides me, sat Madhu still a bit stunned.

'There has to be a better way to do this,' Madhu cried, getting up.

'No, there isn't,' I answered. 'That nut of a mayan has made sure there won't be.'

Inspired by Maya, the asuric architect who had constructed the mythic Indraprastha, Talab had painted the department's walls with sharabha's bile, which made it invisible to humans. He had also insisted on putting the gap in between the pathway and the window that we'd just jumped from, to make sure that humans, unless suicidal, didn't drop by for a cup of tea. It worked well, but unfortunately, not for humans. Even my septifocals wouldn't have helped me here, for the office was protected from all kinds of vision checkers.

'To see is to abuse,' was one of his bloody sayings in one of his bloody many philosophical moods, 'In the dark, we are all the same, just flares of shakti.'

Bloody sup-lover.

The early morning corridor was crawling with all kinds of pashus and mayans, who might have arrived here at night and now waited for their stamped pieces of paper to get into the city. Rakshasas, yakshas, dasyus, looked at me with lazy eyes, unseeing and disinterested, waiting for their name to be called. I stepped over a half-eaten dog lying next to a chandaali, who slept with her hand cuffed to the wall, and walked on. Madhu followed, gasping at something every now and then.

'What are these creatures?' he asked me, as we walked along the corridor with damp and filthy walls, a layer of grease splattered on them. The corridor stank of piss and shit and was littered with enough cups, broken plastic bottles, pieces of clothes, bones and stale food to almost hide the tiles of the floor.

'Immigrants from outside the city, waiting for a passport from the immigration office,' I replied.

'Immigration? Aren't they Indians?'

'Hah. The Indian government doesn't recognize them. The tantriks who do, want them to get immigration stamps if they come in highly concentrated human spaces like cities. Which is where the immigration office comes in. Without the papers and a human identity, the supernaturals can be arrested and put into the Tazaak's rotten prisons.'

The Immigration Department was a sham created for the sole purpose of bringing all sups under the control of tantriks. Before CAT had been created, cities were free spaces where any sup could move to. As long as they didn't reveal themselves to the humans. But now, with the recent creation of the association, things had been getting organized. For the supernatural community, that meant carrying their identity papers at all times in the city, without which it meant imprisonment or slavery camps outside the city. The move had only increased illegal immigrants who had no documents and had to pay corrupt tantriks to give them fake papers and human identities.

The Rights Commission office was at the end of the corridor, after the immigration office. We walked in to see a shrivelled tantrik sitting behind a big table.

'What's this about?' he asked, looking at us.

'We're here to report a nishada's death—'

'Nishadas have been recently demoted to pashu level. You should head to the Pashu Department for filing a complaint.' He waved his hand to dismiss us. I counted till ten and thought of nice things like taking a snag off a beedi.

'Why was Talab transferred?' The tantrik looked up, his lips stretching.

'Happens. Government offices, you see. Next,' he bellowed to my angry, stiff back. The Pashu Department was at the far end of the corridor, past a shiny new door with a brand new nameplate outside that read 'Tvasta Tantrik' with the triangular sign of the Kaulas on either side.

The room was plush. Wall-to-wall carpets with frescoes on the walls, each with a different scene of tantrik heroes of myth, killing or battling demons and winning a war against mayans or capturing and saving pashus. Tall tales of tantrik superiority.

In the middle of it, behind a wide sandalwood desk, sat a man with a long ponytail and shaved head. His ponytail was rolled up with rudraksh beads. He wore spectacles on his wide, pear-shaped face and bore a small scar on his right cheek. The strong smell of sandalwood suffused the room, making it suffocatingly sweet and claustrophobic.

'Come, come, please sit down,' he said, indicating two chairs opposite him with his hand. 'How can I help?' he asked, and made a steeple of his fingertips, putting his chin on it. He smiled, a cold but polite one. I introduced myself and Madhu.

'We're here to officially report a nishada's death. It happened late this afternoon. She was found in a hotel suite.'

'Jolly good, jolly good. How did she die?' He picked up a gold-tipped pen and a writing pad of sorts. Scribble scribble, he went.

'We don't know for sure yet. It could be some kind of a drug or something. Her body melted. She was in a lot of pain for an hour before she did.'

'Jolly good, jolly good,' he scribbled some more. 'Are you the owner?'

'Owner?'

'With the new administration rules, with effect from last month, we need the owner of the pashu before we can file any complaint about them.'

'So you just decide to shift a race from intelligent beings to animals? Just like that?'

'It's all thanks to the new administration, elected under the leadership of Rishi Narahara of the Central Association of Tantriks, Miss ... Tantrist was it?' He smiled, nodding his head and scribbling again. 'His aim is to bring out laws to rule the city strategically and in the most efficient way possible. It's for everyone's best.' Scribble, scribble. I wondered what he wrote down considering we hadn't said anything yet. Do you know this nishada's name? Any ownership details?' he asked, looking up from his pad. He readied the pen again, pursuing his lips.

'Didn't get her name. She dissolved before I could ask.'

'Oh, oh. Jolly good, jolly good. And where is the body?'

'Her body melted. If you—'

'The remains are with my forensics team,' said Madhu, placing his palm on my arm to calm me.

'Oh good, good,' he scribbled while saying this. 'I've filled in a formal form. Now you've to sign here and here.' I snatched the piece of paper. It just noted that a nishada was found by someone by the name of Anita Tantrite.

'She wasn't found, you ...' I stopped controlling the urge to define the details of his horrendous bottom, '—she was found *dead*. Can you mention that in your report?'

He took off his specs and wiped them. 'It's all I can do until an owner approaches the department.'

A wail came in through the door, invading our silence. I took a deep breath, counted till ten and then counted till ten again, unclenching my fists. Then I asked him if an owner had reported a missing nishada girl.

'Not yet. There's only one nishada owner in Delhi and she hasn't formally lodged a complaint. I am afraid there's very little I can do to help.'

'We have the melted remains of the body,' Madhu pointed out.

'Well, that you can hand over to me to formally close the case from your end. I understand; these government procedures can get a bit much. It used to be the same with us but ever since Rishi Narahara has taken control of the association—'

'So if the owner's not reported her missing, she doesn't exist?' I snapped, clasping my boneblade in its scabbard.

'Ma'am, you're applying simplification to the law. As I was saying—'

'Can you tell me who that one nishada owner is?' The boneblade pierced in my index finger.

'I'm afraid that's against the law. We at the Pashu Department take pride in protecting the privacy of—'

'*Jabaan khol taal, sach nikaal*,' I screamed, landing a droplet of blood on Tvasta's lips. His eyes widened and he wiped off his lips with the back of his hand.

'What the—' Madhu began. I grabbed his shoulder, pushing him back into his seat and putting a finger on my lip. Then I faced the tantrik.

'Who is this nishada owner, Tvasta,' I asked politely, smiling.

'Jolly go—I do not know, ma'am.'

'I know you're pretty good with your clerk business. Would you like to check your files and tell me, please?'

'Oh good, good.' He shuffled through some papers. 'Miss Saranyu owns them, ma'am.'

'And her address?'

'Triya Art Gallery, Civil Lines.'

'See, that's all I wanted. Glad you could help. Your Rishi sure is trying to ensure efficient administration. Good job!' I gave him a thumbs-up as we walked out, leaving a dazed official behind us.

Madhu wiped off his forehead after we'd leaped off the invisible gap. 'Remind me never to say no to you,' he said.

I smiled, patting him on the shoulder.

In the evening, I wasn't smiling anymore. It was all Shukra's fault. I could be doing any number of things, including finding out who had squeezed Guru B, or what that gooey diamond was. I still didn't know who that skull-wearing creep was, and knew next to nothing about Marty, who'd vanished in the night. Also, why the hell was Ashwa's phone switched off?

All I could do now was sit in an almost empty auditorium in Jawaharlal Nehru University, listening to a professor who had decided that droning was the only way one could impart knowledge. I could've got some shuteye if it weren't for an enthusiastic academic sitting by my side, jabbing me with his rather large, ape-like finger every once in a while, drawing attention to something that the professor said.

I sighed, looking at the only window in the cold hall, which let in the early evening sun. There were better ways to spend an evening. A drink in the bar, or experimenting on the paintbrush we'd found on the nishada's body. I'd already tested it for curses with all kinds of revealing and repelling potions in my Rasayana lab. But it seemed like an ordinary horse-hair paintbrush with a pretty scribble.

'Ooh,' went the ape, almost breaking the chair in his excitement as the professor changed yet another slide of his presentation. 'That's genius, Anantya!' Another poke. 'Madhu was right. The professor is an expert when it comes to clinical pathology. He's the right man for sure.'

I crossed my arm. Seriously, I should've just taken advantage of this ape, got him drunk, banged him to work out the mutual attraction over one night and said goodbye. Now, we'd fallen into that creepy zone of friends-only-but-with-sizzling-attraction, the cringe-worthy camaraderie where you got jabbed in your ribs and patted on your arm and had to go listen to lectures. Ugh.

The droning continued in the same vein for an hour, as we waited. Finally, with all students out, we caught Professor Bodhgaya's attention. He was a squat, middle-aged man with a flat head as if he'd just emerged from a matchbox.

'Professor Bodhgaya, that was quite insightful,' exclaimed Shukra, shaking hands with him. 'What a presentation, sir, what a presentation.'

'Glad you think so.' The professor nodded, his eyes glazed behind his thick spectacles.

'I was wondering if you would give us a moment. It's about a tissue and blood sample I'd sent you in the morning,' said Shukra, looking on either side of us and then whispering dramatically. 'It's for the case for the CBI.'

'Oh, so you are Mister Seventy-two? The one that sent me the samples in the morning?'

'No, sir, Shukracharya, the seventy-six. And this is Anantya, a consultant with the CBI.'

'Yes, it's rather dry. A natural reaction of the cold weather I would say. Was your stay nice, seventy-two?'

'Stay? Sir, I'm Shukracharya, though my friends call me …'

'Tea, of course. Come, come.' He led the way with a meandering, distracted walk, from the auditorium to the biotechnology department. We didn't get into the main building. Instead, he took up to one behind it, disused, and crumbling, almost hidden in shrubbery. The front door opened creakily as we walked into a dusty corridor.

'Sir, about the sample,' began Shukra.

'Apple? I'm afraid I won't have any here. I might have oranges if you would like. Bought a few for one of the experiments.'

'Sample, sir, *sample*!' hollered Shukra.

'Yes, I've seen the sample, of course. That's why you send it to me, no? Most, most unusual.'

We walked past two rooms with broken windows. The walls of one of them was blackened and burnt. 'My temporary lab area. The professors in the department don't use this wing anymore, which is good because if you're experimenting, you might have an unfortunate accident and then before you know, you need to move a lab since the existing one has already been rather … ah … used.'

We entered a small room with a sharp stink of rotten eggs. A table on one side was piled up with untidy books, three microscopes, a few jars of various shapes and colours and neatly labelled. In the middle was another table, brimming with books, apparatus, some weird shaped tubes, baths and needles. The [professor filled a vial with water and put it over a lab burner. He then put on a lab coat two sizes too big for him. I tenderly leaned against a sink, taking a strand of my hair and curling around my fingertip.

'Where did you find it?' asked Bodhgaya.

'The sample? It's part of a case.' Shukra looked at me, as if asking if he should reveal more. I shook my head.

'I have never seen anything of the sort! The regenerative levels of this parasite are quite high. Impossibly so,' he said. 'Come, come, let me show you.' He pulled Shukra by his arm, pointing to a microscope.

Shukra peered into it, with me behind, trying to get a look.

'You look too, lady, come, come,' he said, his grey hair haloing around his face. I peeked at the microscope which had a blackened blob at the end of it, full of golden pinpricks.

'You see, you see? It's quite spectacular!' he cried, bobbing up and down.

'What is?' I asked.

'Fish? No, no, you might have missed it. It's the golden dot-like structures. It's the parasite from the tissue and blood sample that you gave me, and it has already multiplied exponentially. Through a normal microscope all you can see is the black tissue sample with the parasite, which is golden in colour. But if you look at it from a dark-field microscope, which is more powerful than this one, you can understand what's going on.'

'And what is going on?' I asked.

'It's a battle!' His voice thinned. 'There's a parasite in the host's blood stream which seems to have travelled into the host's tissue and, after a while, it began to eat away its host's tissue, liquidating it, almost like a protozoa feeds on the bacteria that feeds on your organic garbage, decomposing it. I tested this parasite on a rat and would you believe it, within four hours, it had eaten away the rat's body, which melted into nothingness. See, here, I have the melted rat. Must be here somewhere.' His hands waved in a general direction.

'That explains the pleasant fragrance,' I muttered.

'Much like the nishada!' said Shukra, horrified.

'Aadas? Are those the creatures whose tissue sample you gave to me?' he asked.

I glared at Shukra as the professor continued: 'What marvellous creatures. I thought it might be a fish or something. There are some jellies which have regenerative abilities like this aada.'

'Nishada,' I said.

'Nishada,' the professor clapped. 'What an unusual ability, a strong immunity system, so strong that it can ward off any pathogens or parasites that might attack it. But this parasite, it is not only powerful in its ability to regenerate and grow, but is also powerful enough to overcome even this nishada creature's tissue. It would have taken longer, my guess is about four weeks in the nishada's case. If it were a human, he would have given in to the parasite within a day.'

'So it's a kind of a disease?'

'Not at all, miss. No fees. This is my pleasure. It's a very special parasite. Just uncontrollable for now. Given enough time and experimentation, and if we can find a demure version, we could possibly even stop or reverse ageing. Who knows?'

'Professor!' Shukra shouted, speaking slowly as one does to a child. 'Can a person infected with the parasite be treated?' asked Shukra.

'Greeted?'

'Treated,' shouted Shukra.

'Treated? Yes, Yes, it might be possible. All I need to do is reverse the effect and it will kill this virus. Give me a day or two with this sample and I'll see what I—ugg,' The professor clutched the side of his stomach.

'Are you okay?' I asked.

'Yes, yes,' He pressed his hands on either side of his hip, his face crumpled with pain. 'It's my apprentice.'

'You mean your appendix?' corrected Shukra.

'Yes. My apprentice. He's giving me an ulcer,' He cringed. 'I think I need to rest. It was nice meeting you both.'

'What I want to know is how she got that parasite in the first place,' I said as we walked out of the department building.

At least we knew why she'd melted. Once I met Miss Saranyu, I would learn more.

4

TRIYA ART Gallery was an old bungalow reconverted to an art gallery. The late night traffic had died down. I parked Chhotu a few houses from the gallery and after a thought, pulled out the nishada's blood I'd brought along. I gulped it down, slashed my index finger with the boneblade and whispered the Dehavyu mantra:

'*Dikhau chhupau mayavu dehavyuh*!'

I felt my skin change to scales. Then I took out the paintbrush, which I'd checked for curses and poisons, and wore it around my neck. After a little thought, I packed my satchel and belt into the chhotu's storage and hid the boneblade in my culottes. That and my yugma locket were my only defence. There were no guards at the gate, but there was a line of people outside, whispering to each other.

'Can't go in ... It's cursed,' said a man, a driver standing next to his car, dressed in white cap and uniform.

'... Rich people, rich—' the companion stopped, staring at me open mouthed.

'Show me those filthy teeth some more and I will sock them out.' I scowled, glad to see him take a few steps back. The paintbrush around my neck glowed green as I walked through the gate. The glowing died down as soon as I was inside. Which meant it was an entry card to this place. Which meant the nishada had come from here. I started to walk briskly.

The garden was landscaped elaborately with a lane of statues of yalis, mythical beasts: part lion, part elephant and part horse with a few birds thrown in. Running along the sculptures, were rills that connected to a fountain and two canals on either side. Lifelike sculptures of makara posed under soft blue lights in the moat between the pathway and the bungalow up ahead, spreading out into canals. Soft blue light lit up the waterbodies. The bungalow was humming with the low murmurs of the socialites gathered there.

'Finally,' said a sleek voice from the darkness beside the pathway. A tall, thin nishada in a knee-length black cowl dress, her greyed hair neatly tied in a bun and a deep shade of red on her lips, approached me. Her scales had browned with age, a few of them broken. She had a pinched, look about her face, like someone had stretched her loose skin one too many times. She put a firm hand on the small of my back, directing me towards a lane leading away from the main path.

'Kokila, where were we? Our heart got crushed looking for us all day and night. Goddess has asked about us so many times! We had to make some excuse.' She hissed, turning to smile at a man who walked past us in a tuxedo.

'This is not the jungles, we hear? Bad things can happen to a youngling like us in human jungles. What if we'd gotten lost? Or worse? But we are glad we reached without Goddess knowing. The excuses we had to make. Hurry, hurry. Time. Time is important in human jungles.'

We made our way backstage, a section which was buzzing with activity.

'We are here,' announced my escort. 'Mitch, heat the thing.'

Mitch, a short human who wore a glittering t-shirt torn halfway to show off his stomach, swung to my side, touching my hair. He made a disgusted face.

'Quelle horreur!' he said in a husky voice, 'I need at least twenty minutes, Baaja dear.'

'Not Baaja, Baza is our name,' said my escort. 'And we have ten.' She pushed me through a door, 'Did we eat after?' She took out a towel, frowning. 'Speak up, youngling! We think we have time to wait around all day for our response?'

I nodded, was handed the towel and shoved into a swanky toilet with its shower running.

'Hurry, hurry,' she said from outside. I quickly showered, changed into the bathrobe, which I had mistaken for a towel, made sure my boneblade was with me and walked out.

'Baaja! Her hair, looks feary feary. Like they saw a ghost and had a heart attack,' said Mitch, towelling my mass of curls, rubbing a white cream into it.

'You want me to slit your heart out?' I whispered, smiling sweetly to Mitch. His eyes widened.

Another woman, with a makeup palette in her hand, painted my face, turning her brushes and fussing on my eyes. A third woman tried to remove my robe, saw my expression and mutely showed me the dress I had to wear. It was a green gown, shining like an emerald, long and slinky and backless. As soon as Mitch stopped fussing, I wore the gown and gasped. The gown fitted my nishada shaped body, changing shape and adjusting. It was a tantri dress. Tantri dresses that fit any one's body perfectly, were royalty stuff, cost someone a rakshasa or two. I'd seen a few, but that too at the Kaula ashram, under strict lock and key and only when I'd been royalty there. What were the nishadas doing wearing them?

'Hurry, hurry, just five minutes! Join the other younglings.'

I was pushed along a doorway, into darkness and made to stand along a wall. As my eyes adjusted, I saw nine other nishada girls, wearing the softly glowing tantri dresses. These too were teenagers. My boneblade was snug against my thigh, reassuring.

'What happens now?' A young whisper. Her eyes shone in the darkness, warm amber, liquid like a sleepy tiger's.

'Don't you know?'

'No.'

'Where are you from?'

'From where we both are, sister. Don't you know us? We are Chiri.'

'I don't remember,' I answered.

'We came from really, *really* far. From our forests of sal.'

'How did we come here?'

'We came together, with our senior. Don't you remember? The bad smell of death. So bad that we were sick. Then we were to drink from the moon goddess in our bleeding days. And senior got Goddess for our protection and benefit. But we don't know,' her voice turned into a whisper, her eyes deepened to a darker shade of yellow, 'now we are *scared* here, sister. There's no sal forests here that whispers, no phutki singing our songs, only stillness, only death. Where are we?'

'Who is our senior?'

'Oh, we don't remember anything, sister. Our senior Baza. Our sister, our aunt, but our senior changes her colours. Our—'

'No talking! Hush!' Baza's sharp voice pierced the darkness. A moment later, we were separated and stood a little distance away from each other, around the room. A door opened and people walked in, whispering in the darkness.

Then the blinding lights hit us. Gasps and claps from beyond it.

'Balls of bulls!' I muttered, shading my eyes. Chiri, who stood a few feet away from me, giggled. In the lights, she looked barely thirteen behind the lavender makeup on her face, her scales shining brightly in her grey dress. A young, innocent kid. Between us was a painting, a slap of red and blue to make a blurry room of some sort. The other nishadas across the gallery, each next to an equally banal painting of a room or a passageway. A few of them were as young as Chiri, scales still forming on their soft black skin.

The room had a high ceiling, tall columns carved with

intricate sculptures of Yali and held around fifteen or twenty guests, all men in tailored suits, reeking of expensive perfumes. The whispers died suddenly as a spot light was turned on. An announcer came to the centre.

'Gentlemen, silence please,' he said in a soft, cultured voice. 'We thank you all for taking time to join us here tonight. Without much ado, we present to you, all the way from the jungles of central India, the shy tribe of nishadas. I invite Lady Saranyu to tell you about the art displayed tonight.' The spotlight shifted to the door.

'Welcome to Wombs of Immortality.' A smooth yet eerie voice. Lady Saranyu glided in, raising her arms skywards. Like a bunch of playcards, all of them fell, the nishadas kissing the ground, the men on their knees, their hands together in a namaste gesture. Her skin was milky white and flawless, she wore a long, pink tantri gown with a high slit. Her eyes were large and liquid, a mesmerising grey, an unusual one which was almost ivory in shade. Her long hair fell on the small of her back, each strand in place, shaping her shapely curves. The crowd looked, captivated, still.

'I am Lady Saranyu, the goddess of the gallery. Today I have brought all of you here to ask for your help for these girls.' She walked towards one and gently stroked her scales. 'As some of you know, my family owns the jungles where these creatures are found, which is why I am responsible for their well-being. The nishadas are a kind-hearted, simple tribe. But because of their rudimentary lifestyle, they live in the jungles, like animals, surviving on roots and raw flesh. As part of our rehabilitation programme, Wombs of Immortality, we aim to bring them back into civilization. We want to empower these tribals, give them clean water, sanitation and education. For this noble endeavour, we need your generosity. Auction for the paintings my sons have drawn with blood and sweat, interact with the nishadas, understand their life. Every artwork you buy will help us raise funds to rehabilitate these poor creatures and give you immortality! If you want to bid for a painting, please hand your bid to the girl standing next to it. Make a bid, gentlemen, and you not only take a beautiful creation home, but also adopt and help an orphan tribe.'

The lights dimmed once before beaming straight onto the paintings and onto me and the other nishadas, making it harder to see with my human eyes. A sea of black came forward, like fat flies to ripe fruit. They were all men, dressed nattily in expensive Armani suits and ties, all reeked of money and power. Some hobbled, some looked thin, some weakened, but all had one thing in common – a hungry, desperate look about them, not as they looked at the paintings, but at the girls standing beside them. You could feel the stare, under the gown, going into the skin itself. A guy came forward, a hairy hand, handing me an envelope. I took it and looked at it. A bid for the painting. Or was it? It certainly seemed like a lot more than an art auction.

One man looked at Chiri, hunger plain in his eyes, scowling, his bald head sweating even in the cold. He walked to her. She moaned. Turning my hand into a claw, I slashed at him, baring my teeth. He staggered back. This time Chiri didn't giggle, she was on her knees, doubled up in pain. I sat on the ground, trying to help her.

'Chiri, what—' A hand cuffed my arm.

'What are we doing, Kokila!' screetched Baza.

'She's hurting,' I cried, jerking her arm away, groping for my satchel, only to realize I had it in my mobike. Chiri remained in the foetal position, her body shivering, a constant low moan emitting from her.

'We will do it, Kokila.' She was now holding my face, staring at my forehead, her eyes cold. 'Go back, what has got into us?' she said, her lips thin lines of blue.

'No,' I quipped. Shock coloured her face, turning it darker. Chiri shivered, still not raising her head.

'We dare defy our own tribe senior?' she whispered ferociously.

'And *you* dare become a traitor to your own tribe?' I said. Her face changed, her skin lighting in shade, till her scales showed black on greyed cheeks. 'If we don't—' she began.

'A conference of aunt and nieces in the middle of the auction.'

Baza's face became a lighter grey, as all blood drained from it, eyes widened.

'How interesting.' I turned to look at the source of the voice, directly above us, and stood up. It was a sub-human male, who shimmered like he was surrounded by sunrays. He had an ethereal quality to him, as if he was not real, an illusion, a beautiful dream. His face was carved from supple white marble, his eyes shone like the sun. His hand rose, touching my cheek. A cool touch, like that of a marble statue.

'Prince!' Baza gushed, groveling. 'We say sorry for this.'

'What a pretty face,' he whispered. 'What texture, what scales. What's your name, lady?'

'This one's name is Kokila, our prince. Prince is so kind to ask.' Baza said. I stood there, more amused. Why was she so scared?

'How the scales of your skin shimmer.' The man's eyes were large and moist, pools of liquid grey, shimmering, like his mother, except there was a childlike quality to them, an innocence. So he was one of the artist sons Lady Saranyu had mentioned. 'Fascinating creature.' He cupped my chin. 'I want to paint you, I do, I do!'

'Yes, brother. Let's paint her now, should we?' said another childish voice.

The two look-alikes stood together – blond hair, eyes like the sun, they were both exactly the same height. Even their bodies looked similar. Both were casually but stylishly dressed, and screamed of elegance except when they spoke, in bursts, like excited children. Enthusiasm or madness, I couldn't tell.

'So curious. You know what I am most curious about? To see what she looks like. *Inside*,' one of them quipped.

They giggled, their laughter was uncanny, innocent and resounding.

'Ask Goddess, princes, and we can.'

'But you won't tell mother, will you, Baza? Else we will paint *you* too.' They giggled again.

'No, our prince, we won't,' said Baza, pinching my hip, pushing me away from the twins. She smiled grimly and veered away, pulling me with her by the arm. I looked back to see both of them, their eyes enthusiastic and shiny, staring back at me, smiling.

'Idiotic monkey! Look what we've done!' She pinched my ear. 'We've made the princes notice us. And Kubja prince is not here to protect us too. Now you stand there and we will take Chiri inside.'

'So what?' I asked, but she didn't answer, pushing me back on the spot I had left and hurrying away. She pulled up a moaning Chiri and took the exit we'd entered from. A couple of men came forward, giving me an envelope. I took them, distracted, still staring at the door. Maybe I should go too. Chiri didn't look too well.

'Gentlemen, we thank you for bidding,' said the announcer about five minutes later. He announced the names of the men who'd bid the maximum, congratulated the new art owners.

'This is mine!' said a big, fat man. He took my arm and pulled me hard, making me stumble. 'I need it now.' He laughed, his triple chins dribbling. 'I will live, I will live!'

I got up, straightened my dress, made a fist of my hand and boxed him straight on his flabby face.

He staggered, holding his mouth, which was leaking blood. 'She … she *hit* me,' he squeaked.

'Touch me again,' I said showing him my fist, 'and I will

mince your jiggly face and make kebabs out of it.' I massaged my head, wondering if I should cut one of his chins.

'Lad—Lady Saranyu …' he squeaked again, scuttling away towards wherever the dinner party had gone to. Baza rushed over to me, but someone stepped in between.

'I have always liked attitude in a woman,' said a sleek, cultured voice. Vajrin Mahendra stood, with his dimpled chin and longish hair that made soft waves just above his broad shoulders. A single grey streak in his hair. I had met Vajrin a few months ago in a case I had been investigating. He was one of the most influential businessmen in the city.

'Vaj—' I began and caught myself, smiling stiffly and bowing, 'I mean, Mr Vajrin Mahendra.'

'How interesting. You know my name when I don't seem to remember meeting you.' He turned to address the fuming Baza, 'Allow me to escort her, Miss Baza, and make sure she gives no trouble.'

Baza, obviously displeased, but with no choice, walked off, fussing over the nishada who was still cringing in pain.

Vajrin turned to face me again. 'I have always been fascinated by women who have sources other than the obvious one of knowing things. Come let's take a walk.'

'I want to treat—'

He took me firmly by the elbow and out of hearing range of everyone. 'I have always wondered,' he began, fingering my yugma locket, so close that I could smell the wine on his breath. 'Miss Anantya Tantrist, whether trouble follows you everywhere you go or you follow it, in a psychopathic need to die early. Why is it that you want to leave this world so desperately?'

We entered another gallery. From the looks of it, the bungalow was divided into rooms with high ceilings and French windows all painted pristine white and making a string of rooms together. Soft cream lights illuminated the galleries, highlighting the paintings not from above but lit up from behind. There were more paintings in the other galleries, paintings of closed rooms, some done up in a gothic style, some in a pastel romanticism and some hardy.

'And why is it that you want to live so desperately, Mr Vajrin Mahendra?' I jibed, touching my scaly skin. He threw his head back and laughed, his voice deep and soft, his curls falling over his eyes. Deliciously.

'Who are these people?' I whispered furiously. He waved at someone who stood admiring a red painting of a room, with shades of maroon velvet curtains and a satin sheet on the bed. It was ugly, too red, too rich.

'Keep smiling, you idiot,' he whispered furiously. 'This is no *joke*.'

The man nodded, and moved away. Over the silence between us, we heard Chiri's moan coming from the dressing room.

'Look at the realism in this one. The way the curtains flow, like they're streams of our collective consciousness, squeezing the very lifeblood—'

'It's a stupid painting of a garish room!'

'*Quelle passion*!' he continued as if I hadn't spoken. 'Stay away from Lady Saranyu if you want to stay alive.'

'I am investigating the death of a nishada. She melted,' I whispered back. 'If you won't tell me, I will ask someone else. I don't have patience—'

'Patience. Yes, I forget how that's something only the long-lived have.'

I turned to move away, walking off, but Vajrin held my arm. 'They are dangerous, Anantya, not people who can be messed with. Drop whatever you are looking into. Believe me. They are above any investigation.' He leaned close to me, too close. 'Above even *eternals*.'

'*Vajrin*,' said a deep, echoing voice called to him. Saranyu breezed in. 'I am so glad you could make it. It's been centuries, my dear,' she said. They kissed each other on the cheek.

'I had no choice in the matter, Saranyu,' he answered with a half-smile of sorts, taking her hand and kissing it. She smiled.

'How time changes everything. You look good in this new avatar …' She fingered his hair and turned her eyes in my direction with a sudden intensity, gorging into my core, my bones, like a diamond cutter. At that second, I knew she knew. She knew me, who I was and who I was pretending to be. My cover was blown. But she didn't say anything.

'All because of your kindness, Goddess,' Vajrin answered.

'Hmm. You seem to have chosen your escort from my girls,' she said, not hurried, not menacingly, but with an edge. 'It's good to know you're helping the impoverished, Vajrin, so selfless of you.'

He smiled. 'So is Manu Maharaj. He has been granted a ministry of his own, for manufacturing miracles for the poor. But you would know that, wouldn't you—'

She froze, her eyes hardening. 'Let's not talk about unpleasant things on a night full of life like this. Unless you don't like the idea of life that is—' She glided her hand towards Vajrin, whose smile had dropped, as had his hand from my arm. 'Come, it's time for din—'

A bloodcurdling scream stilled her hand. For a second we stared at each other. For me, the scream was eerily familiar. The same one that got into your bones without touching your ears. I dashed into the first gallery, taking the exit to the green room. Chiri lay in the middle of the space, bundled up, a thin, alien wail emitting from her.

'Shit of an asura!' Last time this had happened, I'd tried all the mantras. Now it was time for something more drastic. I took out the rakta vial from my yugma locket, opening the lid and dropping the blood to trace a circle around me and her. As soon as the circle was complete, slashing my wrist, I said aloud:

'Kha kaasu kha roga mehikulli aa!'

Mehi was a kulli spirit that drank disease from creatures. She curdled my blood, running from my veins to the boneblade to the blood circle I'd drawn and inside. I felt like someone was scratching the inside of my skin.

'No, sister, no!' Chiri cried, screaming, fearful.

'Stop, witch!'

'Stay out!' I said, knowing I was back to being Anantya and was a nishada no more. Wasting no time, I dug my boneblade into the girl's stomach, slashing it, letting my blood leak from boneblade into the incision. I directed Mehi-kulli, burning my blood, directing her to the girl, to drink up the thing that was boiling inside her. Someone screamed in terror. Mehi poured out, her mouth open and dark, her pendulous breasts danced as she stood on top of the bundled up Chiri and started to howl. She cowered, withered, bawled in pain as the kulli seeped into her.

'… trying to kill her …!'

'… witch!'

The voices came from the people around us. I ignored them.

'Come on,' I said to the girl. Chiri lay bundled up, screaming in pain.

'Bloodied balls of boars!' I stood still, my eyes half closed, concentrating on directing Mehi, which is why I felt rather than saw her glide towards me.

'Guards, please throw this shape-shifter out of my bungalow,' Saranyu said, her voice emotionless, calm. Two beefy hands, on either side of me, pulling me away. I struggled, wriggling in their grasp, my left hand still holding the boneblade.

'Don't! She will—' The guards pulled me away. 'What did you do to them, you bitch!' I screamed as they dragged me away. 'I will come back!'

'You're most welcome to do anything you want, shape-shifter,' she said, turning away. 'Baza, we have told you this before. The diseased are to be strictly kept away from the healthy stock. Heed us.'

'Yes, Goddess,' Baza replied, falling to her knees, 'but we apologize Goddess that we—'

'No!' I screamed. The boneblade clattered on the floor as the guards pulled me. Interrupted, the kulli pulled back forcibly into my body, making me gasp. As the guards dragged me, I helplessly looked back to where Chiri was, in pain, moaning, her body beginning loose its firm shape, her stomach bulging. She burst out, just as I was dragged, melting, becoming a pool of black.

We reached a pathway. Kulli in my blood, drank from me, sipping on the cocktail of my bones and bile. Without my blade, I couldn't do any magic, which meant a feast for her.

'W … wait,' I said, my head muddy, blood chugging. 'What is happening? I … I can help.'

'Why haven't we left the place?' Baza walked in, her face pinched with disapproval. 'Go!'

'What is the disease? I can help them Baza. I am a tantrik!' I said, my voice heavy with bile. She came close and pulled my hair hard. 'We are never to see our witch face again!' She whispered, her lips hard. Through my hazy, getting-Mehi-drunk-vision, I saw her face floating. Something crescent fell onto my lap. My boneblade.

'Help,' she whispered yanking my hair. 'We are captured with Barbareeka. We need help.'

Before I could react, she slapped me hard on the face, making my head rattle. She left with the guards, leaving me outside the gate.

'Listen,' I said calling to the driver and his friend I'd seen earlier. They came forward, worried, confused. 'Who … are …'

I gulped. Words came hard. I clutched his neck. 'Sorry … need … blood.'

'Aiiy!' cried the driver, as I slashed his neck, droplets of red falling on his white uniform and on the boneblade. I whispered the mantra, sending Mehi back. Blood rushed in a sudden roar to my head, clearing off the kulli.

'Sorry about that,' I said, gulping half a bottle of rakpiss, and splattering a few drops on his surprised neck. I dragged myself up, heading to my mobike and zooming off into the darkness before dawn.

Barbareeka. Now what was the rakshasa queen doing that the nishadas needed help with? This case had taken an interesting turn.

5

EVEN AT four in the morning, Bedardi Bar was packed. I nodded at Maiyya, the resident beggar sitting outside the bar, and squeezed through the small slit of a hole-in-the-wall of an old warehouse in Chandni Chowk.

The invisible anti-maya wall rippled, making my skin prickle. Ducking to avoid a pair of drunk and boisterous kravyads as they scurried across the ceiling towards the back room, I called out to Maaki, the giant spider who ran the bar. Usually it was dark and dingy but today, it had been done up with disco lights and balls, throwing sparkles of pulsating light all around the bar, even the dark corners. Drunken sups of all kinds gyrated on the floor, walls and ceiling, moving their hands, claws and flapping wings in a stupor and stomping feet, bellies, buttocks and whatnots on the floor.

The music was loud, the kind I knew Maaki hated. But it was something new that he wanted to try for the bar, to make it more approachable, which would of course destroy the place I knew and loved. Sigh. Where would one go after a night of solving a couple of gruesome murder crimes?

A dasyu, hanging upsidedown, fluttered its translucent wings at me from the far corner. It reminded me of a dasyu I loved but had lost, making me frown back at him.

'Howdy, A,' Maaki shouted over the loud music, his eight arms efficiently serving four different drinks to customers without him blinking any of his eyes. He sploshed a soma-on-the-rocks on the grime-topped bar and flicked his head, his bulb-like eyes staring at a bhuri, who was on top of the disco ball, licking it with its long tongue.

Maaki was the owner and bartender of Bedardi Bar. The flamboyant Joro, his equal-legged partner in this pub, glided by, giving me a quick smile, her eight limbs graceful, smoothly serving drinks to the customers. He pointed to the corner of the bar.

He had called me earlier about Ashwa's presence at the bar. I nodded, paid, gulped and started to make my way to the other side of the bar, a humongous task as I had to weave between a couple of boisterous rakshasas, a tall bloodgrass cudding chitro and a couple of lagins, mermaids who had brought along a mini pool so that they could sit and splash in it. A girl, a human one, stared at me, frozen with fear and stuck to the bar. She looked like it was her first time in Bedardi and I could understand, though I didn't have time to calm her. Fortunately, her date, a muscled kirata, came from behind and they started to chat. Recently I had seen much more dating between humans and other species than before. It was good that sups (and humans) were experimenting, but I wondered how long it would last. CAT had a tendency to go out and put restrictions on anything fun, anything they couldn't control about sups. All in the name of protection. It was complete hogwash. But then, when did anyone not buy in hogwash? Since Bedardi Bar was the only place in the city which allowed sups to be in their natural form and not hide themselves as humans, it was always busy, even though the bar was little more than a hole in the wall. Maaki made sure that no one tried to hide behind a human form by putting an anti-maya spell right at the doorway, which was the public entry. City tantriks kept away from it and hung out at Cups and Sorcerer, an upmarket, expensive pub somewhere in Greater Kailash.

Ashwa sat in a dark corner of the bar, his tall body crouched, face covered as usual. He was seven feet tall and even when sitting, his face came up to my shoulder.

'You went?' he whispered hoarsely, his eyes staring at a couple of kravyads on the ceiling, rolling their warm, fiery breaths into each other's mouths, their mating ritual, lost to the world.

'Yeah.'

'Is he dead?'

'Definitely skinned,' I squeezed by his side, pushing myself into the corner. 'Know anything about it?' I took a long gulp of my soma-on-the-rocks. 'He got a visitor, someone who knew him, who gave him some peacock meat to eat. You wouldn't know who that is?'

'Trouble, he is trouble,' he said, looking down into his glass of Smok Joint, which had a waft of orange smoke with a strong heady smell, emitting from it. He took a sniff. 'We all are. Death,' he took another sniff and then looked at me, his eyes glittering from inside his cowl, 'is the only solution.'

'Who "we"?' I screamed over the loud music. He looked down into the waft coming from his drink. A thought struck me. Though I called Ashwa a friend, I had never seen his face, never needed to. We had met at Bedardi and usually hung out on slow nights, drinking in silence. Our relationship had always been more about silence than conversation. Tonight however, I wondered if I knew him at all.

'You know how precious death is?' he asked, looking at the gyrating crowd around us. 'It's a nectar, a blessing, to die. To give up life, its memories, the *baggage*. To start afresh. You wouldn't understand, Anantya. You with your moment's breath, so full of life, wouldn't understand. Death begets life. The fear of death clutches at your heart' – he made a claw of his hand – 'so that blood flows faster, pumping through your veins, making you run, feel the wind in your hair … without it, there's nothing, *nothing*. There's nothing but a long, long lonely stretch of road. There's nothing but emptiness—'

The kravyad couple above us screeched, burst uncontrollable fireballs at each other.

'Dude, don't talk in freakish metaphors. What the hell happened to Guru B? How did you know—'

Maaki picked up a fire extinguisher and sprayed the kravyads.

'It doesn't matter!' said Ashwa, lifting his head to shine his eyes at me. 'We should all go! *Die!*'

'Who?'

'All of us. *All.* Our souls they're so threadbare, so torn, so tired. How can freedom from life be wrong for us? I don't want to wait anymore for death to choose me. Though I know that's the way, it doesn't seem right. What is my dharma, what's my duty? Can I never choose right? How can something that feels so right, so natural, so much like breathing again, like freedom, cause this pain?' He clutched my arm. His hands were stiff with sores of leprosy. Something crawled above us over the ceiling. 'It was a *mistake*. Leave this, Anantya. Go *live* your life. Forget Guru B or I ever were.'

'I would never—'

'A mistake you need to forget. Before death will make a fool of you as it did of me.'

'What the—'

'Why so grumpy!' cried a voice, interrupting us. It was the same kravyad who had been fighting a little earlier, her face flushed with the fiery drinks she'd had, clinging with her vacuum paws on the ceiling, upside down. She scooped and stretched and pulled Ashwa's cowl.

'Let's … *ugh*!'

'Devil!' she squeaked, falling onto the floor and scuttling away, screaming. I was busy staring at the man before me. Or, rather, at the ancient immortal before me.

I had seen Ashwa's face for the first time ever since I had met him. It had once been a beautiful, regal face, now however, it was marred, by sores and ulcers and remnants of a leprosy attack. His lips were full of sore wounds. No wonder I had never seen him eat anything at Bedardi. As if conscious of my stare, he scratched on a bandage on his forehead, which was wet with blood. A maggot fell out from behind the dressing and onto his nose. He flicked it away.

'Kali's shit! You …' I stopped, waiting for a word to come to me, '*you*?'

'Am unnatural, yes,' he answered, hurriedly putting his cape back on the head. He got up, to his seven feet of height. 'Which is why death is right. We are all evil creations who shouldn't exist.' He rushed towards the back entrance.

'Wait, Ashwa! Wait! I …' I tore through the crowd, running after him, squeezing through the crowd.

Ashwa's bulk filled the narrow passageway with darkness. Just at the exit, he turned, his eyes burning in the shadows of his cape and our eyes met. Mine full of regret, but his polished and hard with defiance. He walked away. I ran into someone.

'Anantya!' screamed a vinaat. It took me a split to realize it was Baal, the vinaat I'd slept with a night before. A single night in the city had changed him. He now wore danglers and studs and had a newfound swagger. I ducked, trying to chase Ashwa.

'I am so glad I caught you!' He grabbed me, kissing me on each of my cheek. If Maaki didn't have a no-magic rule, I would've cut off his snub of a nose for stopping me. 'I got a job! There's a Maut performance, do come.' He winked (yes, winked) at me, leered, and put something around my neck.

I pushed him, running out of the door, but Ashwa was already gone.

'Shit of a shatoot!' I cried aloud, stomping my feet at the darkness. Could Ashwa be him? Ashwathama, the immortal from the times of Mahabharata? But that would be a bit too bizarre, won't it, even for my life where I'd tried to save a baby elephant from a giant ikshugandha, a carnivorous plant in the jungles of Kerala. No, no. Why did I always choose trouble? So if Ashwa was Ashwathama, an immortal, was Guru B … He had been living for a long time and that collection of his seemed to have been built over centuries and not decades. And why would someone send pretas after immortals and how did Ashwa know of *that*? I threw my hands exasperatedly, slinking down alongside Maiyya and taking out a beedi, puffing morosely. The sky had turned dark indigo.

My home, a haunted haveli, lay just a few streets away from Bedardi Bar.

I took a shortcut – a thin, meandering lane with ramshackle buildings on both sides, so close together that their protruding balconies touched to make a canopy overhead. My phone had a couple of messages from Shukra, which swam in front of my eyes as I walked, trying to decipher what he meant by—

Wham. It was a wall, a wall where there should've been a road.

Through the haze of potent soma, I looked up and frowned. There was a wall in front of me at a place where there should have been nothing. No, I corrected myself, not a wall, a whole bloody house. A brand new, bright-red house, right in the middle of where the lane should be, high enough to block out the the sky above. Had I taken a wrong turn?

'Old age,' I muttered, getting up and turning away to where I had come from. I stopped and stared, at another bright-red house, turned again to where I had come from, and stared again. Then I rubbed my eyes. Yes, it was there all right. A red house, strikingly similar to the one I had just seen, had popped up behind me in the two seconds that I had taken to turn. There was just one difference. This one was done up with bright white balustrades that looked like ruffles on its first and second floor balconies.

'Um. Why are you here, houses?' I asked, politely and a bit

fuzzily. Must be the drinks. The bright red house with the frill windows looked at me, forlorn, before its door blasted open.

'We will be assisting you in a second,' a gust of a voice said, hitting me like a storm on my face. 'Please wait for our customer care representative.' I took out my boneblade and contemplated and then turned to look at the red house *without* the white frill windows, who was blocking my lane to home. I looked up to the balconies overhead. The red houses covered not only my way, but also converged above me, making a sort of a canopy beyond the balconies of the houses. I could try and say a mantra and see what the houses would do, but then frankly, I was curious, so I playfully bit the boneblade, waiting. It would get me killed someday, curiousity.

'So you like your job?' I asked to the house without the frills. Its door opened and flapped a couple of times.

'I take it that's a yes.'

Its door did the same thing again.

'Nice dawn, huh? Do they pay you guys well? Or you could be girls for all I know.'

The houses didn't respond, but someone else did.

'We thank you for waiting, Miss Anantya Tantrist,' said a shrill voice. An impossibly thin, tall man emerged from the door of the frilly house, wearing a black achkan. His face was sharp and angular with a long pointed nose.

'I am Chhoti Stratejee, principal secretary of the newly constructed Ministry of Miracles and Healing of Central Association of Tantriks.'

'And I am MBA Tantrist?' I giggled, managing a foul alcoholic burp. He glared at me. 'It's your real name, isn't it?'

'I would like to request you to accompany us to fill in a questionnaire in order to leverage your experiences.'

'What kind of questionnaire?'

'This questionnaire will allow us to leverage your experiences of a certain visit to a certain art gallery earlier tonight. As you can probably conjecture, this market research is important for us to build a strategic policy that benefits and affects lives of maximum races in the country.'

'I have no idea what you just said.'

'It's essential that you accompany us at this point, miss, to understand our strategic plan.' He folded his hands, standing with a polite smile, holding a thin, long stick which had a spiral shaped design on top.

'You cannot legally arrest me.'

'Unfortunately, that fact is factually correct, Miss Anantya. But there has been a paradigm shift so that fact, in fact, might not be able to play a significant role in being exercised. There is an incapability, I share with you, though it can be restructured depending on your response to our request to fill in the said questionnaire.'

'What response?'

'As I said, when our strategic plan can be possibly affected by the actions of certain individuals or corporations, under the aegis of Central Association of Tantriks, we are allowed to apprehend said individuals or corporations—'

'Dude, can you talk in a language that normal people understand?'

'—to fill in the said questionnaire.'

'Wha—' I tried to say. Stopped, took a deep breath and tried again. 'What is it you're arresting me for?'

He looked at me, looked at the house behind me, smiled. 'As we mentioned before, we at the Miracles and Healing Department would like to invite you to our hospice to fill in a questionnaire for intelligent primary research over said matter for the said strategy. Please allow us to escort you to our premises, without any attempt to escape, raising alarm or usage of weapons.'

'I politely but firmly refuse to go,' I said, mirroring his polite smile, that tore my lips apart and firmly suppressing the rather primitive urge to smash and flatten his head with my bare hands.

'We regret that we have no choice but to apprehend you in that event with force, for the said questionnaire.'

'Allow *me*,' I answered, 'to use force against your mind-blowingly moronic self.' I pointed my boneblade. He didn't move or react. Instead, he looked at me calmly, smiling, his eyes dead.

'Please comply.'

'I would rather smell yaksha fart,' I answered, starting to mutter the Visphota mantra which had the power of a mine blaster and could shatter walls and hillocks to pieces with a single utterance. Or at least that's how it sounded in my drunken head.

'Apprehend, please,' said Stratejee, like he was asking for a glass of water. There was a thunder. The houses turned out to be much faster that I would have given them credit for. Before I could even begin to say the mantra, they rose, gaining height, restructuring and transforming in front of my eyes. The door turned into a small head on a massive block of a body, which was at least three-storey high. Their arms hung on their sides, touching the ground, their legs, were rock solid, short and stout. The second red house, with the white frills, I discovered was a female, wearing a tutu kind of a frock in white. They were of massive height, with stone-like skin and resistant to any kind of tantric mantra, which is why I bet the Tazaak had been hiring them. They thundered together, both lunging from each side in my direction, with all the intention of daityas who had been forced to be stationary houses and now had the freedom to move about and grab things with their massive hands or, if not, smash them into pieces. This was no time for magic. I ducked and ran to save myself from becoming minced meat.

6

UNLIKE WHAT most myths and stories would have you believe, daityas or trolls, as people have recently come to call them, are not slow.

They are huge, they are solid like granite hillocks and yes, they have a stony brain the size of a pigeon, but they do not move slowly. In fact they are quite fast when ordered to do something, which is why they make such freakishly brilliant guards. The two of them lunged towards me and I had but just a split of a second before I would be turned into mush. I dug out the Vedara from my satchel and ran, rubbing it on my palms as their hands thundered on either side of me.

They were fast, but Dhuma had made me practice with snow leopards in the Himalayas, who were much faster. I ducked one's arm, skidded behind the other's legs and the ogres crashed into one another, confused, blinking their square eyes. Just as the redbrick daitya was about to catch me with his thumb and index finger, I lunged, grabbing hold of the female daitya's white tutu dress.

Crash!

His fist thundered down on the road, making a cavity in it. Vedara the gum I'd rubbed on my palms, created a vacuum for me, allowing me to climb up the daitya's body with a lizard-like, gravity-defying grip. I swung again, in time to escape the redbrick daitya's finger as he tried to flick me like a fly, and climbed onto the female daitya's tutu. And got on the inside of it, between the white tutu and her rock-hard skin. Then I started to crawl, run, hide, like a rat who was being chased by two elephants, which was what I would be like. I ran and ran, helter skelter, up and down and sideways on the daitya's stomach.

The daitya danced, tickled, laughing out loud, her stomping footsteps making thunderous noises in the tiny street, trying to fish me out of her tutu. She waved her hand, houses on either side crashing down. I was fast, but I didn't have much time. Even if she managed to touch me with her finger, my head would be smashed.

'Indumati, I request you to prevent your dancing,' Stratejee said softly.

'But, it … it tickles,' said Indumati, stopping at the order, even though I still ran on her mountain of a body. She trembled as it tickled, feeling the itch to scratch. Taking my que, I stopped too, peeping out of her tutu. Stratejee stood in front, a few feet away, covered in dust. A couple of houses had turned to rubble while Indumati had been dancing.

Stratejee walked up to Indumati and touched her toenail with his thin staff.

'If you ask them to attack me, I will tickle them again,' I threatened, making a paw of my hand and showing it to him taking short, sharp breaths in order to avoid the odour that came off the daitya. 'And next time you take them anywhere, ask them to have a bath first. It can be quite lethal—'

Fisss. Something leaked from Indumati's skin, a dense mist, with a heavy mix of fart and sweat. I gasped trying not to breathe, gasped again. Losing my grip, I fell through her tutu onto the concrete floor. Stratejee towered above me, staff in hand, smiling politely.

'Miss Tantrist, we request you to come to our ministry's new hospice to fill in a questionnaire.'

I stared at him, trying to keep my eyes open against the onslaught of a giggly kind of sleepiness.

'We are glad you agree with us.'

'Fuck the fishes, that's a hospital?' I asked, giggling at a guard standing stiff in front of the wrought iron gate, who glared back. The effects of whatever drug Indumati's skin had doled on me, made me laugh like a teenager on charak.

Stratejee ushered me in. The daityas must have managed to slink away at some point. I wondered how Stratejee here had convinced those two to do his dirty work in the city. Daityas were notoriously wary of concentrated populations, preferring remote mountains.

Manu Manava Maharaj Maharishi (Miracle Baba for short) had been gifted a newly built edifice of bad architecture in the protected forest area of Qutub institutional area by the Delhi Government. The hospital was called Manu Manava Maharaj Maharishi's Miracle and Medical Facility (6M Hospital for short). It was a collection of buildings of various sizes and shapes, some shaped like a dome, with Islamic-inspired carving, some with tall columns and badly shaped winged horses on top of them. As I entered, my hand itched reminding me it was bare. My boneblade and satchel had been confiscated by Mr Stratejee who had assured me that they would be returned after I filled in the 'said questionnaire'. I wanted to take said questionnaire and stuff it with a pen and other sharper things up his tight ass, while I giggled.

'Long life is your right', claimed one banner. *'Miracles do happen. Get yours here'*, said another.

The entrance was followed by an inverted U-shaped gate covered with banners and garish colours of parrot green, orange and reds and yellows. From inside it, a forty-foot huge cutout of Miracle Baba smiled while sitting cross legged, his right hand raised in blessing like goddess Laxmi. On one side of the gate was an entrance to one of the buildings, this one inspired by Japanese architecture. A long queue of people stood there while, on the other side, with 'exit' on its door, a few came out, in groups, chatting, conversing.

'It's Friday. Maharaj performs free treatments for the betterment of society on Fridays.'

'Ah. Free for a day, paid for the rest of the week,' I said, eyeing the line which had a mix of people – some in rags and others in high heels and designer outfits. I followed Stratejee away from the crowd, to the back entrance of the Japanese building. We entered from a side entrance into a general ward, a long open, high-ceilinged space. Patients lay on either side, on low-lying beds, with family members fussing over them. Half a hall later, was the general sitting space, segregated from the patients, where people sat cross-legged on the floor, singing songs with more enthusiasm than talent.

At the far end, from the crowd and then the line of patients sat Manu Manava Maharaj Maharishi, cross-legged on a golden seat, his eyes closed. His right hand stuck to his body, in paralyses. His left, lay on the forehead of a person who lay in front of him. Manu's lips moved. The body trembled. The chants rose echoing into a din.

'Miracle!'

'Miracle Baba *ki jai ho*!'

'Long live Miracle Baba!'

Manu Manava slowly opened his eyes, saw us standing in the middle of the aisle and flicked his hand. Stratejee took me by my elbow and through another door on the opposite side of the dorm. It was an office, with a low, long desk on one side with a pile of files, stationary and other paraphernalia and a threadbare carpet. Sunlight streamed in through a tall window, making an elongated patch.

'Miss Anantya, we at the 6M Hospice thank you for taking your precious time out with a counter offer of filling in our questionnaire,' started Stratejee, handing in a thick sheaf of papers, almost the size of a thesis. I flipped through, unbelieving.

'That's your questionnaire? This is at least a hundred pages long!'

'This is just the disclaimer, Miss Anantya. Ministry policy. The questionnaire will follow.'

'What do you want from people here? Slavery for the rest of their incarnated lives? No way in Patala's burning bum am I signing this.'

'It's just policy, Miss Anantya. Regularized papers that everyone who enters the premises of the hospital has to sign.'

My lips pressed together. I crossed my arms and tapped my right food. Frankly, it was curiosity that had kept me here for this long.

'Waste of paper,' I muttered, crossing my arms. 'Just ask whatever it is you want to know and let me get the hell out of your policy paranoia!'

'But how can I give you the questionnaire without you signing the disclaimer form? It's simply ministry regulations—'

The door opened, a warm breeze entered and Stratejee went silent. Manu Manava dragged his half paralysed body in, the eye on his normal side of the face, focused on us.

'Maharaj!' Stratejee bent down and kissed his feet. I sat in the corner, wishing I had a beedi. The bugger had taken even that from me.

'Stratejee, get some tea for our guest and maybe a beedi. She looks famished and tired.'

Stratejee slunk away, leaving the two of us alone.

'Stratejee has been my assistant for years, but he read up a few books on management before we started our ministry and has never been the same,' Manu said. His voice was calm, soft with a whisper of comfort. 'Thank you for coming, though I know you were forced to. I have heard of your name in Delhi and your penchant for causing trouble. And I've also heard that you're becoming really interested in what's happening to the nishadas owned by a certain woman called Saranyu.'

'How did you find out about that?'

'I know you were there at the art gallery, I know you tried to save Chiri, but even with your tantrik prowess, I don't think you could have. What they suffer from is a disease, not a natural one, but an ambition-induced one.'

'Whose ambition?'

'The ones who own them. They want to use the tribal creatures for an ugly purpose. They don't see them as living beings with hearts, but things to be used for power. It's a shame—'

'Maharaj!' The door flew open and Stratejee ran inside. 'You're needed! That boy from Banaras!'

Manu stood up and raced after Stratejee, waving me to follow.

Stratejee led us to the back of the two buildings and into a patch of forestland. We stopped after a few minutes at an old warehouse with a broken door. Something within sounded like a dog being gutted.

With a speed I wouldn't have thought possible for a half-paralysed person, Manu zoomed in stopping in front of a man, old burnt scars on his body, who lay thrashing on the floor, wailing, his eyes rolling, his hands and feet whipping uncontrollably.

'Ratan, have you given him the blood?' Manu asked a nurse, who was standing nearby, his voice calm.

'Yes, Maharaj. He has not stabilized.'

'Transfusion then!'

'But it's been just been a week.'

'Do it.' He struggled up, as Ratan and another nurse took hold of the man, putting him on a low bed and administering blood through an intravenous syringe.

'This is our old facility, where we started before we got too famous,' he said, seeing me look around. The warehouse had a long, railway-platform feel to it, high airy roof with small ledges halfway up, which were accessible by stairs. Eyes peeped at us from every corner, about forty or fifty pairs of them. 'Now we treat non-humans here.'

The wailing man fell silent as the blood flowed in. Manu walked towards the other end of the building, where there was a small shrine to Lord Dhanwantari, god of Ayurvedic medicine.

'Who is he?' I asked, eyeing the patient.

'An injured bird we found with twelve others of his flock in Banaras a few weeks ago. Injured with something we've not been able to diagnose till now. They've been abused, all of them. Cruelly. When Lord Dhanwantari came to me in my dreams and told me my purpose, I thought I could heal this pain, this suffering! But healers are just a handful of sand in an ocean of cruelty.' He crouched, touching his forehead to the ground in front of the shrine.

'You're the Kubja prince aren't you? Saranyu's your mother?' He turned, eyed me for a moment and nodded.

'So this whole nishada issue is a territorial tussle between a mother and son who can't decide who should get the slaves?'

'No one owns them!' Manu said, inching up, his warm, soft voice acquiring an edge, his palm up. 'They're not *things*! They're people! Living beings! I—' He stopped himself, taking a moment, a deep breath, bringing his right arm down. 'I am sorry, Anantya. I just … I've seen those poor creatures go through so much, for far too long.'

'Why didn't you do anything?'

'I … I guess I … failed them. I couldn't act against the woman who had given birth to me. When Lord Dhanwantari came into my dreams and gave me the power to heal it was a blessing. I had the power … to heal creatures, their misery, their pain, their sadness. But, I … I couldn't help my own. I couldn't help the nishadas. How can you stand up against your own mother? That's my biggest failure! Today, I heal using the Lord's knowledge of herbs and nature and potions, but people think it's a miracle. Even the government and the Tantrik Association think I'm performing miracles. They put me on a pedestal, make me a god, call me Miracle Baba, sing bhajans for me, but it means nothing. Nothing! This power is not mine. It's Lord Dhanwantari. I am just the medium for it. And I failed to use it for my *own* people. They are suffering, Anantya! And I can't do anything about it.'

'I … Why not act now? Stand up against her.'

'No, no … I can't, not openly. I am sorry. I just … please help *them*, Anantya. I have already filed for their custody in the Pashu Department, and I should get their ownership in a few days. But it will be too late by then. They're being killed *now*! Please, save those poor creatures from the evil of my mother. Just meet them, see that they're safe!'

'You know you're asking me to do something illegal.'

'Yes.' Manu looked at me, his eyes honest and clear, the paralyzed side of his face twitching. 'I will compensate you for this.' He waited, as I bit my lip, undecided. But only for a split second.

'I will do it.' Shakti's ass. I was getting into trouble. It felt good though.

'Thank you!' The right side of the face lit up, lips twisting grotesquely. 'Come!'

We walked back to the entrance of the old facility, the eyes from the ledge on us. A man bent down to touch Manu's feet. Manu held him up by his shoulder, bringing him up.

'You know those thirteen unfortunate boys I'd been talking about, he's one of them. Poor thing, they took his tongue out.'

I stared, and gulped and then stared again. There was something familiar about those eyes, those eyes that had once been like clear pools of sky. The light blue eyes, which I knew darkened when they felt love.

'Neel?' I whispered, not ready to believe it. The eyes remained blank, icy blue, without feeling, without recognizing. I didn't understand. I rubbed my eyes, shook my head. 'But, but you were dead. You …'

'You know this person?' asked Manu.

'But … I saw you *dead* … how can it be?'

Neel kept on looking at me, mute. I walked to him, took a deep breath, and slapped him across his face, hard enough to make him stagger. 'What in Naraka's ass are you doing here?'

'She's gone off her topper!' cried Ratan.

'Seven years, Neel,' I screamed, 'Seven bloody fucking years and you couldn't bloody tell me you were *alive*? Give me a call? Let me know? What the fuck am I, an idiot grieving and feeling guilty for having let you *die*?'

'Umm, Anantya,' someone tried to say but I wasn't willing to listen.

'Where were you? In hell, stuck with Yamaraj? In heaven, flirting with apsaras?' I shook him, shaking with anger, 'Where were you Neel that you couldn't even give me a fucking call that you were fucking alive? Tell me!'

'Umm Anantya, he cannot tell you.'

'Shut up!' I turned furiously, to look at Stratejee, who was distracting me.

'Anantya,' said Manu from behind, his voice gentle, 'he can't talk.'

'Why can't he?' I screamed.

'You see, he has no tongue. Show her, Neel, show her your tongue.' He gently pried Neel's mouth open. A cavity lay there, a dark cavity with yellowed teeth and no tongue.

'Fuck my ass to Swarga!' I exclaimed. 'Where did you find him?' I turned and grabbed Manu by his neck. There were a few gasps and angry shouts and movements, but I didn't move. 'What happened to him? Tell me or I'll burn everything down!'

Manu looked deep into my eyes, calm. 'I've already told you. We found him with twelve others in Banaras. Only Lord Dhanwantri knows what they've gone through. We are trying to treat them here.'

My hands dropped, as I slumped down onto the floor, trying hard not to cry.

'I want to take him home. My … home.'

'That's simply not possible!' cried Stratejee. 'He … he cannot be spared, Maharaj, for how will we continue the life support?'

'What life support?' I looked up.

'Neel has faced a trauma in the past causing stress to his heart. He needs blood transfusion every week,' said Stratejee. 'That's the only way we can ensure that his heart continues to beat.'

'My dear secretary, what your MBA didn't teach you was that mental health is far more beneficial than physical one. Maybe this lady can heal our grieving stranger in ways we cannot fathom and so help our aim. Let him be taken.'

Manu looked at me with his childlike eyes and brought his hand in front, expectantly, palms up. I placed my hand in his. They were soft, like a baby's. 'I can see you love him. Maybe that's a cure. Take this potion. A single drop when he has the fits, which he will every now and then. Also, try sexual intercourse, it's known to help,' he said.

For the first time in many years, though there was no reason for it, I blushed like a newly blooded thirteen-year-old. And frankly, it wasn't so bad.

7

IT WAS just before dawn. The night's rituals had ended and all the tantriks slept. The ashram was at its quietest. She peeped through her room, making sure no one heard her and stepped out, slipping through a small alley, a shortcut she knew that connected the women's quarter to the main courtyard. He was there, waiting, sitting under the peepal tree, his monsoon eyes staring into nothingness.

'Neel,' she whispered, running to him, forgetting caution in her hurry. 'Neel!'

He kissed her wet cheeks. She didn't know they had been wet, when had she started to cry? She couldn't imagine life without him. She couldn't imagine herself without him. He held her tightly, smoothing his hand over her hair. Her shoulder tickled as she rested it on his hairy chest. She looked up and saw his eyes soften into a deep blue of desire.

'I am ready,' she said. 'Let's do the ritual.'

'No, my darling,' he answered, softly, kindly with a feather kiss on her cheek. 'It's not a ritual. It's love. We make love. Let's do this right. Let's wait for your friend to come. Let's leave from here and unite.'

'I can't wait any longer. I want you!' I breathed in his sweat, the heady odour that came from his sweat, and my heart hammered, wanting to tear his dhoti, wanting him then and there.

'You will have me always, silly,' he answered, gently kissing her burning forehead. And so they waited. They waited for her best friend to come, to find them and take them to the safe place.

Only he never did. Instead her father came, he came with an army of others. He forced them apart. She cried, and begged and shook and wailed but nothing stopped them. Neel looked at her with his blue, blue eyes. 'Goodbye, my sweet,' he whispered as they led him away into the rising sun.

'Neel! Neel!' she shouted, but they held her, their eyes were pinpricks of fury. 'Neeeeeel!'

My eyes opened. Blue eyes stared down at me. The lovely face I remember, scarred now, emptied of everything. Neel leaned on top, so close that I could see the emptiness, the void in his cold eyes. His expression was empty too, not full of love as I remembered, not soft, but hard, hardened by years of who knew what? I touched his scarred face gently, tears filling my eyes.

'What happened, my love,' I asked gently, 'What happened to you?' He looked, blinked, stared and turned, moving to go sit on the couch, in front of the television, not touching the remote, staring at the screen. Zaazee wasn't here, off to hunt rats or peddle potions. The television was switched off. But that didn't bore Neel. He stared, still, calmly looking at the telly screen. I had to do something.

'Here,' I said, switching the television on and handing him the remote. Neel blinked, the only sign he gave that he'd noticed, staring at the gyrating figures of a Bollywood item girl. I waited and when he didn't touch it, changed the channel. The hateful face of Rishi Narahara came on, screaming in a panel defending the requirement to change ancient tantrik laws to suit modern cities. Changing it back to the girl in throes, I headed to the kitchen to put on a masala tea, bringing it back in two cups. Neel held the cup I gave him with both his hands, like a child, staring at the television, his lips parted slightly. The afternoon sun showered from above us, filtered by the broken shaft in the ceiling. I studied him, his scarred face and arms. The way his sharp nose was dented as if wounded in battle. The Neel I'd known was a soft-spoken, wise person. This one looked like he had been fused together with broken bits. But perhaps he would say the same about me, if only he could recognize me.

'Seven years,' I whispered more to myself than to him, tasting the years. It felt like a vast emptiness. I took his cold hand in mine, bringing it to my lips to kiss it softly, crinkling my nose. He reeked of things that he had no business being in. I pulled him up, took off his dirtied shirt and pants, till he was naked.

'Great. The first time I see you naked is when you're all covered in shit,' I muttered, taking him like a lonesome child into the bathroom. Making him sit on a stool there, I washed him, scrubbing him, each part of him, thoroughly, wondering what my life would've been like if I had run away with him, if our plans had succeeded. Wondering if this was what I would be doing for the rest of my life now, taking care of him, having his blue-eyed kids. And if it would be so bad.

My phone rang, interrupting the rather prolonged bath. Forcing his clothes onto him, I called Madhu back, updating him on my meeting with Manu Manava, leaving out the bit about the blue-eyed boy. That was my business.

'You trust him?' Madhu asked.

'No, but I definitely don't trust his mother. That Saranyu woman looked like trouble,' I answered, getting up to find a few biscuits to grub on. 'Those girls need to be somewhere safe.'

'Dr Bodhgaya has figured an anti-dote to the virus,' answered Madhu, 'but without her permission, we'll have to keep it—'

'Unofficial. I know. It's best you don't get involved. Your uncle—'

'Grrhat? He won't help—'

'—his dying mother if it wasn't for money. But he owes me a big one, so he will.'

'I wish I could come but I'm banned from Lavana.'

'Yeah, half-rakshasa bastard that you are. Don't worry, I've got a plan.'

place?' I shifted closer to Stratejee. His shadowsword danced, ecstatic, weaving the embryo and closing it.

'No creature can come here in his physical form,' said Stratejee, who stood on the same spot. 'Nothing alive, only dead. You foolishly expired to come here.'

'But that's the thing,' I said, reaching for Stratejee's shadowsword and grasping it. It fumed, flickering. I pulled back the shadowsword and jumped on top of him. Moving like a shadow, I plunged it into Stratejee's face.

'I am not quite dead. Yet. So you see, I can kill,' I said twisting the shadowsword in his neck. I took the sword out and pierced the other head too – Bodhgaya's head, just to be safe. The nagamani fell, clattering on the floor. A black wisp escaped the broken skulls. One rose, the other zoomed at me, screaming in silent fury.

'That,' whispered Bhairava, 'was not a good idea.' He flicked a blackened hand, wielding a shadow staff and sent an army of pretas my way. As the pretas attacked from all direction, I evaded, slashing them to pieces with the sharper edge of Stratejee's shadowsword. It went through them like butter.

I twirled, slashing and cutting and gashing and slitting the wisps that attacked me. The shadowsword proved to be worth it but there were too many of them, biting and pinching and eating and slicing. They fed on bits of my prana since there was no blood or body here. 'Who will help you here now, Bhairava?' I cried. The pretas wound around me – tighter and tighter such that I couldn't use my hands or legs for anything – nipping on the edges of my shadow and soul.

'You skull cup of stupidity. You missed your only chance to get your lover back!' he zoomed up into the centre of the cavern and then fell down. 'You want to see who will help me? Here! See!'

Everything twisted and churned and emptied. In the darkness was a stage made of crumpled pieces of human bodies.

On it stood, naked and beautiful, as I first remembered him – not as the wraith-like creature I had last encountered – Neel, my Neel, his eyes blue like diamonds. His smile warm and innocent. His hair wavy.

'Anantya? he said, running towards me. '*Is it really you I ... What are we doing here? I don't remember.*'

I struggled and raged against the pretas who bound me, their hold tightening, my heart, oh my heart aching like the bones of an old man, tears rolling down my cheeks.

A laugh rumbled in the womb.

'Don't give in to him, Neel! Don't let him control you. Fight!'

'Soppy and sad. Like a loud TV drama,' Neel sneered, his voice changing. 'Or,' the voice echoed in my shadow ears. 'If you'd thought about it a bit more, you could've gotten *her*.' As if on a remote switch, the person shimmered and changed, turning into a brown skinned woman, her hair wavy and falling till her buttocks. Her eyes black with flecks of smoke.

'Mama?' I whispered. A cruel laughter filled my blood. 'Dear daughter, I'm dead. Or maybe not,' she mouthed. 'Do you even care?' She walked towards me, tiptoeing around as I struggled with the pretas.

She slapped me on my face. 'Do you?' She pounced on top of me, her mouth opening wide. Dark smoke released from it, a gaping hole of nothingness and fear. I screamed, horror and dread and anguish dancing together in a macabre rave.

'No,' I said, but no words came out. She laughed, a maniacal laugh, her face changing, flickering, to Neel and then to her, her eyes growing bigger and then leaking. I felt weak, weepy and things I had not felt in a long long time.

'You're a mere puppet to my power, Anantya Tantrist.'

I stretched, screaming or whispering. *It's not her, it's not her.*

Prana leaked feeding the hungry shapes. I swatted, weakly, as a wounded deer, trying to keep the jackals at bay. It was pretty in a way, the darkness that swirled down, like stars with their lights off. 'My little swirls of darkness will feed on you till there's nothing. Not even bones. No one to remember you by,' the darkness whispered. *It's not her.*

How the fuck does he know her? How much does he know about me? Collecting the remainder of my prana I screamed, struggled, swatting, and crawling. My hand touched the stone, the nagamani. I grabbed it and pushed it into the throbbing embryo. With a thunder of needles, the embryo uncurdled, releasing its captives like an unwanted abortion. The immortals fell, on the floor made of bones, splashing and spreading. The unexpected smell of flesh and blood brought in the pretas like a swarm, biting and screeching, eating their flesh. The pretas flew away, distracted, howling and wheezing, excited, for they could feed on something more real than mere shadow.

'No! Not there! Her!' The scream echoed all around, making the womb tremble with fear. 'That's the thing with minions,' I said, getting up and grabbing the shadowsword from the floor and slashing in through a few pretas around me. 'They never really do what you want them to.' I headed to the embryo and slashed it off.

'Save yourselves, you all,' I cried, running to the far end of the cavern and trying to pull a skull from it. My hands went through the skull, unable to touch it. Shit. The womb throbbed and turned, fear alive in everyone.

'Anantya!' Neel stood a few feet away, his form wavering. 'I will help. Don't leave me with him. Set me free!'

'Shh. It's okay,' I turned to him, kissing him lightly on his trembling lips. 'I promise I'll free you, Neel.' Tears of shadows streamed down my eyes, blurring everything. I kissed his brow. The first, then the other. Then I took my shadowsword to his neck and slashed it. 'Goodbye sweets,' I whispered in his shadow of an ear. 'Go, rip the sky up.'

23

A CHINK. A chink is all it takes for the storm to enter. And what are spirits if not whispers of rain and hail and snow? Neel's soul, his spirit, freed from what bound him, soared, soared into the sky, through the womb, leaving a miniscule rip in that enclosed space. A teeny weeny slash. Enough for the beings of Naraka to enter. And so the womb thundered and screamed. I ran back to the immortals as gushes of hungry pretas and betalas and spirits entered, ripping the fabric of the womb, invading. Bhairava screamed in fury, but his voice drowned in the gush of the broken dam.

'If you live, I will get you,' his shadow whispered, sending his army of pretas towards me. The fabric of the womb unravelled further, falling apart. Beings of darkness hurled down towards us, filling in the space as air fills vaccum.

'Someday we'll meet you shit of an ass,' I said, moving, gliding, slashing on the way. 'Someday!' The skull wall crumbled, scattering with a thunder like autumn leaves. In puffs of smoke and screams the spirits that had been trapped escaped, their fury directed towards the shadow of the tantrik.

'Get up!' I cried to Ashwa, shaking him. I also shook the others—Hanuman, Guru B, Parashurama, the twins, Saranyu, Avvaiyar, Markandeya and Vasuki. 'Find the mani, save us!' Skinless, they were raw and bleeding, the smell attracting the pretas and bhutas. I pounced, panther like onto the pretas, slashing and ripping and wounding in all directions.

'I don't want to live!' cried Ashwa. Turning I slapped his raw face.

'You self-absorbed mopping imbecile immortal!' My hand slipped through him like a shadow. 'If you want to die, can we figure a more efficient way than killing humankind with it too? Find the nagamani!' Slash, rip, wound. The pretas ate from the rest of the immortals, beginning to take them away. They were too weak to fight back.

'Avvaiyar with diamonds in the sky!' cried Parashurama, holding up the nagamani.

'Para! Give the mani to Ashwa!' I shouted. Slash, rip, snip.

'The shine is mine!' he ran and jumped as Ashwathama tried to grab it. I pounced on him. He punched me. The womb began to disintegrate and scatter as hungry bhutas and pretas from Naraka leaked in, like ink. I grabbed his dreadlocks and pulled him, snatching the mani. 'Mine!'

'You silly poetic poop!' I screamed as the ground shook. The womb fell apart, undone at its seams.

'Get us out of here!' I cried, giving the mani to Ashwa. The ten immortals held each other, grabbing hold of me too. The floor under us thundered as we shortened and expanded. My stomach shifted and soared. The mani expanded, like a white bubble and became a balloon, expanding till it filled all of us inside it. I closed my eyes, tired, floating, falling down or maybe flying up, and tumbling through the chaos that ensued. It fell with a hard tug. I gasped, unable to breath, unable to see or hear or feel, thrashing panicking in a dark dungeon of a thing. My wrists burned and thrashed as I lost consciousness.

'I will kill her!' screamed a voice, a while later, piercing through my darkness.

I opened my eyes. I was on a floor in the room. My hands had been bandaged. A gust of light, sprinkled with dust filtered in through a slit of a window. Above me, a skinless ugly face loomed, twisted in anger and hatred, held by two others, equally skinless. I got up, reeled, bit my lip and struggled.

'Glad … you're … feeling better … Saranyu,' I managed to say, my hand trying to locate the vial of rakpiss on my neck. Missing.

'*Rakpiss* …' A cool thing poured on my wrists, stopping the burning. Someone opened my eyes a bit.

'Das, Nas! Take her, paint her!'

'No one but Maut will take her, Saranyu.' Hanumanji's calm voice. 'Here.' A skeletal face loomed in front of my face. 'This belongs to you.' I nodded, still not sure I could speak as I took a thirsty swig of rakpiss and lay back, staring at the ceiling with its paint peeling off. The House of Horrors was certainly not meant to be seen in light. During the day, it just looked like an old unkempt room.

'A kindness you showed us, by bringing us out,' said Avvaiyar, shuffling on her toes. 'If there's anything I can do …?'

'Get me a beedi?' I said, getting up and walking outside. For suddenly, I wanted to feel cold air on my skin.

Cold moonlight slanted through the trees, dappling the funeral pyre. The fire roared high, burning yellow and orange, burning the corpse of a person with blue, blue eyes. The immortals, worshippers of Maut, danced around it, each in their own style. Parashurama had his damru and hit it vigorously.

Hanumanji hopped and rotated on a single foot, Meera jiggled, Markandeya banged his head, Ashwa moved sombrely, almost in a trance, Avvaiyar moved her head side to side. They all wore skins of the dead, human skins, complete with faces and hands and nails. They all sang, hummed an ancient tune together, the ode to Maut, heavy and haunting. I lit a beedi off the pyre, nodded to it once and turned away, ignoring the way my legs shook as I walked. *Walk away, quickly, before you sink to the ground.*

He listened in silently, interrupting me a couple of times.

'Hope it works. I'll deal with Wizam. He's giving me a hard time for the case transfer still, telling Nandan again and again that he's the one who busted the prostitution ring.'

'And? You would rather *you* get that credit?'

We fixed up a time over a guffaw and disconnected. I walked back into the courtyard to find an empty couch.

'Neel!' I cried and turned, looking around, running from one corner of the haveli to the other. The main door was still locked and he wasn't behind the stash of broken furniture at the other side. He wasn't in the rasayana lab too, or in the bedroom, or the kitchen. 'Neel!'

'Hai, hai! Djinn! Djinn!' Nawab Sahib floated down, panicked, as out of breath as ghosts can be, running through me in his hurry to get away.

'Fuck a farishta!' I cried to him, grabbing my boneblade and running up the broken staircase two at a time. I was ready to murder Nawab Sahib's ghost all over again except he stood in a corner, looking rather confused. Neel lay flat on his back, on the dusty corridor, thrashing like a fish out of water. Turning the cap on the vial around my neck and grabbing him by the shoulders, I put a drop of rakpiss into his mouth. His lips trembled and he gulped, continuing his epileptic journey.

'*Hai, hai! Djinn hai ye! Hai, Hai!*'

'Stop dancing, you ancient dud! He's not a djinn!'

'*Aiiy! Aiiy! Djinn! Djinn! Aaaii!*' Nawab's voice rang in the house as I scampered back and upturned my satchel, spilling its contents and grabbing the potion that Manu Manava had given me. I dashed back, held Neel down, and put a drop on his lips. He trembled, continuing to thrash, but stopped a few seconds later. I sat back, panting.

'Djinn! Djinn!' cried Nawab from whichever corner he was sulking in. I pulled up Neel and took him down, making him sit on the couch again and sinking into it beside him. He was

calm again, staring at the television as if his sudden attack hadn't happened. Not taking my eyes off him, I started to put in things back into my satchel. I picked up a card, remembering Baal who'd given it to me the night before, when I was trying to chase Ashwa. What had he said? Something that was quite important. Maut. It was an invite to a heavy metal performance, with a group of teenagers dressed with peircings and rings in their noses and eyebrows, and Shakti knew where else, and called themselves Maut. One of them, a girl, had her tongue out, showing a stud inside. Their hair were spiky and their black leather costumes, full of studs. I let it flutter onto the ground and then stopped and stared. Something flashed before my eyes, making me pick up the invite again and look at it.

'Bali's burnt balls,' I exclaimed, staring at the boy who held a mike to his face, screaming into it. He was dressed like the others, in a studded, black leather costume with kohled eyes and gelled, spiky hair. He wore a ganji and had a tattoo of a fish in a fish in a circle on his chest. Yup, he was the same boy, the boy I'd helped pick up corpses at Guru B's library. The boy who was supposedly a corpse collector and a … heavy metal bassist? I looked at the watch, looked at the now calm Neel staring at the telly. I had time before I met Grrhat. Quickly packing my satchel, I checked my boneblade, septifocals, locket and rings. Dragging Neel up, I got out, kick-started my motorbike and was off in the evening light, with him sitting behind me.

The last rays of the sun tore through the evening sky sinking desperately. An army of teenagers walked towards the amphitheatre. They all wore black t-shirts and had piercings, their favourite metal group frowning on their proud chests as they walked, trotted, dashed to the amphitheatre, their heart one with the loud thumps of music that shook the road in Pragati Maidan.

A couple ahead stopped to take a break from the long walk, about a kilometre long, to kiss each other on the lips, ignoring the friendly jeers of their friends. Their jokes were carefree, their smiles innocent and my heart twisted as I dragged a silent Neel. We had never been given a chance to do this – have fun, scream at the world, think we were kings and queens. At seventeen, at the age when I should have been doing stupid things like getting drunk, experimenting with drugs, kissing boyfriends and attending rock concerts, I had been learning vajroli, the art of sexual reunions, of tapping into shakti, to become a vessel of shakti for my patron, the man who would rape me to tap into my power. And Neel? He had been confused, convinced that tantrism was not something he wanted to follow, stepping towards protest a bit closer each day.

I shook my head to scatter those memories. I couldn't change the past, but I could definitely try and give Neel a better future. And I would, I thought turning to see Neel, his expression dead, walking like someone under a spell.

Hamsadhawani amphitheatre was a semi-circular space with planks of stone steps facing the stage in the bottom. The stage was done up with a large banner with a woman's severed head, with her eyes popped and her tongue out, both deep red, and with 'MAUT' written across her blood-sprouting neck. The concert had already started. The space shook with the loud beats of the drum and the heavy strums of the base. Whatever empty space was left, was filled in with the screams of the two vocalists. Teenagers screaming at the top of their voices, head banging, chest thumping, their hands raised in the Devil's sign. In the open air, with their hands raised, it almost seemed like a ritual in itself, a ritual to call, to demand the presence of an entity much stronger, in their desire to fiddle with darkness, with danger, with the unknown.

The music throbbed in my head as I began to wade through the crowd to reach the stage below, dragging Neel with me.

I craned my neck, parted a couple of teenagers who seemed hell-bent on stomping the earth into mush, and finally saw Marty. That quiet boy I had seen in Guru's library had completely changed. He danced in the middle of the stage, thrumming a bass guitar, screaming. He wore a leather jacket and tight leather jeans, their back studded with rivets and metallic chains. His hair was spiked, his eyes kohled and his lips and eyebrow were pierced. As if filled with occult energy, he danced, frenzied, hopping from one end of the stage to the other, carrying the mike and alternatively turning his spiked back to the crowd whilst revving up the drummer and bassist behind him.

'Ooh yeah!' I screamed back at him, joining forces with the raving teenagers around me. Getting into higher spirits, I pulled Neel back up the amphitheatre. Now that I was here, might as well enjoy the show before I spoke to Marty. I climbed back up, finding us a ledge to sit on.

Oh this called for a bit of charak, I thought, taking out one from Dhuma's special beedis, opening it up and putting a drop of chandaali rakta on top of it. I rolled it back, lit it up and took a long drag.

'Want some, Neel?' I asked the statue standing beside me. He ignored me, staring up at the sky, silently pointing at something I couldn't see.

'You like it, don't you?' I whispered, gently weaving my fingertips through his hair, wondering if I should take him to Dhuma. She would know what to do, how to heal him, bring him back to me. Yes, I would do that tomorrow, I thought, jubilant for some reason, my heart pounding, my flesh tingling. I got down, joining the crowd, as animalistic as them. I had lived with a few tribes in the jungles of central India and remembered the headiness one got as the beats of the drums and the songs of the tribal priests and priestesses melted together, communicating with the dark spirits of the jungle. My eyes fell on a figure at the very edge of the amphitheatre. He was tall and covered from head to toe in a sleek black cloak and looked familiar.

'A horny toad's sting!' I cried, fishing out my boneblade and looking at Neel. What does one do with a dazed boyfriend along on a case? Add to that a group of kids on one side, and a couple of boys, screaming at the top of their lungs.

'Hey!' I cried, tapping one of them on his shoulder.

'Get off, old crone!' he screeched, laughing with his friends. I grabbed his right hand, slashed his wrist with my boneblade, watching his eyes widen. I tied a mayan rope around Neel's wrist, and then his, and then spat on the wrist. He tried to scream but couldn't.

'Be a doll and babysit my boyfriend for a few minutes.' He tried to take off the rope. 'If you try to take this away, your wrist will burn and fall off. As will your balls.' I smiled. He stared at Neel as if he was a ghost, his eyes as big as rakshasa balls.

'But …' he started, looking at Neel as if he was a serial killer. I put my boneblade on his Adam's apple.

'He's not dangerous,' I said, smiling, 'but I am.' He gulped, his Adam's apple bobbing almost grazing itself against the blade.

And then I turned and made my way through the sea of frenzied teens, my eyes on my prey, on Ashwathama, the legendary fighter, son of Dronacharya, the immortal. He stood away from the gyrating crowd, talking intensely to an old woman who was simply dressed in a white cotton sari without a blouse and had a long staff in her hand, with a jhola tied to one end.

'… it's time Avvaiyar for us to …'

I tapped his shoulder. 'Hey, Ashwa! What a coincidence,' I said.

He turned, stiffened, raised both of his hands and gave me a hard push. I fell as he turned and ran into the bobbing crowd.

'Balls of bulls!' I cried, back on my feet and taking out my boneblade and chasing him. He used his seven-foot frame to jump stairs, fly over groups of stunned teens and push past them. Cries of surprise, fear and pain followed him. I dodged the youngsters who fell towards me, ducking and jumping over bags lying on steps. We were headed towards the stage. Marty was still screaming, in throes, thrashing and stomping.

'Stop or I will stun you!' I screamed to no avail. He knew I wouldn't risk a mantra, not in such a crowd. He jumped over the stage with one heave, a height of about six feet. Marty's voice faltered and he squeaked in terror as Ashwa tripped on a wire and pushed past a surprised bassist before running backstage. For a second, the whole amphitheatre fell silent.

I heaved onto the stage, waved to Marty. 'Play, play, I won't mind missing a song,' I said and ran towards the backstage exit. 'Or two.'

Ashwa's trail was clear from a lane of boxes strewn to either side, to the makeup room where artistes were peeping from behind the mirrors, to drinks which had been spilled by surprised revellers in makeshift celebration rooms. I ran and panted, reaching a lawn. It was beginning to get cold, misty.

'Stop, Ashwa!' I cried to the shadow which still dashed before me. 'I won't ask your age!' He turned, for a split second.

'Leave, you moron!' he cried, his voice raw. I lunged the next few metres, my fingertips clutching his cape. He shoved me away. I tried to cling, clawing, grabbing anything. He picked me up, grabbing my neck and twisted my body, like it was a papier-mâché doll.

'Don't force me to feed you to Death!' he growled, dropping me suddenly.

'What did you want?' I screamed, getting back on my feet, seeing his shadow dissolve in the darkness.

'Death,' he answered, faintly. As if on cue, the heavy metal song stopped playing. The shouts of excitement were silenced abruptly, becoming whispers like a stadium of cicadas in meeting, and then abruptly rose to crescendo with screams of terror. I rushed, heading backstage again. People were huddled together in the doorway, silent, horrified by whatever it was they were peeping at. On stage, the musicians were silent spectators, standing, looking at somewhere in the middle of the amphitheatre.

'What happened?' I asked Marty. He calmly pointed with his index finger towards a vortex of swirling darkness. Not the winter mist, but a dense, smoky darkness. I dropped my septifocals on top of my eyes and whispered the Drishti mantra. The world livened in a dirty mustard haze.

Pretas. Not one, not two, but a swarm of them, as if Naraka had opened. They formed themselves in a circle in the middle, sucking in and out in a rhythmic fashion In the centre stood another figure, a figure that showed indigo through my septifocals, which meant it thrummed with shakti. What was it? A person or a spirit? As if fascinated by the darkness, the audience surrounding the cloud of darkness went closer towards it.

'Looks like we will get a new job tonight,' said Marty. The wail started suddenly, surprising the audience around it. It was a beautiful, anguished song.

As if a stone was thrown into a silent pool, ripples of panicked people started to run away from the scream. I jumped off the stage and ran up the stairs to the circle of darkness

Struggling through the terrified crowd, I reached the vortex, slashing my right finger with my boneblade pointed towards the pretas, hitting a solid wall I didn't see through my septifocals. I removed them to find a circle of men and women with one thing common: all of them were dead, and rotting.

'Get everyone out of here!' I cried to a couple of guards who stood there, frozen. 'Go!' The two guards hesitated, before pulling people away from the space. Through my septifocals, I saw the pretas on top come alive. Each corpse hung, suspended by the dark breath of a preta that perched on top, sucking their brains out with its sharp teeth. I slashed my vein and pointed the boneblade towards the wall of dead flesh.

'*Ghoom aa phata jaa*!'

Pieces of maggot-infested skin and flesh, jagged pieces of bone, and layers of mud flew into my face as the Visphota mantra hit. A jagged hole opened up, two of the corpses blown off and half of a woman's corpse and a man's on my right, limping, their one leg and hand blown. No one screamed, no one felt it. The woman's wail continued from inside. I walked into the circle of corpses, pressing my treta ring.

Inside stood a being made of shadows, his form burning a dark blue. The pretas mingled with him – filthy yellow on ink blue. He stood on top of the old woman, who was crouched on all fours now, her wailing song still emerging from her lips. Pretas tumbled around them both, circling in a frenzied, dance. I gorged an eye out of a corpse behind me and pointed the treta ring towards the pretas whirling around the woman.

'Kha jalaa, sokhna, nimagna!'

The shadow turned, his eyes burning black, a third eye, a beam of light, a bright diamond, pointing at me from its forehead. He was formless, only a shadow, his mouth yawned open, increasing in size, till it became a fist, a plate, a window and then a door of nothingness. Pretas flew out, streaks of black on yellow flashes. I pulled up the mandala and screamed the Nodha mantra.

'Bhuta pishacha darke bhag!'

It was just in time to deflect the onslaught. The tantrik's smoky eyes glittered, darkening to black. Blindly, I ran forward, my mandala in place, deflecting the pretas. With my left hand, I slashed the shadow being, aiming for the face.

Clank!

Something fell on the ground as his form wavered, perhaps surprised by my attack, the pretas scattering. I jumped to the woman. Her wail had become stronger, piercing my ears with its knife-like sharpness. I reached her, took out my mandala and, pointing to her, screamed:

'Bhuta pishacha darke bhag!'

The sucking pretas fell away and for a second I could see the old woman, writhing on the floor, white hair spread out of her bun, her sari askew, her staff lost. She was the same one who I had seen speaking to Ashwa earlier. Her eyes were closed and she swooned, as if in a trance, screaming and wailing her song. A whisper from the side made me look back. The blue-black form looked at me, his pinpoint eyes narrowing, and pointed a shadowsword in my direction, muttering. I fell on my back, pulled up my mandala – and just in time to see the gush of shadow-fire yawning in my direction, licking, consuming everything before and behind me.

I turned, my hair singed. The smell of burning flesh filled my nostrils as the corpses behind me caught fire. But the shadow-being wasn't interested in a duel. Ignoring me, he pointed his sword towards the pretas who reformed around the woman, started to suck. She sang, weaker this time, softly.

Flesh burnt and with it hands, blackened and burning, grabbed me. A broad and tall man, his eye gorged out (by me), his other hanging by a lean meat thread, and his shoulder and torso burning, held me in his bony, hands. I slashed blindly on top of him, at the preta I knew was giving him its weak life breath. Another pair of hands grabbed my legs. A woman's corpse, fallen because of her missing legs, grabbed mine. I kicked the woman's blackened face. Another attacked, then another, burnt, fleshy corpses, grabbing my hands and arms and legs and shoulders. They grabbed, clung, pinched and held with their rock-hard hands and rotten teeth, sinking into my flesh. My boneblade fell as the corpse of a little girl sank her teeth into my arm. Some of them burnt searing hot, some were cold as if frozen ice.

I squirmed and wriggled but there were too many of them. Helplessly, I watched as the tantrik called upon the pretas who fed on the woman. Her screaming stopped abruptly. A darkened hole opened up somewhere to the preta tantrik's left side. The pretas whooshed, in rank and file, into the yawning hole, taking the woman with them.

'Don't!' I cried helplessly as a corpse climbed over my back, pulling me down. There were too many, too heavy. I fell to my knees and then sank to the ground. The black hole began to close as the tantrik stepped inside it and while the corpses climbed on top of me. Then, like puppets without their puppeteer, the fell dead again.

Darkness, with the smell of burning and rot, surrounded me. Someone grabbed me from behind. I turned, ready to claw a throat. Blue eyes, staring down at me, expressionless. Behind him, the terrified boy I'd bound him to. He squeaked, as if his throat was too tight to scream.

'He won't stay!' the boy whispered. I scrambled up, pushing off the dead weight of corpses on my body. The dead girl lay a few metres away from me. Bent on top of her was Marty. Screams and cries started to fill the night as a few spectators came back.

'Get away from her,' I bellowed, kicking off a corpse, scrambling to find my satchel and boneblade.

'Zombie, she's a zombie!' A bunch of boys surrounded the spread of corpse, their phones held up.

I found my stuff below a dead man's burnt hand.

'Bro, take a pic!'

'Don't let her bite you! It's infectious. I saw a movie on that.'

'Stop or I will shear your balls,' I growled, pointing my boneblade. They made themselves scarce. The boy remained, shivering and tied to Neel's hand. I slashed the mayan rope open with a swipe of my boneblade.

'Thanks for taking care of him,' I said. He muttered a welcome, turned and ran as if a sharabha was chasing him.

Nothing remained of Ashwa's friend, but a sack of her skin, wrapped in her old sari, an outer covering left as she'd been taken to wherever that portal led. I picked it up. Something on the slackened face glinted. Using my boneblade, I scraped it. A drop of diamond, exactly what I'd found at Guru B's library. I got up, looking around for the locket I had snatched off the tantrik before he'd gone to whichever hell he came from.

'Naraka's piss,' I whispered, putting the diamond blob into a pouch and pocketing it. I headed to the place where I'd seen Ashwa speak to the woman earlier and found the bag of cloth, stuck to the wooden staff. There was nothing in it but another old, faded sari and a diary full of writing.

I quietly put it in my satchel.

'Was she your friend?' Marty stood on the other side, eyeing me like he was looking at a mannenquin at a mall.

'No, I don't know her.'

'Then why fight so hard?' he asked, his bowl-shaped hairstyle was spiked and gelled, studs in his nose, eyebrow and tongue.

'Because.' I stood up, walked to Marty, and held the boneblade to his neck. 'There have been two such incidents now and you've been around both. Too much of a coincidence?'

'So have you,' said Marty, 'The only person you see standing here and you suspect him. If I had something to do with it, why would I be around taking selfies? You think of me as an idiot? What kind of a detective are you anyway?'

I sighed, controlling a surge of anger. He's young, I told myself, and probably will enjoy it if you turn him into a sewer rat.

'Maut concerts always attract corpses. Always have. I remember that night at the funeral home—'

'These … these … are from my graveyard.' A slight man stood a few feet away from us, shaking in his chappals. 'How … how did they get here?'

'Walked by the looks of it,' quipped Marty.

'But *how*?' he asked.

'Happens sometimes. See, they don't realize they're dead,' he answered. 'Here, I am from Maut, a funeral home. We specialize in these kind of deaths. May Maut grant them death. I suggest—'

'Marty,' I said in a warning tone, putting a little distance between the corpses and the man by taking him to a corner. I sat down on one of the concrete ledges, along with him, taking out a beedi. 'What did you see?' I asked.

'Darkness … I was sleeping and heard a rumbling noise. When I woke up, they … they were *walking*.'

'Burn them. It might help,' I answered, unsure, taking a long puff. 'And what will you tell the police?'

He shrugged, his eyes wide, unbelieving. Thirty corpses, risen from the grave to be fed to pretas. Had to be the work of a tantrik. And it was the same one who took Guru B. But there, I'd seen just a few pretas, leftovers after he'd come and just three corpses. Today however had been much more elaborate, almost like he wanted to show off his power. Making one corpse rise with a preta was powerful magic. But thirty? Together? And with more than that – pretas? Pretas might be lost souls but they were stubborn spirits and took a lot of power to control. And here, all of them had been formed, like an army, doing the tantrik's bidding. Who was this powerful being? Where was he? What did he want from Guru B and this old woman? And Ashwa? How did he fit in into it all? Was he the one who was doing this? But why?

A bunch of teenagers giggled with Marty, taking selfies in the backdrop of the corpses. He posed, making faces into the smartphone cameras. I finished my smoke and walked back to pick up the woman's skin. Except it wasn't there.

'What in Naraka's name!' I exclaimed, looking around. The dash of white in the darkness, held the skin, flapping around his shoulders like a cape. 'Stop, you!'

He pounced. The teenagers who'd been taking photos, ran, helter-skelter.

Slashing my wrist I started to scream a mantra for a bhuta when I saw the flash behind Marty. The being I'd seen at Guru B's place, wearing a human skull, grabbed the boy and with a blade, slashed his neck, pushing him onto me. Marty fell with a fountain of blood erupting from him. I grabbed hold of him, laying him on his back.

'What the fuck did you do that for?' I screamed. The skull-wearing stranger vanished into the night. Blood frothed out of Marty's mouth. I quickly opened the rakpiss vial and put a drop into his neck. Blood oozed from the slash in his neck, his body thrashed like a fish out of water, stilling and slacking. In the distance, I heard police sirens. There wasn't time to do anything else. I stood up, lit a matchstick and and spoke the Agni mantra, directing it at the dead bodies spread around.

'Jal bhun bhasm ho ja!'

Soon there was blazing fire in the middle of the amphitheatre. About five odd youngsters came in, throwing arms and legs into the fire, laughing crazily and dancing around the pyre, part of another dark ritual. I took one last look at Marty's body, now still, and grabbed Neel by the hand and left, slipping into the dark night. Once out, I made a quick call to Madhu and then to Shukra. There were many questions left here, but I had a feeling that the police won't appreciate me being around a dead body. No one with any authority ever did.

8

'WELL, WHAT'VE you found out till now?' I asked as soon as I entered Shukra's kitchenette, flopping myself into a sofa. I looked out the window, seeing Shukra's reflection looking at Neel who sat on the carpet.

'Who's the vagabond?' asked Shukra, handing me a cup of green tea. I put in a dollop of rakta in it and gulped, thankful.

'Neel.'

'Neel, as in your ex? *The* ex?' Shukra's spectacles popped off his face. He grabbed them like a fly and put them back on.

'Yup,' I answered.

Neel sat on the carpet, playing with Shukra's iPad, mute, his blue eyes taking in the flickering screen. My heart expanded with tenderness. I shouldn't have taken him with me to the concert, what if something had happened? What if he'd died on me all over again?

'The guy you thought was dead?'

'Yup,' I answered, sighing. 'So what did you find in the diary, Shukra? I've to go.'

'The guy who you hadn't been able to get over for seven years?'

'Yup.'

'You fell for *this*?' said Shukra. 'I mean, I am not trying to be impolite or something, but he doesn't seem right, does he. In here.' He pointed his index finger to his own head. I looked at Neel again, who now leaned on a round white table, flexing his hands up and down, his expression blank, as if he had not even heard what Shukra said. I was desperate to go to him, hug him, cover him, protect him from the things he had faced.

'Don't be silly, Shuks,' I answered, picking up a thin rod. A current passed through my finger and I dropped it. It clattered on the cold floor.

'You, monkey, get down from the couch,' cried Shukra, muscles rippling.

'Stop it, Shuks. He's *perfect*. Did you look at his eyes? By Kali, the first time I saw his eyes I knew, I knew that he was the one. You know, the first time I met him was on a full moon—' I stopped, gulping. My heart grew heavy as I remembered that night, the night which had just recently come to me in dreams. Such a perfect night it had been, the full-moon night with everyone there to witness the vajroli. All I remember was him though, his eyes. Standing across from me, over the couple who conjugated in front of both of us. That stark blue colour, like the monsoon sky, drenching my soul. He had just entered Kaula Ashram as a young man, brought in by one of the seniors as his apprentice. He was tall, muscular and flawless. But that's not what had completely melted my heart. It was his eyes, the blue eyes brimming with kindness. That and the smile he had given me. Though I wasn't a virgin, at that time, I used to think of sex as holy. That you couldn't waste shakti on lust, or on love. It's only purpose was to harness spiritual power, to achieve siddhis for your male partner. Sex could only be used to gain power. But Neel, he had changed my mind. And how.

'It's your hormones talking,' Shukra was saying, 'Are you ovulating? I read a study which said that many a women tend to mistake the urge for intercourse with love during—'

'I am not horny Shukra!' I retorted, eyeing Shukra. Why was I so conflicted? 'All I feel is—' I stopped, the word 'tenderness' unspoken. It was like an ache inside of me that I had thought had died years ago with the girl I used to be. But then that's life. The moment you feel you are finally a hardass bitch, it comes and bites you hard on the ass. There, Anantya, you arrogant bitch, you're not so hard anymore are you?

'He's my *love*, Shukra,' I said, not believing those words were coming out of my mouth. 'He's the one who made me realize I can be much more than a mere battery for a tantrik. A woman rather than a sexual tool for power. And I've found him! He's alive, here, with me. I feel—' I got up, not able to contain myself, about to burst, 'I feel *blessed*.'

'Nothing but chemicals messing your brain, Anantya. You *made* yourself. No one did you a favour!' Shukra growled. 'If he's so lovely and all that, why didn't he call you or something all these seven years.'

'He can't speak.' Taking my tongue out, I made a gesture of swiping though it.

'So? Can't he write? I hope he's literate.'

I smacked him and walked to Neel, taking his hand into mine and patting it. He didn't respond, staring at the screen instead, his hand rough and limp and cold in mine.

'I found him at Manu Maharaj's hospital. He thinks Neel has some kind of a disease which is fatal. Are you cold?' I asked softly, looking at Neel. He kept staring at the screen, not even bothering to respond. What had happened to him? He felt like a completely different person. He hadn't shown any interest, hadn't recognised me, hadn't even desired for anything, even food. There hadn't been a flicker of recognition.

'How did he get that scar?'

'I don't know and I don't care.'

'You mean to tell me, you don't care that he might have spent the last seven years in an asylum or a terrorist camp or something crazier? Come on Anantya, don't be irrational.'

'Doesn't matter. He was there for me all those years ago. Now I will be. He's my love.'

'*Was* your love. He drops into your life seven years later and you think he's still the same?'

'We won't talk about this anymore. What did you find out?'

'Seriously, you should check up your hormone balance. It might be that—'

'Shut up Shuks. Tell me what you found about the immortals.' I didn't want any probing questions about Neel, I just wanted to feel his beating heart next to mine. Thinking about things always ruined them. He stopped, a bit shocked at my tone, a bit offended. The kettle sang. He walked back to the study.

I placed Neel on the carpet, where he picked up a tablet. Shukra came and sat on my other side, cross-legged, his powerful muscles peeking through the shorts he wore, distracting me. My heart beat for Neel, while my hand itched to touch Shukra's hairy skin.

'Not immortals, *chiranjeevis*. They just live really long, unlike immortals who are to live indefinitely.'

'What about them, Shuks?'

'According to most of the Puranas and the Mahabharata and Ramayana,' said Shukra, delicately holding his green tea in the hook of his little finger. Even though he'd sized up twice, he still remained poised, elegant. I gulped again, looking at Neel. 'There were seven chiranjeevis: Ashwathama, Bali, Vyasa, Hanumana, Vibhishana, Kripacharya and Parashurama. But not all of them are supposed to live till the end of Kali yuga, that's the age we're in. Those are just four of these seven: Parashurama, who is a master of all weapons both human and divine; Hanuman, the monkey god; Bali who is still rumoured to walk the earth and is a scholar and a wise man—'

'That sounds suspiciously like the person I knew as Guru B. He told me he has been around for a long while.'

'And the fourth is Ashwathama, your friend.'

'Was there any reason they became long-lived? I mean, how does one do that?'

'No text covers that parameter. That's the problem when litterateurs take control over history and science. They drain it of all objectivity; they buy whatever the poets say. There was a thesis written by an ancient surgeon by the name of Charaka who wrote a text called *Charaka Samhita* in which he was experimenting with all forms of potions and medicines that can extend a life. He claimed to have tested one of the chiranjeevi's blood, but unfortunately, none of his studies have survived.'

'What *do* the poets say?'

'That it's a blessing, a boon, a gift by the gods, a curse in the case of your friend Ashwathama, etcetera, etcetera.'

'A curse?'

'Yes. According to the Mahabharata, your friend tried to kill the grandson of the winners in the war of Mahabharata. So he got cursed to walk the earth forever and atone for his sins. Mr Bali, got this as a boon. As did Mr Hanuman and Mr Parashurama.'

'Such bull! Walking the earth forever has to be a good thing. How can that be a curse?'

Shukra pushed his spectacles up, thoughtfully. 'You should ask your friend that question. He has been walking the earth for about 12000 years if the dates doled out by the current academics are to be believed. That's a lot of walking.'

'I wish that idiot had told me before he started running from me with his tail in his ass.'

'You think he's innocent? He hasn't kidnapped these two immortals?'

'He's definitely doing something he shouldn't be. But he doesn't look like that preta tantrik. And I don't know who that ape-thing is who stole the old woman's skin. Why does he do that? This case has more questions than answers! The immortal men and wo—women! There are no women among the seven immortals are there?'

'Chiranjeevi,' corrected Shukra. 'No. The seven are men, though I could find mentions of other species—a crow, a bear, and even a teenage rishi called Markandeya. No mention in the texts of any females though.'

'Yeah, men hate to write about women, don't they?' I took out the diary I'd found in the old woman's belongings and handed it to Shukra. He thumbed through the diary.

'Oh!' he cried, reaching out and trying to take the tablet from Neel, who kept a grip on it.

'Give it to me,' he said. Neel kept staring at the screen, silent. 'It's mine!'

He tried to snatch it and Neel gave a wail of helplessness. 'Let him have it, Shukra.'

'But it's mine!'

I sighed. 'Just use your laptop, will you?'

Shukra stopped, surprised. 'But this *is* mine. He has to be told that he can't own things that belong to other people.'

'Yes, but right now, can we pretend we are grown-ups and figure this out?'

He gave a curt nod, frowning. 'Let me just protest once that this is just not a done thing to do, taking other people's things.' He walked to his study table and sat in front of his laptop, clinking away with furious concentration.

'Duly noted.' I got up and stood behind him, trying not to breathe in too much of his raw, sweaty smell. I looked back at Neel, staring at the screen, my heart skipping a beat. Maybe Shukra was right. I needed to. But no. He won't be a lab rat. I will love him no matter what.

'… is a poetess!'

'A poetess?' I asked, reigning the fuzzy horniness of my body and bringing it back to work.

'Avvaiyar!' he cried, 'Don't you know? A Tamil poetess, all this while … people thought there were many women who took on that name, but she was always the same … the one, an old woman in a faded cotton sari, singing songs of devotion. She had three horizontal marks of ash on her forehead.' He swivelled the laptop in my direction.

'By Kali's tongue. That does look like her,' I answered, looking at the images.

'See.' He scrolled. 'This diary, it's a collection of her poems in Tamil. All original. The legend goes that she was given some kind of a fruit, an amla most likely, by a king to make her life long.'

'So she is an immortal of sorts too? Guru B and now Avvaiyar, with Ashwa on the run. Who is hunting them? And who called this woman at a heavy metal gig to die?'

'You just told me she's Ashwa's friend.'

'As was Guru B, or Bali,' I said. 'I need to find that ever-living bugger! But before that,' I looked up at Shukra, giving him the full frontal, cheerful smile, 'Can I ask you for a favour? *Pleeease.*'

He frowned, stopped, looked down into his empty cup, and frowned some more. 'Yes?'

'Can you *please* keep an eye on Neel while I go meet Grrhat?'

'What? Are you out of your space ship?'

'Come on, man! What are friends for? I can't take him into Lavana! He'll be slaughtered! Just put him to sleep. Give me a little of that green tea of yours, na?' I picked up my satchel, checked the boneblade in the scabbard around my waist and popped the septifocals on top of my head, dashing out of Shukra's place before he could argue further. I loved Neel and Shukra, but there were things a girl needed to do alone. Going to the rakshasa ghetto was one of them.

9

IT WAS my favourite time of the night, when silence filled the dark corners of the city. I grabbed a live patanga, put it in a plastic-wrap and then in my bag, sneaking into Jawaharlal Nehru Stadium Metro Station. The station was closed for the day and I quietly stepping down to the basement station. Grrhat, Madhu's uncle, had chosen to be a teenager tonight, his face pimpled and pouty. He wore a pair of bright red pants and yellow sneakers with a red t-shirt.

'This almost makes me wish I was seeing your true form instead,' I said, fingering my septifocals.

He looked at me, without a quip, standing still, staring on the railings. Grrhat was a true-blooded rakshasa, a rarity in Delhi. He was from royalty and could trace his lineage to Madhu, the one who fought with Brahma. His family, with Barbareeka as its head, ran the biggest underworld supernatural business in Delhi, giving a cut of the hefty profits to the Association to make them look the other way. Illegal immigrants, sups for sex, herbs, and skins, everything magical that reached Delhi came through the rakshasa clan of Barbareeka.

'It's a stupid plan,' muttered Grrhat, as he flicked his hand. We jumped onto the rails, walking towards the opposite direction of the metro line. 'Why did I agree to help you?'

'Because just a few months ago you used me for your own stupid plan.'

'That was just a joke. Buy a sense of humour will you?'

'If you call being chased by a crazy bitch who shoots venomous snakes a joke, this one's going to be a real PJ.' I followed him through the track. We were headed in the direction of Jangpura Metro Station. He stopped and crouched on the side of the rails.

'Hope you're earning to keep eighteen generations of your community happy,' he said, opening a small shaft in the ground to a stairway heading south. 'You'll need those on your blind eyes.'

I pulled the septifocals over my eyes, whispering the Drishti mantra and followed. The world washed in a rainbow haze.

'It's not about money—' I began, looking in front to see the stairs. Grrhat took off his clothes and changed into himself, in diamantine body of lean black muscles, his eyes green. He walked ahead, butt naked, staring at the stone wall of the stairwell. I touched the wall, engraved with sensual motifs, curves changing into creatures in throes of passion, dressed in fine gold. Trees branching out into exotic creatures of the lush jungles.

'Anarth!' said Grrhat. We stopped in front of a two-foot high, finely made metal sculpture of a tantrik, dressed in black dhoti. 'Of course you're *that* kind. The good kind. Tell me something ...' He stopped in front, stood for a short second and peed on it. The statue melted, becoming a pool of dark, glistening water. 'This was my idea. I like using latest biometric technology,' he said winking.

'Somehow, I don't see you fitting into Swarga. You'll be bored and boxing those self-righteous buggers in under a minute. Naraka, now that's where you'll fit right in. So why bother with noble? Forget about the case, let me give you a night you'll remember,' he whispered, standing close to me, so his body touched mine from behind, his breath fiery on my neck. Electricity passed my body, making it shake. A natural reaction to a rakshasa's touch, which was like electricity in water. 'What say, Anantya?'

'Until your kriti has increased beyond your puny body, there's nothing of interest for me here.' I patted his penis. He pushed his head back and guffawed.

'Oh, I like you too much to lose you to those stiff Swarga dwellers!' He grabbed my ass and as I was ready to hit him in his nether region, jumped with me into the melted pool of black water. For a moment we were suspended, in nothingness, in vacuum. A second later, something coiled around my legs and I was jerked away from Grrhat's hold.

'Lookie, lookie, what is that Grrhat?' a thin piercing voice called out. The coil pulled and flipped me like a cloth in wind. It uncoiled and I was suspended again, rotating, upside down. A cold, damp touch on my shoulder.

'A manavi?' screeched the voice, 'Yummy —'

With my left hand, I grabbed my boneblade and slashed the thing that held me.

'Eee!' My shoulder was drenched. The metallic smell of blood. The coil released me and I fell on my back on hard rock.

'It cut me!' The septifocals shimmered and the darkness melted away into a rocky cellar, just in time to see huge, gnarled roots shooting my way. I ducked, tumbling, and my back against a corner, touching cold, rough-cut rock, my boneblade ready with a mantra on my lips. The monster screamed in annoyance. 'I will suck it dry!'

'Stop being a drama drone, Madalasa,' said Grrhat in an amused voice. 'It was just a love nip.'

Madalasa, a giant rakshasi, thundered towards us. Her hair, which wove around her dead-tree-like gnarled body, looked like a woven mesh of thick branches. Piles of roots danced around her trunk-like body, weaving and snaking, their edges shooting to where I stood. I twisted, fell on the floor, escaping one only to have my foot snagged by the other. I swung my boneblade to slash—

'*Stop*. She's mine!' growled Grrhat before I could begin. Madalasa dropped her hair, which retracted back to the top of her head. The word 'mine' had ownership weight attached to it and rakshasas respected it.

'Does she ever have a good hair day?' I asked, touching a strand of my own unruly hair. They were tame lambs compared to Madalasa's.

'Have you seen yourself lately?' he asked.

'Once you are done sexing,' Madalasa growled from behind, 'I shall make her dessert I *swear*.' The voice boomed behind us, as we left through a cave, which looked like a yellowed jaw of a monster, its long teeth pushing out of its gums, excited, about to consume.

'Two seconds in Lavana and I've already made friends,' I muttered. The path curved like a snake, oozing stalagmites and stalactites, so we had to duck and jump, our shadows trailing long and thin on the ceiling. I muttered the drishti mantra again, sharpening the red vision through the septifocals.

The constricting wormhole gave way to a vast cavern, rising up like a billowing monster, its walls and floors pogmarked in stalagmites and stalactites, it's ceiling invisible, though a few upside down mountains remained, looking down like inverted lactating breasts. As far as the eye could see, the cavern was full of camps, makeshift tents, made of leaves, barks, on the floor, on the ceiling, alongside the lake in the middle which might have been beautiful once but was now reeking with garbage. It was a dirty, dank place with the putrid smell of sulfur and dead things. Voices and wails and shouts and screams coloured the stale air. Supernatural creatures of all kinds huddled in spaces between these tents: kinnaras sharpening blades, pulindas sitting in huts made of bones, yatus hanging in the shadows of the cavern, the tree-like sharavaras bunched up together to make a dried up, tired grove. One corner was completely filled by daityas the rock-shaped cousins of the two I had met a couple of days ago. Mixed blood offspring played in between makeshift paths. From the floor to the wall to the ceiling, everything was covered. Some sups lay on the floor, some drunk, some dead, some having sex, some eating raw flesh. Some like dasyus and yatus hanging on the ceiling, playing cards. Some had even created a middle layer, crossing ropes where they could claim home.

'You selling this?' asked a pulinda, his leery eyes on me. I showed him my boneblade.

'Only if she agrees,' said Grrhat. We walked along a muddied puddle, a remnant of what must've been a beautiful lake, its water blackened with overuse and garbage, spread out ahead of us. An impromptu market had begun on its banks. It bustled with all kinds of cries, screetches of a shavara, sneers of a sarp and billowing farts from a pard, which is how they communicated. Sups sold food, pieces of human meat as kebabs, eyes of frogs, snakes and other pieces of charred meat and bones.

Before it was a ghetto, Lavana had been a city of famed beauty, a vast network of underground caves. Legend had it that the city was covered with gold and jewels. Hell, rakshasas used to be so rich that they shat gold and precious jewels (as per a rather imaginative saying in tantriks). As with any ancient city, this one had fallen to bad days, conquered by a tyrant, its treasuries looted, its people killed. Now it was a ghetto with a population of refugees and illegal sups rather than a city of traders. The only trade here was illegal and run by Barbareeka, the rakshasi queen of the royal blood of rakshasa.

'It's worse than I saw before,' I said as we passed a six-legged pingala who had just chopped off its own leg and was offering it for coin. I'd been here two years ago looking for gorochana, for an amulet, when I was fucking a half-rakshasa. 'Why are there so many of them?'

'The hungry CATs,' Grrhat spat.

'Oh yes. The Association made it mandatory to buy maya potions from licenced re-sellers only.' Zaazee had been making good money on the side selling vials of the potion at one-fourth the price. CAT had not only made it necessary to buy from licensed sellers, but also increased the price.

'Bloody tantriks,' Grrhat spat feelingly, pushing away the pingala. We walked up, away from the lake, leaving the cavern through another connected cave, climbing uphill. 'Poisonous, addled potion, gets into your bones, making them ache. And prices touch Swarga! Everyone here's too poor to live up-ground and pay Barbareeka meagre coin to live here.'

'And they can't go back to their homes.'

'Where's any left? The jungles are crawling with manavas, their hungry mouths consuming everything they see. And they call us greedy.'

'And Barbareeka? She can stop the supply of rakpiss to tantriks.' Rakpiss or rakshasa piss was easy money for all blueblood rakshasas. It healed most wounds in humans and tantriks, and hakims who knew about it, paid through their throats for rakpiss. Grrhat snorted.

'And how will she buy her wine?' Most from the pure-blood family drank a lot of wine to make sure they had a ready supply of rakpiss, which supplied them enough money to continue drinking. Vicious circle. And Barbareeka, being the head of the family, made sure she got a percentage from all her cousins and children. Grrhat was a distant cousin to her, but Barbareeka was the most powerful in the blueblood clan. For one, she was a female and an older one. Rakshasa clans were matriarchal. The trade she ran had its tentacles not only underground but also up-ground. She provided passage to new sups who entered Delhi illegally, controlled the supply of rakpiss from everyone in her family, supplied exotic pashus and rakpiss to tantriks across the country. Everyone who needed anything kinky or illegal or rare from the supernatural world, came to her. This was her domain. No one, even CAT or CBI had any power here. And I was planning to throw desert dust in her eyes, in her domain. Nice, Anantya.

'Ooh, Grrhat, want to fly with me?' asked a musical female voice. A bhurunda, with a cherubic female face and the body of an eagle perched on the corner of an alley, a gateway entrance to the queen's sex market. She sat with a series of other bhurundas, ferocious warriors all of them, who also doubled up as escorts for clients to the sex street.

'Hira, my beautiful bird!' answered Grrhat, walking close, clutching her feathery back and tickling her side, 'We will fly. Come show us the way!' He went close to her ear and started to whisper.

'Welcome to the linga bazaar. What would you like to pick, mistress?' Hira asked me. The bharunda was one of the escorts of the street, who made sure that clients got what they came here looking for, no one died, or if someone did, was picked up and disposed of.

She escorted us through, taking one alley after another, till a broad cave with scoops of niches on both sides of the cave. There were rakshasas, daityas, kiratas, dasyus, chandaalis, all kinds of sups, male and female and without gender in corners, alcoves cut into the rock. Some were completely naked, some completely covered, some covered with knives or leaves. Noises surrounded us at all sides, a cacophony of sighs, screams, orgasmic giggles and growls.

Barbareeka ran this market, though not all of them were slaves. Some had been forced by family or circumstances, some liked it, some were blood-bound to another and had no choice.

'Doesn't this street lead to one of the Lodhi monuments?'

'Yeah. Used to, long, long back when the royalty wasn't so peevish that they had to hide who they were sleeping with. But that's been filled up now. The only other entrance is the manava one.'

I nodded, walking ahead. Last time, drunk, a half-rakshasa had brought me through there for a threesome from another entrance, a little cub in the hole from a seedy South Extension basement from where humans and tantriks entered Lavana.

'Get back here, you whore!' From an alcove a shavara scuttled, a pumpkin-like sup with a marble smooth body, followed by a man. Both giggled. The man who followed was butt naked, flailing his chubby arms, his naked drum of a stomach jiggling as he ran. He grabbed the shavaras and rubbed his tummy, laughing.

'Justice Kanthak?' I said. He turned, his eyes glazed, his ponytail open, the rudraksha beads scattered.

'Umm …' He smiled with a glazed look, unrecognizing, pushing the shavara back into the alcove. Hah. No wonder the Tazaak stayed away from any raids in this place. Looked like the head of the tantrik police was a regular visitor to its charms. We walked ahead, till the creatures thinned and not many alcoves could be seen.

'Doesn't the mistress like anything she's seen?' asked Hira. We were almost at the end of the long street now. It had thinned as most of the creatures there had already found what they came for and chosen their thrill for the night. I turned back and slapped Grrhat on his face.

'I came here looking for nishadas and instead you show me a few *bastard* creatures?' I said, lips thin.

'Nishadas?' said Hira. 'But … but we have none, mistress.' I pulled out my boneblade and held it on Grrhat's neck.

'You promised me, Grrhat,' I sneered. 'Show me some or I loosen hounds of Naraka right into your fucking blood.'

'But, madam, we don't have—' Grrhat took Hira on the side and whispered something urgently in her ear. It was all planned of course, even my slap had been. 'She has a bit of a fetish, wants …' I felt a twinge, just a little twinge mind you, of guilt at not telling him what I planned to do. It was important, more important for him than me, that he didn't know. It was better this way, yes much better. Knowing always led to questions and then cautious advice and then a lot of delays. I didn't want any of that.

'But we can't! It's the bounty—' He held her claws and kissed them repeatedly, begging.

'Grr, it's impossible ...' She said, softly, undecided. I smiled. There were very few who could resist Grrhat's sexual charm. Hira nodded a second later and whispered to Grrhat. She looked around, toward both our sides. We were at the other end of the street, with three smaller exits. The centre one, I knew led to the South Extension. Grrhat held his stomach and started to scream, scream so hard that his voice echoed in the cave, stopping a few of the grunting noises coming our way. Clients, and guards gathered around us, curious, concerned.

'We have to take him to the infirmary!' cried Hira to the few other escorts who were there with the clients. Grrhat, in the mood, lay on his back in the middle, thrashing. Working on instinct, I stepped back, pretending to be horrified and pulled out the patanga from my bag, tore two of its wings and stuck them to the entrance of the middle cave.

We held a doubled-up Grrhat, pushing our way through a meandering cave at the end of the linga bazaar, away from the other exit which was the human one and led to South Extension. As soon as we were out of sight from the bazaar, we turned away from the cave that led to the hospital, instead taking a detour and heading down, a steep downwards incline, which let to a subterranean space, damper and darker, foul smelling basement. After a few minutes of walking, Hira stopped, signaling to an alcove on her right, locked with a wooden door. Hira opened the door with one of the keys jangling on her waist, turned and whispered. 'Just for two minutes, mistress. Because Grrhat promised you.' I nodded and entered, my heart thumping.

'Where's that flying you promised me, Hira?' said Grrhat from behind.

'But, she shouldn't be left alone.'

'Oh, she will be fine. It's just a moon minute, what's the worst that can happen? It's I who needs all your attention.' Grrhat took the giggling Hira to a corner, tickling her feathers.

The room was dark and damp, a familiar smell clung to it. The nishadas sat huddled together in one corner of the room. In front of it, a black lava-like formation glistened, like the lake I'd just seen. Sobs of fear escaped their throats, raw and quiet, as if they were too tired to even cry.

'Don't be afraid,' I whispered, 'your sister Baza, sent me here.'

'Are we leaving, sister?' she asked.

'I cant take—' I stopped.

'Please sister, help us sister! We will all die like our sisters, vanish into the dark pool!' cried one.

'Please sister, take us sister! Take us from here to under the sal trees. Let us die there.'

'Hells of a roach's ass!' I cried. This was so going to get me into trouble. 'How many of you melted?'

'We were three times ten. The princes came and took some away. Then we were two times ten and three more, but then we melted. Now we're ten and six more. The Pretty Princes told us to wait here.'

'Do you have an eldest?' One of them came forward. A tiny girl, her scales bright black in the dark cavern.

'We are eldest,' she said in a soft voice. 'We are Tataiya.'

'Tataiya, now you listen up carefully,' I said, walking up to her, holding her by her scaly shoulders.

'You all can get rid of the disease. We need to treat you. But this is a bad place, so we'll have to sneak out with magic.'

'Yes. Magic, yes.' She nodded.

'All of you, stand together. You'll need to go upground right now.'

'But … the princes …'

'Kubja prince sent me to help you,' I said. They looked at each other, they amber eyes larger, full of fear. 'I promise to keep you safe, sisters.'

Tataiya nodded, her tiger eyes sombre. They all huddled together, stuck to each other. Breaking a mandala, I made small pieces of bones. Plucking strands of my hair, I tied the bone to each of their wrists. Finally, opening up the powerful rakta, I put a drop of it on each of their heads, and whispered:

'Shareer jaa, saans jaa, sugandh jaa aur preta
Chhup jaa, so jaa, ojhal ho jaa.'

The Ojhal mantra shimmered around them, till none could be seen. 'You're now invisible to all beings,' I whispered to the empty room. 'Not completely for they can smell and hear you. Just not see you, so don't speak when you head out.'

I groped and took a hand, placing a patanga on the palm. 'Follow him, for he searches for his wings. The cave where he finds them, will lead you up-ground. Go up and wait for me. Go, now!'

I opened the door, to find Hira with her wings crushed on the wall as Grrhat humped her. She screamed, delighted. Rushing to them, I hit Hira on the head with the hilt of my boneblade. She slunk on the floor. It took a second for Grrhat's passionate expression to change into a completely furious one.

Slashing my wrist, I whispered: 'Sorry, Grr. *Aim Hreem Sthuli ooli laake aa!*'

Swack! Swack! The sticky bhuta slapped from my boneblade onto Grrhat's face, like a splash of unseen chewing gum. It spread on his body, sticking itself like gum to his natural kriti. Grrhat squirmed stickily as it wrapped itself around him like a vaccum sealed pack. I dragged the unconscious Hira into the alcove.

'Come,' I whispered to the nishadas, closing the cellar door after the last one had come out. The nishadas led the way, a hazy group of murky shadows now, cloaked in the invisiblity spell. Grrhat followed, floating before me, directed by my boneblade and me. The boneblade sometimes squished his body, like a jellyfish. He wriggled, his adamantine body flickering with furious streaks.

'Halt!' a voice called out from behind. I turned, as a screech echoed through the constricted corridor. 'Shit of a medieval ass. *Run!*' I whispered to the girls, turning and standing in the middle, with Grrhat beside me, his expression furious. Three bharundas zoomed in.

'Who're you?' asked an eagle-faced bharunda. I bent my neck and sat on a knee. 'Slave, mistress. Human slave who accompanies her master to the Linga—'

'That's Grrhat!' said another, with the face of a squashed sparrow. 'Get her!'

'*Ghani bhavati*!' I cried. The bharundas flipped, hanging upside down like bats, the mantra's power missing them by an inch. Still there, they emitted a screech, like that of an owl, except it was multipled by a thousand.

My boneblade clattered on the floor, as I slipped onto my knees, my hands reaching out to cover my ears. They rang still. The screech entered my blood, making it swell in my veins. Panicked blood ran out of my ears, the onslaught continuing. My sight darkened, the noise continued. No! I wanted to say. Stop! But no words came out, only bile and blood.

'That's enough,' someone said. The horrible voice stopped as I slunk on the floor, breathing into the space. 'Arrest her and take her to the queen.' Someone dragged me up. Darkness reigned, though my septifocals were still over my eyes. Shakti, there was none left in me, even for the business-as-usual Drishti mantra.

'Take everything off her,' grumbled Grrhat, 'Even clothes, except for her VISION, for she should see.' Through my hazy vision, Grrhat thrummed red with anger. They tore together, the bharundas as Grrhat watched.

'Grr, I'm sorry—'

'Don't speak, devil manavi!'

Tearing at my clothes and grabbing my satchel, he left and the two bharundas on either side dragged me uphill and then down, through burrows and shafts to reach an entrance, made of a daitya's ribcage, leading up through a stairway made by layers of bones, skulls, skeletons and jawbones stacked up. The staircase led to a hive of sorts, constructed completely of skulls of daityas piled on top of each other, making a pyramid of daitya skulls. Smaller bones from neck, fingers and joints, jutted out from the ceiling to make pavillions and courtyards and even a central fountainhead.

'Have you been to Barbareeka's Palace of Bones?' asked Grrhat, his voice gritty. 'She built it last year to reflect the cultural integration that she's found in her business. Keeps adding raw material as when. And did I tell you she loves soft, juicy human bones of arrogant tantriks who steal from her?'

'They add to her personal bed.'

'Grr, I didn't mean to—'

The bharundas dragged me into a dark damp room made out of a daitya's skull and covered with skins of various animals and sups. A fire burnt in the centre, indigo through my septifocals. On either side, stood bharundas of all types, fowl faced, blue like a kingfisher with a shapely body, a tall crane-faced lady, a hummingbird who hovered at the very end of the room and a few little ones. All of them carried weapons of all kinds, long swords, short knifes, spears, lances and even old style guns. At the very end of it all, sat Queen Barbareeka, a humongous rakshasi, her legs spread apart, her pale skin cozied with theee white-green fur of a yeti, her uncombed hair falling in a tumble behind. She had two heads and four hands. She fed one of her heads meat, while with one of her hands fed a drink to the other. One of the bharundas who'd captured me, walked up to her and whispered in her ear.

'Cousin Grrhat,' her non-eating lips spoke. 'It's been a while.'

'Chomp! A stealer!' the eating-side lips spoke. *'Chomp! Chomp!'*

'Queen of Magical Creatures,' Grrhat bowed low, his nose touching the ground. 'Yes, it's been a while. She is Anantya, a female manava from up ground. I got her in for she desired sex-flesh at the linga street, but she … I had no idea she'll steal from your generous coffers.'

'I didn't steal. The nishadas are not hers. They're free creatures.'

Both her heads looked in my direction.

'You're supposed to protect your people! Not sell them to greedy tantriks for coin and blood diamonds!'

'Fire. Chomp, chomp. Roast it.'

'Bhina go find the bounty before our delivery date is due,' she sniffed. 'Manavi do you bleed?'

Grrhat frowned.

'Yes. I moonshed.'

'Good.' Both of Queen Barbareeka's heads grinned together, all four of her eyes rounding up above her broad noses. 'We always like a bit of blood on our dessert. Better than corpses sprinkled with bloodwine. Nira, cover her with daitya piss and roast her while we dine. We will finish and then have this scrumptious dessert that our cousin brings.'

Nira turned out to be a bhurunda with an owl's face and a female body which would have made an apsara insecure. She also had a strong elephantine grip. Before I could act, she grabbed me, splashed piss on my body and along with another bhurunda, this one with a sparrow's back but a woman's face and legs, picked me up, tying me around a tall bamboo stick, like a lamb about to be skewered. They put the bambooo stick on top of the fire which had been burning in the middle of the room and then stoked it. Fire burst upwards, burning my naked back.

'Ugh!' The stick was rotated, the fire licking my face and breasts and singed my pubic hair. The fire burst up, burning my shoulders and chest and hair. A scream emitted from somewhere. I realized it was me.

'Come, join us for a drink, cousin,' said Barbareeka. 'We shall share the dessert you bring.'

10

THE DUNGEON room burnt, as Barbareeka's sharp voice sounded above the sound of a chirpy chorus. The party was in full swing. In a haze of drums, backslapping and laughter, I heard Grrhat's voice.

'But, Queen-who-is-cousin—'

'Is there a difficulty? Do I not offer you good food?'

'A thief! A manavi! Blood bursting!'

'I—I'm dieting, Queen of Dire Supernaturals. So no dessert for me this night,' said Grrhat. My scream of pain turned into a guffaw.

'She's no queen!' I cried, through clenched teeth. 'She's a peddler … A *dirty rat* to the CATs.'

'Calls us a rat, she does! Chomp, chomp. Kill her.'

'Let her burn for a bit more. I desire a well-roasted dessert tonight,' said Barbareeka. The bharunda rotated me, bringing my face straight into to the fire, my hands tied from one end of the stick as were my feet. I wriggled and screamed: 'You're nothing but a two-legged ass licker!' I cried. 'You sell your kriti to upground taunts! You exchange saliva with taunts!'

'Falsity! Liar!'

'Aerrrgh!' screamed Barbareeka. 'She insults our kriti!' She thundered up, kicking the fire in fury. 'We will chomp you now!' I shut my mouth as coals flew upwards.

'Queen of Thousand Elephants, don't heed her!'

'You're a taunt mouthkisser!' I screamed. 'Toe licker!'

'ARRGAH!' She burst towards me, her four hands grabbing my body and like a twig, pulling it off the bamboo stick. She opened her mouth wide, moving her fat heat and pointed teeth to my side. I squiggled out of her iron grip, grabbed her hair, and jerked away, swinging like a monkey. She swatted her four hands, like trying to get rid of a fly. I swung, getting into her hair, blindly grabbing one root to another, moving constantly, trying to avoid the thunderous bolts of her smashing iron fists. 'ARRRGH!'

'No! She's a tantrik!' screamed Grrhat. Holding tight to another strand, I swung around, snatching a sword from a bharunda frozen in surprise, and landed bang in the middle of her face. I slashed my arm and my blood falling on her face, screamed: '*Dhoop dhan roshan kara!*'

The Dhoop mantra soaked the sunlight from my skin and spread like wave of bright sunlight, spilling bright and blinding them all for a second. Barbareeka screamed as her pale skin burned, hitting her face, her fingers trying to grab me. In the confusion and screams, I lodged myself into a cosy corner in Barbareeka's neck, pressing my blade right on top of a ticking vein.

'My lady,' I said, 'Let's take a walk to the up-ground exit, shall we?'

Barbareeka roared, a blinding sound of fury. I pushed the blade a bit, blood oozed out of the cut.

'And ask your guards to refrain from the urge to sing mournful songs. Before I dry up your blood.'

'Go!' said Barbareeka. The bharundas stepped away, letting us out.

'Grrhat, my bag,' I said without taking my eyes off Barbareeka. There was a reason rakshasas were scared of tantriks. They might have the magic piss, but it was tantriks who knew how to use it. We walked, me still lodged in Barbareeka, till the mouth of the up-ground exit. I somersaulted and jumped out of the open exit, smashing the door shut before any of the rakshasas or bharundas could come through. Not that they would, considering it was daytime. Rakshasas were creatures of the night and hated the sunlight which burned their ethereal bodies.

'Sister,' Tataiya said, 'what do we do now?' The girls huddled together, cells of one organism, waiting, still.

'Eat something,' I muttered, my stomach rumbling. I fished out my phone called Madhu, giving him our location. He screamed, then stopped and heard. I clicked the phone, took out a beedi, lit it and dragged. 'Have you girls tried chola bhatura in South Ex?'

Her hair spread across the dawn sky, latticing the dimming stars. Two blue sapphires twinkled below her, burning, brimming with desire. What is it about moments which flicker and die? With her hand clutched she tried to steal this moment, this second, steal it from Kala, the god of time and keep it safe within her somewhere, hidden in her womb. Somewhere that no one could reach. Not even her father. Neel laughed, teasing her, tickling her, his eyes softening and making her melt too. She felt his heart, beating, skipping and then beating again, under her warm palm. They laughed softly under the buttercup tree, hidden from everyone at the ashram. Their space, their world, the world where they were not playing a part in the order, where she wasn't a princess and he wasn't a pupil, a world where they had no commitments, no promises, no encumbrances. Nothing except them and the stars and dawn and the crisp bed of autumn leaves. They tumbled together, laughing and kissing, their hands and feet intertwined. He picked up a strand of her long, impossibly curly hair and rubbed his face into them, sending a tingling sensation through her nerves.

Her throat was heavy with emotion, so heavy that her tongue froze. She couldn't tell him how much her heart burnt, how much her stomach churned, how much her head thundered every time he touched her skin. She wanted to be his, fill him with herself, become his power, his shakti, his life. She wanted him to consume her, to own her, to suffuse her, to make her do his will. She pounced on him, demanding him to give her way, to take her, to consume her. He accepted her, desiring her body, her soul, her shakti. It was heaven. Except it smelled all wrong.

It smelled of filth, of ruin, of decomposing, of death. Neel opened his eyes but his sapphires were lost and only black holes remained from where maggots crawled out, clutching his sockets with their tiny, clasping claws. They came through his eyes and his ears and his mouth and his nostrils. She screamed, in terror, trying to brush away the maggots from his empty face and hands and feet and chest and eyes, trying to stop them from eating him alive as he screamed. But there were too many and her shakti didn't work. They crawled out, eating and gorging, and shitting and consuming, Neel and the stars and the dark-hued sky and the autumn leaves and the buttercup tree. The maggots spread from the dark, dark trunk, like smoke they spread, consuming the autumn leaves, the buttercup tree, the stars and the lightening of the sky at dawn.

Then they turned to her. The tree and the leaves and Neel, all rose and trickled together, weaving and raising and spreading all around her, before her and behind her, above and below. Till they made a cage, a fortress around her, a mesh of millions of maggots covering her from all over.

'Hold on to me,' cried Neel's lips, stretched and covered with maggots. She groped, a sighted human in darkness, her hands becoming claws, becoming long-fingered.

'I can't,' she cried.

'Please! Don't let go of me. I am scared!' said the lips. She waved her fingers, her arms, her head and her body clutching the wispy forms of the mesh, which started to rotate around her or maybe she rotated, revolving, going around and round, revolving around an unseen axis. Dizzy she cried his name again and again, but the maggots had him and they were nothing more than just wisps of darkness dancing

around her, their wisps becoming claws becoming vines, becoming ropes, twisting, turning, rotating around her.

'So powerless, but power thrums in you,' the wisps whispered. 'Find me, my darling. Let's become one.' Wisps of darkness and vines of maggots combined, becoming a form of sorts, a form with black holes for eyes instead of warm sapphires. 'Come, my darling. Don't you love me?'

'Yes, *so* much.' I said, desiring him, aching for him, with not only body but my whole heart too. He pulled me close to him, touching my body with his wispy hands. Maggots jumped and crawled and wriggled and brawled on my skin, owning it, etching it and making it his. 'I never want to leave you.'

'I ache for you,' he answered, his left claw twisted and clutched my right breast, clutching, hungrily grabbing the flesh, the ribcage and the heart below it. 'I desire your beating heart.' He tightened his grip, clutching, squeezing, pulling her heart out of the chest. 'I desire your life.' The maggots all started to scream and screech, clawing, biting, nipping and eating my flesh away. The dark threads rotated around, faster and faster, consuming, clutching, drinking my soul, my power and my being.

'No!' I cried, my eyes opening wide. It was dark and the maggots wriggled, eating into me. My hands wouldn't move though I ordered them to pick up the boneblade. They still grabbed onto Neel's dark neck, clutching not wanting to let him go. 'Oh, don't make us do this,' my hands cried. I ordered and screamed at them for misbehaving. 'We love him so. Let them have us,' they sang conniving with my legs to plan my destruction. The pretas sucked on me, making wet noises, clawing and sipping and sucking.

'No!' It shot out from somewhere deep inside of me, a protest, a struggle, a desire to remain alive, to not give in to these sucking hungry dark monsters. The mesh stretched like goo, pulling away but the mantra was just not strong enough. '*Vajni ghanti apahanti*!' I cried, putting together my remaining strength, pushing away from the fluid dark death, pushing away from the darkness, to life, to live. With more mental than physical strength, I shoved it away. Neel fell on the ground, thrashing like a fish out of water. I twisted and reached out, took out my bone mandala and pointing it at him screamed.

'*Bhuta pishacha darke bhag!*'

'No!' I cried, as he continued to thrash. I realized I was too. I could feel the icy cold hands of pretas still touching, clutching, clawing from inside my bones, making me gasp. He fell on the floor, as I tried to run, falling as the pretas sipped my inside. 'Sharmila's shit!' I inched and crawled and lay and crawled again, clutching onto the sides, toppling several bottles and potions and pulled myself up. The dust-covered bottles of mottled chandaali rakta, at the far end of the cabinet. I reached out for it, but by then my heads refused to accept my dominion. 'Do!' I tried to speak, but my lips didn't utter a word. My head lolled and the mantra remained on my lips, unspoken, unpowered as the pretas fed on my entrails. My legs failed, making me fall on the ground helpless, like a vegetable. I closed my eyes, feeling the hungry growl, like a beast eating me from inside, opened them again and reached out. This time my hands accepted and picked up the bottle. Holding it by its noose, I hit the glass bottle on the floor. The vintage rakta, more powerful than fresh chandaali rakta spilled, splashing on the floor. A waft of green muck rose like a doomed cloud. The pretas, invisible to the eye, spilled out of me like vomit, attracted by the blood. I grabbed a knife, slashed my index finger and screamed.

'*Um hum dhum pretam narakam!*'

This time my lips accepted my command and the pretas swooshed into the rakta, which turned black. I ran back to Neel, spilled some more vintage rakta by his side, and screamed the Bhutpresh mantra again, banishing the preta to Naraka.

'Of all the snide, cheap, acts of the world,' I cried, still gasping, still out of breath. Neel thrashed about, epilectic. I got out the potion that Manu Manava had given me and gave him a drop of it. He thrashed for a few seconds more, before steadying. I wiped off the blood from my face, spat the bitter vomit taste in my mouth and stood up, shaking, sat down, wiping sweat of Neel, who was breathing harshly still.

'Kali's ass. Attacking us while we slept! That cheap-balled, fat-assed cowardly tantrik,' I shouted. 'I will hound him to the gates of Naraka for this!' I put on my septifocals, cried the drishti mantra. The room was clear of all pretas. I pulled it off and shakily went to the rasayana lab. It was time to track the hole full of preta shit down.

'I will shave off his head and use his skull for a tea cup!' I cried, spitting again.

11

THREE HOURS later, I was headed nowhere. The mad laughter of the preta tantrik still echoed in my head and the doughy shiny ball lay in front of me, on the table, keeping its secrets firmly to itself.

'Shit of shaolin asses!' I cried. 'Where is Zaazee when I need him?' The shiny dough sat there, staring back at me. I went over to Neel, who had plonked himself on the couch, staring at the telly with unblinking eyes. He looked better after the potion, his bruises less prominent. I touched his hair, weaving my fingers through it gently. There was no reaction, but there was still hope. He had come to me while I was sleeping, he had wanted to lie with me. I would have opened my eyes to see his blue sapphires glittering on top if it hadn't been for that hell-forsaken tantrik. I needed to find that worm. I called up Shukra, convinced him to be with Neel, packed my back and after a bit of cajoling headed to Jama Masjid.

Agana Dawakhana was right there, behind Jama Masjid, on one of the busiest streets of old Delhi, but no one saw it really. Not because it was hidden by a magical firewall, but just because it seemed like a place that not many would like to venture into. It was squeezed between a stress causing kebab joint and a knick-knacks shop which did bustling business and took all the attention of the street with its gaudy streamers and a rather enthusiastic sales person who called out aloud to every being who walked on the street. Even with my height, I had to crouch to get through the door, which was three feet high, climbing down a few steps into the half basement. It was cold here, colder than the December afternoon outside. I shivered, touching its damp and dark walls, my footsteps squishing in a watery, mulchy mess on the floor. Two staircases later, I reached a small room lit up with a dull bulb, throwing dirty light on old wooden damp shelves with bottles and jars and vases, skins, teeth and bones.

Hakim Mikaz was a vaidya, a doctor of ancient potions and poisons, one of the rare ones remaining in Delhi. He nodded from behind the grime-crusted counter and nodded, his way of saying hello, as if he had customers lined up and was superbly busy. Mika was half-naga and half-human – a human's face, torso and arms with a coiled long snake-tail instead of legs. He had a head full of white hair, neatly oiled and tied up in multiple plaits, like white snakes around his face. Even though he was barely two hundred years old, about forty in human age, he was the fattest naga I knew. His stomach hung outwards, so that he had to stretch his tail behind him, or his hairy belly would drag him down.

'Sss hisssna Anantyasss …' he said, greeting me in his sticky sugar-syrup like voice, scratching his belly with his human hand.

'Ansssih Mikaz, have you seen Zaazee?' I answered.

'Nazo. Hasn't comes here since awhiless.'

I took out the squelchy diamond from my satchel and put it carefully on top of a velvet platter he had put there. 'Tell me who this belongs to.'

'Sss …' he grumbled, 'Don't buzz around like a flea. Let me sssee.' He picked up the nagamani and touched it with his forked tongue. In and out. His forehead frowned. In and out again, tasting the chemicals emitting from the mani. His white brows touched each other in disapproval. He shook his head, brought his long tongue out again and then slithered away to the extreme corner of the room, muttering to himself. He slithered to the other end of the room, stooping, his hands wriggling to the far corner of a cabinet. Few seconds later, he emerged, slithering back to the table, his pot belly wobbling. 'Where you findss?' He said, wearing a monocle and peering through the gem.

'What is it?'

'Part of a nagamani. Where did you find it?' He asked his eye enlarged by the monocle.

'It was … it belongs to someone I'm trying to find,' I said. 'Can it be used to take people to another plane?'

'Yazo. That and more. Hissna Anantyass, with right power, nagamani is powerful enough to give *life* to the dead or bring *deaths* to life itself.' His head bounced, making his white plaits dance. 'Our maternal ancestor, Kudru, the motherss of all snakess enslaved her sister Vinata, the mother of birdss. To ransom her, Garuda, Vinata's son, stoless amrita, the immortality nectar from daevas and gave it to the nagass. But before any of us drinks from us, the treacherous Indra tookss it back from usss. Till then, it was only the royal family who had touched a drop, which is why the royal family, Vasuki and his family are the only ones whosss venom createss nagamani.' He was silent for a while, muttering something to himself.

'And where do I find this Vasuki and his family?'

He stared, his irises stony. 'Yous can't.'

'They're not alive?'

'Sss.' He started to pour a golden coloured liquid in a small vial.

'Come on, Anssih Mikaz. You have to tell me.'

'Mmfss.'

'Is that a yes?'

'Mmfss.'

'We can play this game the whole day.'

'Only someoness who wants to get killed would think of seeing the Ancient.'

'My psychologist did tell me I have suicidal tendencies,' I said grinning.

'Vasuki isss … not good anymore … not sssafes. Dangerousss.'

'Works for me.'

He muttered to himself, in naga, his hands taking out a rat from one vial, clubbing it to pieces, gutting the brown skin and gobbling it. He munched on his lunch, eyeing me.

'It will cossst you a nest or two.'

I nodded. 'Your skin, your decision.' He rounded his shoulders, wiping his hand and moving it in my direction for me to come. He turned, leading me to the side room. 'Remove all your clothes and leave everything behind.'

'I have to take my boneblade with me!' I protested, getting out of my clothes.

'Nothing goesss to Bhogawati, but nakedss. Sss. Comess. Drink the mani.' He opened a small trapdoor behind his counter as I gobbled the nagamani. It was rubbery in texture but at the same time like a rock. I swallowed, hoping it won't choke me. Large red ants crawled out of the hole, scattering in anger and panic and the trapdoor opened. He picked a few and made them bite me on my wrists.

'Here drink this.' He handed a little micro-condom shaped tube.

'What is it?'

'Don't waste time, Hisssna Aaantya,' he answered turning away. I squeezed the tube, dropping its content into my mouth. It tasted like melted rubber, gliding into my food pipe, thick like lava. 'Ok, now what?' With a flick of his tail, he gave me a hard push. I slipped on the damp floor, tumbled ahead, straight into the red ant's nest. 'Take the path which is the coldest. May Mani shine on you.'

My scream was bottled up by the thick lava-like thing Mikaz had given me, which suddenly grew thicker and thicker or maybe my neck grew thinner and thinner. Angry ants started to crawl on my hands and neck and hair and face, walking on my eyes, and legs and climbing up places I wouldn't tell you names of.

Then darkness became alive and a tunnel rushed up to me and I started to slither down it, falling, tumbling, and slithering, into the dark damp hole full of the metallic smell of red ants.

Phachak! Water surrounded me, immersed me. I glided through it, feeling the cave around, following others like me, snakes all of them wriggling in the waters. Without anyone speaking, I knew it was a busy road I followed. My vision became murky and secondary. It was my skin, my whole body, a black wriggling beast, that picked up the signals, the vibrations, the movement of water, its current.

Water became alive, its temperatures wavering. I felt the current and followed it. The current touched my nerves and told me I was now in the main highway that snakes and nagas took to their city. I followed mutely. Time had no significance so I didn't know how much had passed, but my mind seemed to be the same because I was wondering about time and wondering what the hour could be.

If I was underwater when I changed back to my human form, it would be quite disastrous. Mikaz could've warned me about that.

The path kept meandering, up and down the water body, left and then right and then right again. As suddenly as it had begun, it ended, sort of scattering in all directions into thin faint paths. I hesitated when another body coiled on mine whispering a zing of anger through the touch. I flickered my tongue at the body, angry myself, trying to put in as many swear words as one can possibly in a snap of a tail and forked tongue. The snake shrank away and disappeared in one of the many lanes. I slurped, tasting the water, slurping and tasting it again till I found the current with the coldest touch, just as Mikaz had told me. It was a thin saline trail, almost dry, like a path in the forest that not many have ventured on. The water drift turned cold and colder still, making me shiver, before it stagnated and stopped. I jumped out of the water body and was for a moment suspended in the air, turning, twisting and converting back into my body. My human eyes returned, blinding me as it was dark all around. I walked out of the pool, stumbling, falling and pulling myself onto a landing of sorts, made of smooth cold stone with tufts of fungi. I shivered. It was colder here, colder than a refrigerator and my human body was naked and wet.

'Who goes?' Cold light spread from somewhere on my left, replacing the blinding darkness with blinding light. My eyes squeezed, cringing and I wished I had an eagle's vision instead. Human eyes are completely unreliable when it comes to dealing with sups or places where there's no tubelight.

'A human and a friend of Mikaz's,' I answered to the white cold light. It moved, gliding in towards me. My eyes started to form the shape of a halfling, a snake's body and a snake's pout with human eyes and lips. The halfling slurped, showing me its forked tongue, tasting the smells coming from my body. Behind him were two or three more halflings, formless in the semi-darkness. Instinctively my hand reached towards the scabbard and instead touched naked skin. Without my boneblade and locket and even ring I felt truly naked, defenseless. It wasn't a problem physically but could become a huge problem without my weapons.

'What you looking for, human?' He was naked except for a golden medallion of twisted snakes in a golden string around his neck.

'Vasuki,' I answered. He came close to me, spilling his cold light on my body. It wasn't a torch really, more like a gliding sea animal that he held in his palm, like a lamp. The creature squiggled sending ripples of light. He slurped his fang and then grinned, a strange amalgamation with human lips and a pout of a snake.

'That fangless old fart?' He glided around me, the formless shadows of halflings together, bunched up behind him. 'What does he have that a young human like you is looking for?'

'That's my business.' My hands on my wet hips I scowled.

'Groove with Kooliz instead, *baby*. We are way cooler than the Ancient.' They came forward together, rising up, snaking up, a couple towering overhead, really close to me. I was about to attack when I heard the music, playing behind somewhere. Smiling, I put my hands on my waist, one foot away, cocked my head and smiled. 'Later, *maybe*. You'll have to show you're worth snaking with me, *baeby*.' I said, touching his flattened, half human nose with the tip of my finger. He put his head back, human like and laughed.

'Oo, such a tease,' he grinned, his teeth yellowed and crooked. Unused. 'Do one little shake with us and then we will take you to that old fart Ancient.' I smiled and he waved his neck. 'Let's go snakies!' In sync, they turned, touching me, sniggering, dancing, twisting and turning, their scaly skin and hands touching my body at various places. And as suddenly as that I was part of their gang.

We entered Bhogawati from a small side gate, its intricately carved naga sculptures and busts lying in the carpet of moss, forgotten, broken, a few of the gems fallen, covered with moss. The city inside was the same. Structures which would have been magnificent at one time, elaborate carving on their tall columns and their ceilings and fronts, were half fallen, caved in, broken, some gems still shining from behind the layer of moss, some gobbled up by the damp, squib road that we walked on, lying covered, unused and forgotten. I had heard about the naga richness and their cities paved with gems and precious stones instead of stone, but I had never imagined it this grand. At its height it would have been a glittering, glistening city with ceilings and walls and columns covered from ground to up with intricately carved sapphires, rubies, blue cobalts and violet amethysts. Everything now was broken, and had a clingy damp smell, sort of like a cellar that had been closed for far too long. The round-shape doors to houses on either side were dark and empty, some dangling, some half-open, moss and fungi having taken ownership. Sometimes different types of snakes oozed through them on the road, hurrying somewhere, everyone with an edge of fear, an edge of alertness.

'Who rules now?' I asked. I hadn't really followed on naga politics. Dhuma had told me that the nagas had been a monarchy since the longest of time, before King Vasuki had abdicated the throne about fifty years ago and made it an oligarchy. So instead of one mad king, they were ruled by a bunch of equally crazy nobility.

'Sss. We do.' He made a sign spreading his webbed hand and wriggling his middle finger. The others did the same, grinning in that disconcerting fashion which was both snake-like and human-like. 'We are Sarpstars, the ruling gangsta of Bhogawati Ancient. You're one lucky babe, that you slithered our way. Had you gone to the suburbs, Talaa and Sutalaa, are against any alliance with the 'leggeds. They would've bitten your soft skin and thrown you into the Hataki before you could say "baby".'

'What happened to the nobles?'

'The sadlicks?' the halfling on Kooliz's side slurped, who had introduced himself as Ghetz. 'Them don't care about us snakelings. They tear down their palaces and coin off shiny stones to the legged upgrounds.'

'Sss,' slithered Kooliz. 'The oldking gave away his throne and the sadlicks have been selling the city to up-grounds for fangfix. No one cares about snakelings, so we thought it's time halflings stood up to the nobles. We arm ourselves and fight the other gangstas to protect ours.'

'Fangfix? That's bad quality anti-venom. They would die,' I said.

'Once they have it, their bodies become still, their eyes vacant and their forked tongues slack. They go to some other plane and remain there for a whole revolution of Hataki through Patala. After a while, when they come back to their self, they hate it and want to go to the other world again, slurping some more of fangfix.'

The deeper we went, the further on I felt the decay, the neglect that the city had gone though. Its once gem-encrusted roads were now cratered and filled with murky, marshy growths. The snakes, halflings and nagas went about hushed, slithering as if from an unknown enemy, running away. The Serpstars, however, walked fearless, gliding with a curvaceous swagger, relaxed, without a hurry.

The palace wasn't hard to miss. It was the biggest, boldest structure of its kind, its entrance caved in and covered from one end to another by a thick layer of moss and fungi. We walked inside it through the marshy path, which was now knee deep for me, as I waddled through like a duckling. I was slow and the others smoothly negotiated the marshy land with their slithering, slick skins. Other than us, the path was empty.

'Who lives here other than Vasuki?'

'No one. His sister, Manasa, left him after they had a fight and since then no one.'

'Doesn't anyone attack the palace?'

'Oh, the old king ruled us for centuries. The tongues of all gangstas slacken at the very thought of him. He's an Ancient. No one attacks him.'

The palace was hushed, completely quiet, with not even any noise of insects. Even the moss and marshes covering its columns and balustrades and floors, seemed deferential, quiet as if they were in his territory and knew it. We entered a grand hall, which would have been absolutely stunning in its time, its high ceiling carved with intricate designs of precious stones in shapes of nagas and their daily lives, as were the columns and walls it stood on. Now, some of the walls had crumbled, columns have broken and scattered, and everything was covered by the bright green moss that was everywhere in Bhogawati. The swishes that the gangstas made, and my clumsy waddle, was the only sound in the palace. I noticed Kaniz make the same sign again, the one with webbed hands spread and the innermost finger closed.

'Wh—' Something moved from the side of my eye and before I could react, I was rolled as in a carpet, turned upside down, a snake tail coiling around my body. The Serpstars fell away, becoming smaller as I rose, higher and higher, rotating fast, turning around, heading straight for the ceiling. Just in the nick of time, the tail flicked and like a doll, I turned from facing the floor to standing position, a tail coiled around me from my toes till my shoulders, making me immobile. I stood facing a five-headed naga, his central head more human, its snout flat, becoming more snakehead as it went beyond, their fangs spread in attention. Ten pairs of ruby-red, wine-coloured eyes stared. Above them in his forehead was a bright white light, shining like millions of car headlights.

'Why have you got a manava into our halls, Kaulashekhara?' Vasuki asked, He squeezed me tighter. I gulped.

'My lord,' I said, bowing my neck as everything else was immobile, hoping he could see the nape of my neck, a sign of docility. 'I asked them to bring me here.'

'And why should they follow your command? Their king is still alive.' His voice echoed, booming in the empty hall. His eyes glittered like ruby disks.

'Not a command, a request to see your highness. They had no choice since they are serpbound to Mikaz who sent me.'

'Sss. They still follow the old ways.'

'We all do, sire,' said Kooliz, bowing his head. Vasuki's tail uncoiled around me, dropping me on the marshy ground. I stood up.

'Why don't you listen to our command!' His voice boomed in the hall, crashing a column at the very end. 'Why don't you follow the nobles?'

'They are not go—'

'Silence! We want none of you traitors and terrorists around. *Leave*, before we dirty our hands and commit skinning.'

'Your highness,' I said, raising my voice. 'I come to you for help! You won't send me back empty-handed. That is no way of kings.'

'We are a king without a kingdom.'

'But a king still. And as a king you need to be generous to the one who stands in your hall.'

'You are a human. Our rules don't apply to you creatures.'

'Do they apply to chiranjeevis, Your Highness?' In a blur, he coiled and uncoiled, his tail suddenly there, all around me though not touching me and his ten eyes staring at, blood-red, each one wide as a disk.

'The chiranjeevis are ancients like *us*.' His voice thundered in the hall. My hair rolled back, panicked. I stood with my feet apart, naked, refusing to move, refusing to budge or cringe. 'We have kept our side of the curse.'

'What curse?'

'We are the grand-king of nagas. The Skin-shedders. We are all powerful, royalty from the gods themselves. An immortal race. Why would we be bothered by other chiranjeevis? We are older than all other ancients. They walk up-ground, beggars to the new world, while we still rule our city, the city we built with our own bare hands. Our subjects still love us, shower praise on us, worship us. We are God to them.' He uncoiled moving back into the darkness of the endless hall.

'Then why sell your nagamani to a tantrik?' Silence and stillness and darkness. For a second I thought he had left, never to come again to answer me.

'Our nagamani?'

'Why give it to an up-ground tantrik?' He slithered around, away in the darkness, moving slowly this time, but out of my sight. I could feel him staring, feel it the way my blood rushed forward and backwards, a choppy sea stuck in thin veins.

'We did not. He did come to us for it. But after the Matsya Curse, we would never trust a tantrik again.'

'Then who could've … Your Highness, where is your sister now?'

'That traitor!' Vasuki spat venom, making the ground sizzle to a burnt patch. 'She revolted against us, her own brother, her king! She has lived up-ground for too long. Wants the kingdom to be ruled by *all* snakes, everyone, even the commoners.' He spat again, making a column sizzle this time.

'We've lived far too long. To see the night where a sister, a mere female, refused her brother, her king's command! May an army of mongoose attack her! She is up-ground now, begging to survive. Suits a *rat* like her. When she dies, and we would know, we will celebrate, with a festival that Bhogawati has never seen!' He fell silent then. His ruby eyes staring at me.

I shifted weight from one leg to another. 'I will take your leave then, Your Highness. It's been a pleasure meeting—'

'Leave? Sss.' As fast as lightening, he coiled around me, tightening his hold, hard enough to squeeze me to death if he wanted it so. 'No puny manava may spread lies about Bhogawati.'

'I won't say anything up-ground.'

'Oh but you would. We see you are a female manava and like other females, you can't keep your mouth closed. So we'll consume you. Kaulashekhara, you and your group can leave.'

'Yes, Your Highness.'

'Weren't we a gang?' I cried, squiggling, shaking, trying to get free from the iron hold.

'Sorry sista. When you came here, we knew this was it for you.' Kooliz slithered back, his webbed hand raised with his middle finger folded in, turning to leave with his group.

'You could've warned me!' I cried from behind, my voice echoing in the empty halls. 'At least you got your answers!' he cried.

'We will treat our special guest with a special death.' The king of nagas tightened his coil around my body moving with a suddenness that left me gasping.

12

VASUKI'S VAST body coiled tighter around me. Not hurriedly mind you, as if he had all the time in the world. The blasted cold-blooded beast.

'We want to test how long you can live in our hold.' He squeezed a little more, his scales barely touching my skin now. Squeeze. Squeeze. We were skin to skin. Squeeze. Squeeze. I curled my fists, pounding them on his vast tail. Squeeze. Squeeze.

'Leave me!' I cried. Squeeze, squeeze. I thought about Neel and about how we'd met after seven years, only to be separated again. Touching the dampness of his scales, I spread my fingers and made the varada mudra, palm pressing his skin and shouted.

'*Kadak kaadak vidyutara*!'

A jolt moved through my body, hitting his scales, his grip loosened for a flash and I jumped out, scurrying away behind a pillar. His tail lashed at the pillar as he let out a hiss of madness. I ran, looking for something that could help me. His five-headed hood was in front of me before I could even reach the gate. He opened his mouth wide, his sharp fangs glistening with venom, and right on top of me, dripping death. Darkness surrounded me, glistening darkness of Vasuki's damp mouth. I grabbed the fang and swung around, interlocking my feet around the curved tooth. He moved his head, angered, I swung, my arms firmly around the fang, as the blackhole of his mouth loomed below.

'Out!' he screamed, his ear-splitting voice booming inside his mouth. I wriggled, hitting his venom sack with my dangling leg.

'Not till you let me live!' I screamed back, my voice echoing in the long, endless tunnel that was his body. He thundered, shaking his enormous head. My grasp loosened and I slipped, reaching the fang's poisonous tip and trying to scuttle back. His mouth yawned, crunching on a broken column. Crumbs and stones flew by me, into his tunnelled body. One hit me on the head and I slipped, falling down in his belly, trying to get a hold, grab something.

'Stop, brother.'

'Manasa!' Vasuki screamed in a maddened, deep-throated tone, gurgling. Things flew out around me as his stomach pushed us out, spewed along with other dead things he'd consumed onto the mossy ground. 'You traitor!' he screamed.

Manasa stood in front, her frothing brother above her, much smaller than him, the size of halflings, with a formidable five fanged hood rising behind her human head.

'Where's the mani?' she asked, her voice was cool, like a mint balm on wounds.

'What mani?' cried Vasuki, his tail thrashing. 'You traitor! I'm going to kill you!'

'Quick, Anantya! The mani!' She cried, in a flash, coiling her tail around my legs and dragging me away just as Vasuki's tail slammed the ground where I'd been standing. She slipped with me in a small niche between two columns. Vasuki's scream echoed through the hall.

'Give me the mani!' she said.

'Tell … me who is … the tantrik,' I asked, trying to retch out the fumes of venom I'd inhaled.

'You stubborn human!' cried Manasa. She snapped at my lips with her forked tongue. I felt an urgent need to puke, crouching on all fours, coughing, puking my guts out, just as Vasuki had done. The mani fell on the floor, like a piece of rubber, it's light blinding me as I continued to puke. Manasa grabbed the mani, turned and flung it towards the entrance of the hall.

'Do it. *Now!*'

The streak of light travelled through the hall, lighting up Vasuki's five heads as they turned to the mani. The two columns thundered, crumbling on top of us. I crawled and tried to run, only to be bound by Manasa's body which coiled around me, squeezing my body, arms and face. 'Don't do anything stupid, Anantya.'

From the shadows, a tall person emerged, the mani cupped in his hand, its light streaking his cloak into swishing pretas. *No!*

'Ashwathama,' Vasuki's voice echoed, coiling into a tight angry pose. 'You've joined our sister have you?'

'Yes,' Ashwa answered, his voice gruff. 'We are abominations, Vasuki. We need to die.'

'We are immortals. Wise Ancients!'

'No. We are *cursed*. And we shall be free! Death has come to free us all!' His hands rose, his cloak fluttering like a group of cats on a hot roof. Swirls of darkness emerged from them, as he furled the light in Vasuki's direction, mouthing a mantra. I squiggled free from Manasa's hold, screaming.

'Don't be a drama queen, Ashwa!' I cried. 'Stop—'

Manasa firmly wrapped her body around my mouth again. I bit her. She squirmed, her grip loosening. I bit her again, tasting blood. I struggled with Manasa, attacking her with my hands and legs and teeth and butting my head. We tumbled.

The light from the nagamani turned into a crackle of light. The high hall crumbled and the air screamed. A sea of black fluid floated out, rushing towards Vasuki. Angered, he struck Ashwa's face.

'Come, Vasuki,' Ashwa's voice boomed in the liquid darkness. Taking hold of Manasa's hair, I kicked her in the face, somersaulting and crouching. Vasuki's moan, a thunder of pain, made the hall tremble. I bit my finger, opened the vial of rakpiss, dipped it mixing blood with piss and screamed in the inky darkness's direction.

'Mahayan jalaa mayan agnidah!'

Mayan fire. Bad, bad idea, that. The all-consuming, uncontrollable fire flashed through my mouth.

'Stop, you imbecile immortal!' I cried as Ashwa's form diluted, surrounded by the inky darkness, floating as if in water, mixing, vanishing, like it never existed. He vanished, leaving Vasuki's shedded skin behind. The mayan fire raged, gorging everything in its way, the discarded flesh, the moss, the pillars and the ceiling. Without my boneblade, I had no control over it, so it ate, burning the mossy patch, climbing up the broken columns and the fungi, spreading on the knee-deep waters, climbing walls and columns and ceilings.

'Anantya! Stop this,' cried Manasa. 'Before you burn down my city!'

'Get away you suicide-inducing ulllu!' I cried, hitting her body, wriggling.

'You stupid stubborn manava!' Manasa cried, her heads rising suddenly. Her voice echoed in the hall, razor-sharp now, like icicles falling all over. 'Listen to me!' she hollered.

'Why in Naraka's name should I?'

She wriggled and slapped both her hands on either side of my ear. My head rang.

'Because I'm your friend. Zaazee.'

And just like that, I knew it. I staggered back, falling on my back, my tongue numb, making me gasp. The mayan fire raged, outside and inside burning red and blue and yellow and green.

'Zaazee? You're a fucking *princess?* But ... but, you don't have a beard!' I said sounding lame even to myself. The hungry mayan fire poured, burning us. Manasa screamed as the fire caught up with her, burning her fangs. I jumped up.

'I need blood,' I cried. She threw something in my direction. I deftly caught it. My boneblade. I looked up, our eyes meeting, nodded, grabbed her, slashed her wrist, into the cup of my palm.

Dipping my boneblade into it and feeling the Shakti cursing through my veins.

'*Ghani bhavati*!' I turned around, splattering the blood in all directions. Blood flowed from my hand to the boneblade to the air, dousing the fire. It was a slow, tedious and tiring process since the fire had spread quite a lot, but at the end of it, it died. I fell down in the knee-deep dampness, exhausted. Manasa wriggled to me, frowning. Manasa, the princess of Bhogawati, Vasuki's sister, an old naga who had the bloods of Kudru running in her veins. She just happened to be Zaazee, my bearded naga roommate, who I'd rubbed the tummy of for two years now.

'Fucking grass!' I cried, kicking the burnt out moss.

'Are you—' Manasa reached out for me. I got up and slapped her scaled face. She stepped back, shocked and angered.

'You are the *silliest* snake in the history of nagas! If you still had a beard, I would've tugged it till you had tears in your eyes,' I screamed, angrily hitting the boneblade into a broken piece of ruby and breaking it into smithereens. The cavity in the middle of her forehead deepened as she frowned. She quietly handed me my satchel and sat down. I took a deep breath, opened my yugma locket and took a swig of rakpiss.

'You used Ashwa to get rid of Vasuki,' I said. 'Without realizing that both of you have played into a tantrik's hands.'

'My Queen, the nobles are—' A bunch of nagas, standing at the entrance.

'Tell them to wait. I will come in a few night-minutes.' I took out a beedi, lit it and took a long drag, cringing at the gummy aftertaste. The dark carpet of the giant naga's burnt skin spread out before me.

'Ashwa trusts the tantrik.'

'Ashwa's an imbecile. Why in Naraka's name would you trust a tantrik of all creatures? Haven't you lived with me long enough?'

We sat in silence, I simmering with anger, she lost in her

own thoughts. The nagas, who had been gathering, hissed softly, whispering to each other.

'Bhogawati needed to be free of him. His mind had withered away centuries ago, though his body remained undying. He needed to die, he needed to end so that we, the rest of the nagas and snakes, could start afresh. Creatures, they should die. Immortality is not natural. What's born should die and Ashwathama agrees with me. When he told me he'd found a way to bring Yamraj to my brother, I didn't think twice. I scooped out my nagamani and handed it to him. I didn't—'

'Why didn't you come to me?'

'I didn't think—'

'Yes, you didn't. The preta tantrik is not running a fucking NGO here, offering euthanasia to immortals for societal benefit! He's out there, planning something much more creepy with all the immortals he continues to add to his collection. And you've gone and handed him the most powerful fucking amulet in the nine universes! And in the process, taken the only fucking friend I'd made in this crazy city in *three years*!' I got up and dusted my buttocks. 'Now, I've to go and save that idiot immortal's ass.'

'I—' Manasa began, looking at the bunch of nagas who had gathered together on the gate.

'Yes, go. Build your city! Shakti knows it needs a fresh coat of paint. I'm off, trying to save your stupid nagamani, a 12000-year-old tantrum-throwing toddler and my own fucking city.' She turned, slithering to her people. My heart plummeted, all anger drained.

'Zee!' I cried, before I could stop myself. She turned back around, her eyes glistening with tears. 'You—' Words failed me. She slithered back, touched my face with her webbed fingertips. I gulped, leaning my cheek into her soft, delicate fingers. 'You need to collect your things,' was all I managed to say. She nodded, holding my hand, assuring me as I had assured her all those years. Manasa. My naga roommate, with whom I had a pact of never talking about the past. And now her past had destroyed whatever semblance of home I'd built up in this city. There had to be a irony goddess laughing her head off somewhere! We reached our – my home – heading inside. Shukra pounced on me like a tiger.

'Anantya!' He jumped on top of me, smothering. 'We have to go. There's been—' He stopped, took in Manasa and asked. 'Who's this?'

'Shukra, meet Manasa, the latest version of Zaazee.'

'Zee? You're a girl?' exclaimed Shukra, his mouth hanging open, his eyes popped out.

'Not a girl, a fucking princess,' I said, dumping my satchel. 'Where do we have to go, Shukra?'

'Oh, yes,' he pushed his specs up his fat nose. 'Madhu called. He told me to get you to JNU immediately.'

'Storm-hitting-shit. Why didn't you say so? Zee—Manasa, will you be with Neel?'

She nodded. I grabbed my satchel, kick-started my bike, packed Shukra's bulk behind me and zoomed into the morning sun.

13

TO SAY Professor Bodhgaya's lab had been ransacked was like saying a tsunami had hit a well. The lab had been butchered, turned upside-down, with malice and an intention to destruct. Books were scattered and torn, the apparatus broken, even pipes wrenched from the walls. Everything methodically smashed to pieces with a blunt weapon. Even the furniture had been broken, deep craters left in the floor.

'He called me two hours ago and told me that he had given the antidote to the girls, that they would soon be free of the virus,' said Madhu. He looked haggard, like he hadn't slept well. 'And then mumbled something about his appendix and having some trouble with it. I rushed to his lab and found him like this. Why would someone do this to him?'

'Shit,' I said, gaping. What Madhu referred to was the body of the professor which had been cut into pieces, an arm here, a leg there and nailed to the wall. The same had been done with his hair, grey and wiry, spread across on top. Even the spectacles were there, placed delicately. It was a collage of sorts, painted over with excessive skill with blood, a sort of an abstract of the professor.

'I will take a few samples,' said Shukra, his voice heavy. I quietly wore my septifocals and muttered the drishti mantra. The world came alive, as fire all around me. I walked from the lab to the other room, where Madhu had told me Bodhgaya had put the nishadas. Nothing. Nada. There was no one here, nothing alive that is. Taking the septifocals off, I walked around, aimlessly, crouching every now and then to look at the broken things that lay strewn everywhere.

'Did anyone see who came?'

'No,' answered Madhu. I walked around, looking, poking. A familiar glint caught my eye. 'I made sure no one saw the nishadas come here, but Bali's Naraka, how will we stop word about this from spreading now? My boss will—'

'I am sorry I put you into this Madhu,' I said, picking up a piece of thin, long wood, familiar from before. 'A fucking paintbrush,' I said. My fists clenched on the piece of cloth. 'Saranyu. How did she find out so soon?'

'Let's find the nishadas first. We'll deal with the how later,' said Madhu. 'Shukra?'

'I'm done. Will go back to the lab,' answered Shukra, packing the samples into his neat leather bag. 'Hey, Anantya, by the way ...'

'What?'

'It's Neel. I ran a blood test on him, a basic test which just checks his lipid profile and—'

'Wait! You ran a test on Neel, without my—You think he's one of your lab rats?'

'I didn't think you'd have a problem with—'

'You. Stay. *Away*' – I fished out my boneblade, jumped up and pressed it on Shukra's thick hairy neck. The same neck that I had been so tempted to touch all these months – 'from my boyfriend.'

Shukra didn't move, instead he gently put his wide hand on my shoulder.

'Anantya!' cried Madhu, coming behind me. 'Can we focus—'

'Your boyfriend?' said Shukra, 'You think he's your boyfriend? I am not sure he's human! Will you at least look at what I found?'

'You're not to touch him!' I cried. 'Ever! Do I make myself—'

'You're too emotional!' cried Shukra, 'You're being irrational and acting like a hormone-controlled teenager!'

'Anantya!' Madhu pulled me back. 'What is wrong with you guys? A friend just died and you're bickering like schoolchildren?'

'And you're acting like the cold-hearted worm that you are!' I cried back.

'Guys!' cried Madhu. 'Shukra, go back to your lab now and test out all these samples. And Anantya, do you want to save these nishadas or not?'

'Just keep him away from me and Neel,' I cried, storming out.

'I hope I'm right in assisting you with your rather unusual methods of investigation, Mr Madhu Tripathi,' said Wizam. 'For this,' he casually waved his hand, 'concoction of vile smells sure doesn't look like a good way to find the kidnapped creatures.'

His reaction was quite normal, I stressed to myself, taking a long drag of my beedi but it was his arrogant smirk that made me want to box him straight on his pointed chin. For some reason, Madhu had thought that letting the arrogant shit into the plan was a good way to make sure that this became official. After all, he'd reasoned, Wizam is handling the prostitution ring case, and will be able to give us official support. More than what Madhu seemed capable of. Whatever that meant.

'Fif me the fufume—' I said, my voice electronic as I had put a clasp on my nose. Madhu quietly handed me the perfume. The evening light ran from the rough pentagon I had drawn on the concrete surface. The abandoned building where the scientist had been killed just a few hours ago, loomed in front, half hiding the winter light behind it. I muttered the mantra again, slashed my middle finger this time with the boneblade so a drop of blood fell into the pentagram.

'Rajni Gandha.'

The whisper travelled over the treat I had collected last minute from a yatu hakim I knew in Connaught Place, the only one who would have anything of the kind. Three raw pig livers, three dried eyes of toads and three of lizards, mixed up with sprinkles of crushed butterfly and locust wings and heady bright purple ooze of the greedha plant from the highlands of Himalaya. It was sprinkled liberally with yaksha's poop or a god's fart, a smell that could hit your head with the force of a flying truck and put you in a coma. The smell was strong enough to bring in any gandhas, those lucid smell-hogs, from the whole city. I chewed my lower lip, trying hard not to think about Shukra. Fuck, why did my friends always betray me like this? Why couldn't I find one, a single friend, who would just not do something stupid?

The air above the pentagon shimmered with a fat spread, like a monsoon cloud over a grey sky. Soon the food started to lose its colour, fading into a pale, transparent grey before turning into blackened spots. I took a silent sigh of relief. Rajni, the best-smelling thing in town, was here. I would find the girls. Someone gasped in relief behind me as the intensity of the smells reduced. I'd asked all eight of them to keep this nose strictly pinched. One had apparently not heeded, for he lay flat on the ground. Yaksha poop. It did that to you. The gandha solidified, his way of a burp after a meal, misshapen the huge wart on an equally humongous pair of nostrils concretising. So as to not disturb his post-dinner ruminations, I just said a casual hi.

'*Gulabo ki kasam*! Not again, not again!' it exclaimed, its nostrils flaring. 'Anantya Tantrist, yes?'

'And hello to you too,' I said rather cheerfully, aware of Wizam's stare.

'Next time,' Rajni Gandha said, his nostrils twitching upwards from the pentagram, sniffing at me, 'instead of trapping me with smells, why don't you just call me instead? More professional and quite easy.'

I snorted. 'As if you would come.'

'Oh, didn't I tell you? It was my Gulabo's idea. She says, "you're so good with smelling people's things, why not do family bisniss with it?" Enough smells on the table for the whole family. So I start bisniss of smells. To find something, ten smells, to find someone, twenny. And no more trapping. Tantriks and sups call, I do the smelly work. Simple. No need for traps and blood bonds. I smell for smells in return.'

'Twenty!' I exclaimed, 'That's daylight robbery!'

'Price of the best, is the best smells.'

'I want you to find someone right now.'

'That costs you extra. Five yaksha-poop dollops. My smellies, all four of them, they love it. As does Gulabo.' The nostrils flared. 'But you will give it. You stink of the sweaty greasy thing that you tantriks always smell like. *Desperation*. So that's my price. Twenty smells and five yaksha-poop dollops.'

'Fine,' I answered. It wasn't me who would be paying him anyway. I quickly gave him the shred of red I had picked up from the lab. 'I need her location. Right now.'

His nostrils narrowed as he sniffed the cloth. 'Ah, what a rare, rare smell. I would decrease the price for it, just for the smell of these delicate creatures, but then what would my family eat, I say? What would Gulabo eat?'

'Where is she?'

'Nishada. So rare. Many, not one has secreted on this piece of cloth I hold. All different ages. Fifeen years, twelve, thirfeen-and-a-half. But something else I smell upon them.' He sniffed it again. 'A disease in their veins, an organism, alive, eating into their insides. It's raw, like silvermoon, raw and powerful.'

'Where are they?' I asked. He sniffed the cloth and then in all directions and started to hover, ready to leave.

'Follow me, all,' I said. Once Rajni had the trail he didn't like to wait. I started Chhotu as his formlessness perched on top of my head, and hit me hard on the nose. '... the hell' I mumbled wiping off my watery eyes.

'I follow the trail. Your nose follows me. My motto,' he said gliding off.

'Snotty sprite,' I grumbled, rubbing my nose which had already begun to itch and kickstarting the bike. Wizam, his six lookalikes and Madhu squeezed into an SUV and followed a puny, noisy Chhotu through the fast dying evening. Rajni Gandha led me, a bit surprisingly, right outside the Triya Art Gallery. The move to murder a scientist and bring nishadas back to your own art gallery was either horrifically stupid or audaciously arrogant. And Saranyu and her children didn't come across as stupid. I wondered if I should've called Manu and updated him.

'By Kali's tail,' I muttered rubbing my nose. 'You better be right today, Rajni.' We entered from the gate, walking down the courtyard with the canopy of yalis above us. The evening sun had set, leaving behind a soft smear of blood red, like the paint on the wall.

'Are you sure you'll find those creatures here?' asked Wizam.

'No,' I spat, again to hide the fact that I wasn't sure. 'I am just taking a stroll in this rather charming garden.' A giggle escaped someone from behind, making Wizam turn in fury. I walked ahead, trying not to feel the hammering of my heart. What did these people have to be so unafraid?

The art gallery still rolled the same exhibition whose launch night I had attended a few evenings ago: Wombs of Immortality. The now familiar black-scaled face of a nishada girl stared at me, naked and helpless, plastered on the big poster outside the first gallery.

The twins, both of them, together, stood in the first gallery, their divine faces shimmering like dying sunrays, a beautiful bygone dream. They greeted us all with a polite but fake smile.

'Where are they?' I asked quietly, after the introductions were done. My hand curled up subconsciously on the boneblade in the scabbard on my waist.

'Who do they ask for Das?' asked one to the other, leaning against a wall.

'No clue at all, Nas,' answered the other, leaning on the opposite wall, in exactly the same way. They looked at each other, looked back at me, and then said in a musical chorus. 'We don't know who you ask for.'

'She asks for the nishada girls.' Madhu frowned.

'Oh, you want the tribal girls?'

'Why didn't you say it before?'

'Come, come!'

They led us inside, from one gallery to the other, until my nose had stopped twitching. We stood in the main gallery of the art house. The one where I had stood a few days ago, pretending to be a nishada.

'Here they are!' toned one of them, pointing to the paintings on the wall alongside us. 'We painted them ourselves!'

'Voila!' said the other pointing to the paintings on the wall facing us. They skidded and skirted, putting their heads back together.

'Now, most of them are taken already but if you want to buy, this, this and this,' he said moving from one painting to another, 'are available. It's easy. The paintings don't have little red dots. Mother makes it quite easy.'

'Where are the girls?' asked Madhu quietly.

'We just told you,' answered Nas. 'But you can't buy, for the gallery has closed for the day.'

'Great, so you won't mind us searching for the whole place, would you now?' Wizam, his men, Madhu and me scattered in all different directions. I headed to the green room where Baza had taken me that night and where I'd seen Chiri melting. I gulped, a deep anger beginning to thrum in me.

We scanned the rooms, the halls, the galleries, one after the other, peeping into store rooms, and even the two offices and toilets. No room was big enough to hold sixteen nishadas. I roamed about in Triya's galleries, looking behind curtains, behind boards, even behind paintings, wondering where it was they could be. But somehow the confident malice in the twins' eyes had convinced me that no one would find the nishadas here. Had Rajni been wrong? If not, where were they hiding them? I looked at the paintings, still there, some with red dots and some blank, for sale. The nishadas drawn in them, one in a red boudoir sprawled on an equally red bed, another lying naked in a dreary hall with a fake landscape on one side, a third in a dungeon. All outsiders in locked rooms. I looked at their yellow eyes, staring at their black bodies and their glistening scales. The artist had drawn them real, bringing out the glint of their bodies as they lay on the sprawled bed, ready, inviting. But for what? What were Saranyu and the twins doing to the nishadas? What were they using them for? How had they become diseased and why was no one treating them?

'I don't think we should've followed your tantrik consultant, Mr Madhu,' said Wizam, loud enough for me to overhear. 'There's nothing here. If they complained to the head for harassment, both you and me are in trouble.' Madhu looked at me, helpless and frustrated. Saranyu walked in, gliding, looking ravishing in a tantri gown which showed off all contours of her shapely body.

'I sincerely hope the CBI has a warrant, or have you not told your boss about this raid on the side?'

'See!' whispered Wizam. 'I told you this was trouble. If she goes to Nandan—'

'Wait,' said Madhu. 'Miss Saranyu, I would like to thank you for allowing us to enter. We haven't come with a warrant since we are still investigating the case.'

'A case which involves harassing innocent people?' she said softly, almost like she was asking someone if they would have more tea. 'Mr Madhu, please leave before I decide to lodge a complaint against you and your misleading staff.'

'I ...' He turned, silenced, helpless, powerless, and swung his hand.

A little later, after we were out of earshot, Madhu said, 'I don't think we can do more, Anantya. Officially, that is.' My lips thinned and I walked off, frustration rising inside me. How would I find the nishadas now?

14

THE GHOSTLY fog was slashed by Chhotu's purple light as we chugged along, searching for the circus tents off Vikas Marg, on the banks of river Yamuna. After half an hour, I found it. A glittering signboard announced that the International Russian Circus was performing there. The signboard was the only thing that glittered. Triangular canvas tents rose up around the main pavilion, a massive multi-layered tent of red and blue. Sign boards and streamers and gaudy fairy lights lined up, some broken, some flickering.

Manasa had met Ashwa earlier this week, here, to discuss their plan. I had been calling Ashwa a friend for a couple of years now, but had never felt the need to ask him what he did when he wasn't at Bedardi Bar. And as it happened, he worked in a circus.

At the entrance, a boy wearing a frilly costume in neon shades of orange and yellow stripes eyed me, asking for a ticket, though it was the middle of the night. I paid and entered the circus ring, a vast amphitheatre inside the main tent. There was a bored audience, some wearing clown clothes, some dressed as acrobats, and some deformed. They clapped unenthusiastically as a dwarf clown in the middle, farted in a microphone and then loudly guffawed. The manager of the circus turned out to be the dwarf in the ring, now playing multiple instruments together.

I took out a beedi and lit it waiting for it to get over, pondering on where the hell all those nishadas had vanished to. Rajni Gandha was a thousand times more effective than any police hound. How could he have gone wrong? I was missing something here. Should I try and approach Kanthak at the Tazaak? With what? He wouldn't care about a bunch of missing *pashus*. Hell, even the Pashu Department didn't care about them. Why was justice so impossible that the only right thing you could do had to be illegal? The clown's performance ended and I headed backstage, removing my goggles.

'Wait for me there,' said Kaka, the clown. Kaka was dressed up in a pair of orange balloon trousers and an equally puffed up and shiny shirt, but he walked with a macho swagger. He brought out a cigar, offered me one, lit one up with his frilly-gloved hand and took a long drag. His whole face was painted white with two rouge spots on the cheek and the lips garishly red. His eyes had a round dirty yellow circle around, making him look like a brightly coloured owl.

'Have you seen a seven-foot man around here?'

'There are two kinds of people I don't like,' he answered in a surprisingly deep and husky voice.

'Quitters and those who waste my time. Your friend was the first kind and you, ma'am, are the second. Remind me again, why am I speaking to you?'

'Because I know who you are.'

'Who doesn't? I play many roles in the circus.'

'But I know the real you, the one I bet no one here does.'

He looked at me, from his owl-coloured eyes and smiled, his exaggerated lips twisting. 'And who is that?'

'A gandharva who has fallen into bad days,' I said softly. 'Last I knew you and your kind were playing heavenly instruments for kings and daevas.'

He turned and faced the mirror again, picking up a sponge and wiping his face with it. 'That era has long gone.'

'And your apsara?' For I knew that gandharvas were never without their apsaras. His hand stilled and trembled a bit.

'She's gone too,' he said softly. 'That era has gone,' he stressed again, more to himself.

'I could put you in touch with a daeva who might make use of your exponential musical talents for his parties.'

He regarded me through the mirror, his stubby hands still working efficiently to remove the paint on his face. Behind the paint, his was an ageless face, brown, weathered, with an arresting animation to it, which might have made him the centre of a kingly stage once. 'I might be a stupid gandharva, miss, but there are two things I am not: a fool and a snitch.'

'Uhun,' I answered taking out a beedi and putting it in my mouth cursing Dhuma for its rancid taste.

'You see me dressed like a fool because my fool who doubled up as an attendant at House of Horrors with your friend, has ditched me. He's gone off to join with that Manu Manava Maharaja. Now I have two acts missing and not enough time. So I become the clown and train another for House of Horrors in my off hours, when I should be drinking. Doesn't make me a snitcher to my friend.'

'I am his friend too. I know who he is and I am here to help,' I said. 'In that way, maybe I can help you too?' He took a long drag from his cigar and regarded me from behind a layer of smoke. Stubbing it, he got up from his seat, paddling towards the exit, beckoning me with a flick of his hand.

'I hope you keep your promise. You will find our mutual friend in his canvas tent, next to the House of Horrors. He's been there since a few hours now, sulking and refusing to come and join our off-time team building activity.'

'What act does he do here?' He eyed me through the cigar smoke. 'Works in House of Horrors. Pretty good, too. All he does is stare and people pee in their pants.' He laughed, in a surprisingly childish voice and winked. 'And cleans the elephants. No ladder required,' he said, flicking his head into the direction of the animal enclosure, where an elephant stood chewing on grass. A series of cages next to the pen had different varieties of wild animals.

'Isn't that illegal?' The gandharva laughed, his cackle sounding like a boy's. 'Yeah, and who will snitch? You?' He showed me the tent and was off. Instead of announcing myself, I entered, deciding to surprise Ashwa so that he couldn't run away before we had our little chat.

The tent was dimly lit with a zero watt light bulb in a corner, throwing more shadows than light on a single mattress on the floor with a small writing table of sorts, the old fashioned kinds, kept alongside. A string for drying clothes was hung above from one end of the ceiling to another. On it dangled a pair of long trousers, a shirt, a cloak and Ashwa's body, or rather his flesh without anything inside, the skin long enough to touch the floor from the ceiling. It hung like any other cloth one wears, drying on the clothes wire.

Breeze through a window, made it flap slightly, his flattened head lolled from side to side. I touched his head, gently unclasping the clasps that helped his skin here. I had been right. The tantrik had betrayed him, taken the nagamani and left his skin flapping like a useless cloth. His desire for death had given the tantrik immense power. I didn't understand the need for death by someone who'd lived for centuries, maybe you got bored. For life, for most parts, was complete daitya's shit anyway.

'No, Ashwa,' I whispered. 'You can choose death, but not on my bloody watch.' It was time to get under his skin. 'You dodo,' I said, laying his skin on the mattress below. Flattened, his skin spread longer than the bed's length itself, about eight feet long. With my bare hands, I turned the skin upside-down, and opened it up, so that his facial skin was facing downwards. A long tear ran in his skin from where he must've oozed out. It ran from the back of his head to his buttocks before dividing into two lines, each for a leg.

I walked out of the tent. Darkness covered the sky, even the stars, too scared to be visible, were hiding their true purposes behind a layer of mist. The last show had finished. Small blurred lights popped here and there in the other circus tents. I headed to the animal pen, which I had noticed earlier. I reached the rusty caravan with a line of cages kept at the very end. They were mostly domesticated cats, dogs, a few rats and mice for smaller circus performances, and a few exotic animals. Enough for me though. I looked at both sides and took out a rabbit from one of the cages.

I went back to Ashwa's tent and opened the cage, not a lock but simply a clasp. Taking the rabbit out, I held it by its neck. It shivered. I brought my face close to his scruffy neck, gently pushed back his white fur, and whispered in his ear: 'Take me to him.' It shivered, a nod or a nay, I wasn't sure, and frankly it wouldn't matter. He had no choice. He shivered and shook as I gently pulled at his ear and made him face the skull cup, upside-down, his neck pointed straight into the cup. With one, practiced stroke of the boneblade, I slashed his throat and let him bleed into the cup.

'*Oh, mother, oh, undead soul,*
fill this skull cup with your whole.'

The skull cup spilled, blood spreading to the mattress and my clothes and Ashwa's skin. I gently laid the rabbit's writhing body on one side and slashed him whole, from neck to stomach. His innards oozed out, warm blood flooding out. I pulled my hand in and took out his heart, still, but warm. Adding it into the skull cup, I whispered.

'*Maa jalaa aatma kapala bharaa.*'

I poured the freshly minted blood into Ashwa's skin, spreading it with both my hands from face to the legs, like a balm on the bark of a tree. Plop. The heart tumbled in. The blood had already started to congeal, solidifying into a dark red. There was still a little blood left in the skull cup. Adding in a chunk of the bleeding heart, I put it to my lips and drank the blood, chewing on the heart, gulping down the liquid and forcing the raw meat to stay down my throat, some of it spilling on my neck in the hurry. The Soul Shadow ritual was not very difficult to perform, but it always left me exhausted. When you dealt death to other creatures, something within you died. But then you got used to it. To death and bringing death to life. I was trying to get life into an immortal who wanted death, by killing an innocent beast. I crouched and slipped into Ashwa's skin, lying face down, my face in his empty face's skin. I stretched my hands, clutching the beating heart of the rabbit and muttered.

'*Kaali khleem, chhaya hreem halkatta aatma kreem*!'

The scent of the rabbit's blood changed, reducing its pungency, becoming more like my odours, more like me. My skin pinned downward mouth to the inside of Ashwa's face, chest to chest, my arms and legs barely filling his much longer arms and legs. I breathed him in, the blood between our skins connecting us, like a river flowing between two shores, physically apart but one, flowing with the river. The rabbit's heart beat fast in my hand, as mine stopped beating.

'*Kaali khleem, chhaya hreem halkatta aatma kreem*!'

I contracted, and shortened and then elongated, spreading into the skin, spreading like nitrogen, spreading with the blood, becoming the blood, becoming one with Ashwa's skin. My skin.

I was 13,564 years old. I felt tired, of living, of survival. There was an ocean of sadness which drowned me, taking me into its heat. My feet had sores as did my heart, worms infested my body, lice and insects and blood ticks and pests and beetles. They all crawled inside my skin, making me itch and prickle and burn as I walked along the Vaitarni, the river of the dead, longing for its waters to consume me. Then I flew, I flew hard and fast like a hurricane, at impossible speed, being sucked by a womb with big blackhole eyes, its hungry mouth open. I was desperate, desperate for the womb, for the death it would give me, for the numbness of not standing on my sore feet.

A cave made of gnarled roots, long dead, blackened and withered, squirmed and withered, sucking me in, like a mass of goo up a giant nostril. I became part of the withering roots, turning, twisting and floating in, like wisps of dead clouds. We went in together, into the darkness, into the damp coldness of death. Bliss. Whirls of darkness we were suffocating on smoke, floating in. But something was wrong.

Claws appeared on both my sides, dead gnarled claws that clutched and pinched on my tender skin, making me scream. They were joined by something more powerful than life: death. The pretas were a whirlwind, around the tantrik who stood in the centre. But he wasn't the same as I'd known before. He wasn't my friend, the wise one who could understand my pain, back from the dead, without judging my past actions. He wasn't Charaka, my ancient friend. He was a human, a manava, a tantrik from Banaras, still alive and burning with greed and hunger. Hunger for power, domination and authority. He controlled my friend. The same hunger that had eaten my family and friends, gorged them and spitted me out, like a wastrel bone, onto the dry lands of humanity, to roam alone on sore feet.

'Who are you?' I tried to ask.

He laughed. 'I am what you craved for, Ashwathama. I set you free from life and in exchange you give me your curse.'

'NO!' The word reverberated through me as realization hit. My soma friend had been right! He was after the Matsya Curse, his sweat reeking of dust and desire and ambition once it was lifted. What had I done? My desire for death would hurl the curse down on humanity. NO! Not again.

The tantrik sniffed, his sweat smelling of a sharp fear. 'Who do you bring along, Ashwathama?'

And just like that I knew. My stubborn friend had tagged along for the stroll into Naraka.

NO! Not you too. My dead heart stopped. The tantrik saw her, a shadow clinging to me from the plane of humanity. His dark claws reached out, sucking and drinking me up, stretching my soul, pulling, pushing, closing in, attracted by the one thing that they did not have:

my life and hers. Together we fell, like a whirlpool, a hurricane into the dark hole of the cave, till we stopped falling and rose instead. She screamed, as did I, made one by her stubborn spell. The darkness clouded my eyeless eyes.

'Ashwa!' she cried. Knowing I had felt her touch. She came, a tall familiar cursed form, like a nagin. She was denser, a shadow made of life, bones and flesh and living blood. Worms and maggots and lice oozed out of her skinless forehead.

NO! I screamed, my voice bursting through like a water cannon, worms crawling out of her eyes. Go back! I grabbed her shadow face and clawed on it, desperate, grabbing and grappling with her smoky self, with my own self.

A burning fire shot through my smoky body, shooting up from the place where he had touched me, spreading to my shoulders, my chest, my legs and arms, fluid with the fire. No! He had screamed, with panic. His icy hands wound up around my neck till I couldn't breathe. I was just a doll of china, helpless, which could be broken easily. Blood curdled in my body, my corpse gasping for life, that trickle not found in the land of in dead. I writhed, crying, pain shooting through me like a million stars on a dark night.

Ashwa fell away, plunging headlong into the tantrik's world of betrayal. I staggered, clutching my chest where a poisonous pain started to spread, where he had touched me. The walls and the ground collapsed into each other like a closing duct. I started to fall, tumble, downhill, faster and faster till I was shooting back, back into my body. Thousands of scorpions bit me and a scream rushed out of my physical mouth. I opened my eyes and struggled up, ordering my body to unclasp Ashwa's dead skin, my head reeling, and fell back, blood leaking from my face and chest and arms. Mine or the rabbit's, I wasn't sure anymore. I staggered up, taking off the top from my burning chest. I looked down at my itching breasts, wet with blood.

Though upside down, the branded symbol was clear: That of a fish in a fish within a circle. The same one that I'd seen on Marty's chest a few days ago.

For the first time in so many days, Neel smiled, his blue eyes lighting up like twin lamps. He rushed forward and took me in his arms. 'Anu, Anu, Anu!' He kissed my forehead, my lips, my wet cheeks.

'You remember?' I asked, not wanting to believe. His blue eyes turned dark like the rainy clouds.

'I missed you, I missed you.' He kept repeating this, like a mantra, like the fluttering wings of the heart, kissing my forehead, cheeks, ears, hair, his warm fingertips tracing my cheek bones, fingering my hair, my ears, my eyebrows. 'Don't leave me, don't let me die!'

'I will never let you go!' I promised, wounding my arms around his warm body. My hands clutched his waist, the hands going together, trying to clutch, to clasp, to bind him, to hug him tighter and tighter. But there was nothing there but emptiness. I screamed, in panic, in desperation. 'Don't leave me, Anu! Don't leave me alone! I am scared! Give me your life, give me your soul.'

My hands clutched him tighter and tighter and tighter, clasping him, trying so hard, so hard to keep him, but like a wisp of wind, smoke from a candle, he slipped away. He rose, there but not there and he started to laugh.

'You and me, me and you, we are the same, Anu. Come with me. Together we can do so much,' He glided towards me and I gasped, for his face, his body and his form were exactly that of Neel's. But he was not.

'How do you know ...' I whispered to myself, 'my name?'

He laughed at my expression, his Neel face crumpling, scattering to the winds like dry leaves. My heart leaped and he noticed, a cruel smile in the scattered face. Maggots started to walk out of his eyes and crawl out of his mouth and ears, spreading out.

'Neel!' I screamed. 'Stop it!'

The laughter thrummed, like millions of ants on my body. His face crumpled, dissolving and forming again as Neel's. 'Do you want it?'

'What?' His hand snaked up, hand sliding between my breasts, my neck and then trailing smoky fingers on the nape, turning to my left breast. 'Immortality.' He squeezed again. I pushed him away, turning, though my feet refused to, forcing myself to turn and walk out. 'Think about it. Think about what it would be like, you and him, together, forever. In eternity. Nothing will tear you apart again. No heartbreak, Anantya. Your heart,' he touched my left breast delicately. 'Will stay intact.'

A dark cloud surrounded me, bubble wrap of claws and pincers and stings. 'Let me go!' I said, scratching and tearing at the bubble wrap, pushing myself forward. 'Awayaaai!' Thump. I thrashed on the cold floor.

'Sorry.' A man bowed on top of me, a broom in his hand. 'Sorry,' he said, looking at me as I shivered, from the cold, from the cold nightmare which had been so real. 'But this is a morgue. You will need to go to a hospital if you're not dead yet.'

'Of all the creepy maggots in the world,' I whispered, turning around, breathing hard, my heart screeching.

'Yes, infestations can get to you, can't they?' the man said. 'I have a rather special mix for maggots, the kind that we get on rotten flesh here. It can kill a whole continent with just a single spray. You would like to try it? I will give a discount.'

I turned to look at the creature. He had six limbs, ending in claws with one head and four eyes. 'Just …' I said taking a deep breath, 'Where's Puma?'

The caretaker nodded, screaming for Puma. The light wavered and the creature's face came into focus in its fuzzy yellow circle. Puma was another kirata, one of the few loyal tribes that the Tazaak got to Delhi from Banaras when they first came into power in Delhi. He looked like he'd been freshly bitten all over his lithe body (which might be a fetish, I don't judge). We had known each other from Banaras when I used to live in the Kaula Ashram, so I had called in a favour.

The Tazaak morgue was a long cave in a dungeon with a pit in the centre, about twenty feet diameter and equally deep. It had a pile of bodies in it, some lay carefully, some thrown in, like a garbage dump and smelled like yakshas had pooped in fear all over the place before dying off. All the supernatural bodies that were found in the city, came here, as part of investigation, to be dumped, to be chopped to pieces and fed to the hungry poor sups who came their way. It was a job that Puma and his friends did quite well. Some bodies, which were under investigation, would stay on small mattresses along the pit, to be checked by the Tazaak investigators before they were thrown into the dark pit.

'Did you find the dead I was looking for?' I asked, rubbing my eyes, sitting cross-legged, the bloody preta tantrik still bright and real in my eyes. I chewed my lower lip, wondering if there was a route the tantrik was taking to come into my dreams. I needed a charm against it. I took out a beedi and lit it up, my hands still shaking a bit.

'No one with too much kajal on his eyes came here. But still, we can look again. There's too many dead here and is easy to miss one or two. Only once a while, tantriks like you come to ask. He must have just fallen off into the pile or the corpse collectors who come here sometimes, they take them. That Balsa is also mindless only, he sees a body off the mattress, thinks "oh well, investigation done! Feed for vultures!" and sweeps and piles it on his cart without bothering to check with me or not and then takes them away to the table inside and hacks it into pieces and dumps them back into the pile. Feeds the bratrats. I don' stop him, is good in a way. What to do with the bodies otherwise? We can't keep them piling up in the sides. The stench don' bother me too much, but if we can use them to feed the bratrats and the chikats, then good only it is no? Food shouldn't be wasted I say. And Balsa is a good lad and feels the same. He is not like others who are younglings. They waste so much and don' listen to their elders and don' hunt, but live off on begging from tantriks. I tell you, ma, we were much more ourselves in my times. We lived off the land, under no one's nose. And now, we do nose-digging them bastar taunts only. You see this—'

'Puma,' I said, cutting off his rambling, 'it's important that I find him, dude. The dead are walking the streets!'

'May Maut grant them death,' he said using his index finger to do a sign of cutting his throat. 'The dead walking the earth is never a goo' thing for the living now—'

'Hold your horny horses. Why did you say that?'

'The dead walking ...?'

'No. May Maut grant them death. Maut, who—'

'Maut disciples say it all times. They're good. They make sure dead stay dead. That's a talent.'

'Where can I find them?'

'The Maut gravediggers? I don't know—' He turned. 'Balsaa! Remember them that came here to pick up the undeads who refused to stay under the earth? What were their names?'

'The Maut gravediggers?'

'Yes, them. Where they come from?'

'I don't know,' he screamed back. I stomped my foot in frustration, slinging my satchel. 'They took them and left. Outside I heard one of them arguing with a rickshaw fella. He wanted to take the rick till the end of the road behind Yogamaya temple and the rick was asking double, so he just said forget it and then grumbled that it was all the other fellow's fault that their hearse wasn't working.'

'Blind mother's ass!' I said, kissing Puma on his bitten face and pecking Balsa on his smooth cheek before running out of the morgue. 'That bloody immortal leech!' I kick-started my bike, and started off towards Mehrauli.

15

I RODE through the midday traffic, and parked my bike behind the Yogmaya temple at the end of the road, next to a garbage dump. A small arched gate stood there, hidden from sight by the pile of litter. It had a decrepit wooden block with the sign of a fish within a fish inside a circle and the words: *'May Maut grant you death.'*

The arch widened into a small courtyard with a banyan tree spread in the middle of it. The afternoon sun streamed from atop, filtering through the leaves onto the empty graves. They rose like benches, dead soldiers in parallel directions, names scribed on each of them, scooped and bare, without the dead. I walked around weaving through the graves, crouching to study them. Each of them were weathered, as if they'd been here for many years, a few marked with the same fish in a fish in a circle. There were names, in an ancient script that I couldn't understand, with roughly scratched symbols.

'These are all reserved!' A human swung upside down from one of the banyan tree, rotating and jumping, landing softly on his bare feet. I stepped back, taking out my boneblade. He was dressed in a human's skin, his hair very, very white, his face very, very weathered and wrinkled and sunburnt. He raised a wooden axe and pointed it towards me. 'You want new grave? You want, you want? We shall chop you and feed you to goats!'

'Over my dead body!' The skin he wore looked quite familiar. 'That's Guru B's skin!' *The skin stealer.*

'Rama, ama, lame-wanna! Fight, fight, fight!' He shook his beard and dreadlocked hair, sending out a gust of dust. He opened his weathered lips about to say something, then shook his head again.

'Why did you steal those people's skins? Guru B and Avvaiyar?'

'Mine!'

'You're freaking nuts!'

'Fecund female, without a tail.' He jumped up, rolling on his head and shoulders and reached me, hitting me with his wooden axe. 'You are eighty nine crore forty four lakh, thirty eight thousand, six hundred and sixty.' I folded my arms across my chest. 'No I'm not! And if you hit me again, I will slash your throat!'

'Feed them to the goat!' He jumped up and sat on his hunches, giggling and swatting flies around his face. Jumping again, he scooped his wooden axe, wove it like a hunter and lunged at me, moving much faster than I would have imagined, making me yelp as he deftly hit the axe on the small of my back.

'You don't need an axe, your creepy poetry is enough to kill me!' I ran after him.

'Perr … fectly true.' The owner to the soft, sing-song voice was a petite lady, stately, dressed in human skin, a man's hairy body wrapped around her petite one like a sari. Her long hair were plaited neatly and covered with a human skull. 'What have I told you about manners, Para? Take permission before you sing. And we have a dead one to prepare. Why don't you help the others?'

Para swatted his head, but agreed, heading to another arched gate at the far side of the courtyard.

'I apologize for him. He isn't used to seeing strangers. Usually he lives too high up in the Himalaya. I am Meera. May Maut grant you death,' she said folding her hands together and bowing. Though her skin was smooth and young, but her eyes, they looked like they were really really wizened, though they were also warm with kindness, a quality that made me trust her completely. 'You must be the woman Markendeya mentioned?'

'Markendeya?' I said.

'Yes. I think he calls himself something else now. He changes his name every few decades, so it's hard to keep up.'

'Of course,' I said slapping my forehead with my hand. 'Marty is Markendeya, the boy who is blessed to be a teenager eternally. And who are you, madam? Meera Bai the immortal singer?' I said my tongue dripping in sarcasm. She turned back, her eyes widening like blooming lotuses.

'How did you know?' she asked. I blinked and after a pause asked, 'And that nutcase back there is … Parashurama?'

'Parashurama, the poet, yes.'

'Wasn't he a legendary warrior?'

'Yes. Legends tell of times long past, don't they? He became a poet sometime last century.' She tapped the side of her head with a finger. 'Unfortunately he hasn't been able to improve it much. Come. We're in the middle of a funeral. You will need to wait.'

'So you all' – I waved my hand around aimlessly – 'are immortals?'

She laughed. 'Hardly! I'm quite young.'

'When were you born?' I asked.

'It was the thirteenth era according to the human calendar that I was born. Can't remember the exact year.'

'So in our terms you are atleast seven centuries and five decades old.'

'Yes, somewhat. Come.' She led me through the same half door, where we both had to crouch. 'One of the youngest here. Though it's Markendeya who looks the youngest.'

'Why did Parashurama steal those skins?'

'I think he always liked Guru's skin,' Meera answered, walking us through a thin long hall into another courtyard. 'Work's increased recently. So many undead. Come.'

'What can I—'

'*Shhh.* They're singing the ode to Maut,' she whispered.

I stopped, to hear a hauntingly beautiful hymn that emerged from the wild growing bushes before us. In the middle of the bushes, surrounded by trees on all sides, lay the corpse of a sharabha, twisted and gnarled with age or suffering. About six or seven various kind of people embalmed the body, their hands yellowed from rubbing a yellow paste on the body. The men were a strange mix, of old and really young, of tall and really short, of deformed and handsome. They hummed an ancient tune together in a soft cooing voice, as Parashurama danced around them, cackling and rotating his damru with a madness. They all wore skins, human skins complete with faces, skins they'd torn off cadavers, before disposing them off. Once the embalming finished, the oldest one picked up sharp knives, their tips glistening, and started to scrape off the dead's skin from the body. Meera stood with the others, in a line, their heads bent, humming the same soulful, heart-wrenching tune. Tears formed in my eyes as for some reason as I was reminded of someone who I had thought was long dead, but might not have been.

It took half an hour for the ceremony to be over. They pushed in the giant body into the ditch, filling it up. Meera came and sat cross-legged on the forest floor, looking up, wounding a blade of grass on her left hand's index finger. 'Sometimes I wish—' She stopped, not sure how she wanted to complete her sentence.

'You know how many humans want this? Eternal living? They will murder their own mothers for it.'

'It's more infernal living,' said Meera, her voice soft. 'To go on living. But let's not be so dull about things. It's so good to talk to another woman! It can get quite lonely you know with only men around.'

'How did you turn into an immortal?'

'I have no idea!' said Meera, touching the skin that covered her plaited hair. 'My husband's family had just poisoned me because I liked music of the other kind, and I was angry so I just walked out of the palace and kept walking. The next thing I know I am lying in a hut belonging to someone who was about to burn me assuming I had died. I got up, this guy started to run crying "Ghost!", so I just walked out, again. I kept walking, going from one place to another. Sometimes I thought I was a ghost, cursed by my family because I was different. But I needed to eat and people could see me and talk to me and even tried a few smart things, thinking of me as gullible. Then somehow I came to Delhi, met Hanuji and have been with these boys since then, waiting for Maut to come to me, to take me in her arms.'

'Aren't any of you curious to understand how you became immortals?'

'Well …' she hesitated, 'there are *rumours*.'

'What sorts?'

'Some say we are experiments of an ancient asura. Rumours mention Mr Bali but I'm sure he would have told us if that was the case. Some say we are gifts from gods to the mortal world, some that we are soulless children of a dark being, or the undead who can walk in daylight. They say our souls have been trapped and so we continue to live. Some moderns have also compared us to vampires. I've seen vampires and well' – she shrugged – 'I don't feel the same way. I love to eat mutton and rice and don't really like human blood too much.' She made a face, touching the skin on her plait, as if reassuring it. 'Who knows but Maut?'

'All those empty graves inside, are for all of you?'

'Yes! We wait. We worship her, we beg her, all of us, to take us. Someday, I know Maut will come for me too.'

'You're all nuts. Like Ashwa.'

'Oh, dear Ashwathama sir. Do you know him?'

'Yes. He sent me here. With a message for the monkey.'

'And the monkey listens.' The voice, gruff with rough edges, came from above. I craned my neck to see a furry white creature perched up on one of the branches above the tree we sat under.

'And hello to you too, Hanuji,' I said. The monkey immortal, Hanuman, perched on the branch, his thin legs crossed, his body covered from head to toe with white fur. He smiled, his brown eyes lighting up, and scribbled in that impossible position on a papyrus, which shone gold.

'What is it you seek?' He jumped down, sleek, without any sign of age, his body covered with a human skin, like the others. He rubbed his hands on his white haired face, making them stand like a halo of white lines around his bulbous face, scratching on the papyrus again.

'I seek answers, Hanuji. What is the Matsya Curse?'

'The Matsya! How can she know—'

'Stop, Meera. Not a word more. We can't reveal it to a tantrik.'

'I am no *tantrik*,' I spat. 'I am a friend. Trying to stop the preta tantrik from taking all of you to his world.'

'We welcome Maut to our shores. We worship her, wait for her eagerly. Look at that. He was a friend of ours. For centuries we roamed together, seeing earth go from lush to parch. And finally, he has gone too. You must wait for our celebrations! For when Maut comes for one of us, we celebrate!'

'That's what Ashwa thought, when he was contacted by the tantrik. He thought it was Charaka who had come to give him death.'

'Ahh. Charaka. The tantrik came to us a few centuries ago, promising that we would meet Maut. What confidence he had. Ashwathama has been so impatient for Maut to take him that he decided to accompany Charaka to his rasayana lab. In exchange Charaka wanted his blood to test out, in his desire to prolong human life. Many experiments he did, cutting humans, transfusing our blood, drinking it mixed with other potions, injecting it, or inhaling it, but nothing worked to increase human lifespan. He even created a virus, raaka. But all the patients he tried to give it to, died, withered, taken by Maut in mere flashes of decades. And every decade, he grew old, getting wrinkles and joint pain. Till finally he was consumed by Maut too. Ashwathama was heartbroken. His chance to die had been snatched from him. Charaka's apprentice, Shushrut too tried some experiments on Ashwathama's blood. He succeeded to a little extent before he was snatched by Maut early in his human life. It took a century for Ashwathama to get over that disappointment.'

'For some reason, Ashwa believed that Charaka has come back and was helping him. He got him the nagamani and helped him get both Guru B and Avvaiyar. But then the tantrik took him too and he realized its not Charaka but a preta tantrik, someone from Banaras, who is really after the Matsya Curse. What is it? What can the curse do?'

'Our duty to humankind is over,' said Hanuji. 'It's best that we leave it alone.'

'Well, my duty to humankind is not. If you're suicidal, fine. At least tell me what the curse is! What does it do?'

Parashurama hopped in from the other side, sitting in a hunch and gobbling up the food in front of him. I watched him warily from the corner of my eye, still speaking to Hanuji.

'It doesn't matter, let's just tell her,' said Meera. 'She will leave anyway.'

'Tantrik vantrik!' cried Parashurama.

'I am more human than tantrik,' I answered. 'And a female. We're different, believe me!'

'Doesn't matter,' said Marty, who'd walked up to our little group too. 'She's mortal. Think of her as a wasp. The next time you meet her, she will be dead.'

'Yeah, well. Thanks for shattering my immortal aspirations,' I dripped sarcasm. 'And really nice, the way you pretended to die. Funny.' He smiled, his eyes lighting up. 'Yes. You all are immortal, I am not. You won't even remember me next century. So you can tell me what this curse is.'

'Do you know Matsyendranath?' Hanuji spoke up and everyone else hushed.

'Of course I do. What else do you learn in Kaula's history books? I know praise songs for the dude. He was one of the strongest tantriks of ancient history and founded the basis of tantrism as we know it today. I was taught about his legends in our first class at the ashram. He's called so for he was born of a fish.'

'He's the one who created a curse against tantriks.'

'A curse against tantriks? Why would he curse his own kind?'

'He knew and understood the growing power of tantriks, the darkness that hid in that power. He could see the future, the destruction they'll bring on all kinds. Their desire, their craving for power, would swing nature's balance, destroying life, courting death. He used his powers to put a control, a lock which forbade the tantriks from ever ruling the humans, though he didn't do the same for other kinds.'

'But, but that doesn't really happen. Humans are ruled by tantriks—'

'Never. They haven't ever been. Tantriks are powerful yes, but they are forced to take on a cloak of secrecy to hide that power. The moment they show it, a ritual, a power, openly to the world, to the humans, their power diminishes, becomes cursed … *dies*. And that is the Matysa Curse.'

'But what's that got to do with you? The immortals?'

'Matsyendranath knew that he would move on eventually, being mortal. And with him, the power of the curse would diminish too. He didn't want that to happen, so he decided to leave a part of him, his blood, forever in this plane so that the curse is as powerful today as centuries ago, when he first created it. He came to us then, marking ten of us with his symbol, to carry his blood and his curse within us forever. And the ten we remain.'

'The fish? You mean Matsyendranath's blood runs—'

'Runs in our immortal bodies, yes. Each of us carry the Matsya Curse in our veins. It's power, its hold on tantriks is because we still walk this plane. And as long as even one of us stands here, on this plane, alive, the curse is effective.'

'Who are the ten?'

'Hanuman,' they sang together, as a whole, 'Ashwanthama, Saranyu and the Aswins. Parashurama, Avviyar, Vasuki, Markendaya and Bali.'

'Saranyu? The twins? The people who run Triya Art Gallery? They're immortals too? Part of the curse? I knew there was something unnatural about them. But … they took nishadas. Wait! I am getting confused here! Wait. You're the only ones who stand between tantriks and total supremacy? And you haven't put a single protection around this place? I could simply walk in! Why has he picked all of you now? At present? Why not three or five years before?'

'Who knows how a tantrik thinks? Maybe he was looking for the right knife?'

'Or if he thinks at all. Crawcraw!' It was a raven, double the size of most jungle ravens, perched on Marty's shoulder. 'That's Basudi.'

'… What we have to do is put up protection charms around you to stop—'

'Time stops everything, even a power hungry tantrik. We don't interfere with mortal greed.'

'You helped Matsya!' Parashurama looked up, his brows and beard bristling, but he didn't say anything, munching away, dripping some kind of liquid on his beard. 'This guy is going to haul all of you back to that infernal hell I visited through Ashwa's eyes. Believe me, this place is much nicer! And who knows what he plans to do once this curse is lifted from tantriks? He was powerful—'

'Everything and everyone dies. Maut will take care of him

too,' said Hanuji. I got up, shaking with anger. 'And now we are off to our celebration!'

'Why not just *confront* him, make the threat go away? Use one of those siddhis you all are known for!'

'Oh, but we are not powerful in the mortal world anymore. We have no powers,' said Meera. 'Except one that is.'

'Fie, fie, keep mum.' Parashurama sat on his hunches, screaming. 'Don't roll your Maut's drum! Give me a chance, give me a noddy, and I will remove her head from her body!'

'We don't kill mortals anymore, you poetic poop,' said Marty. 'Violence is so last century! Grow up!'

'Stop, not talk, you thing of nails and rock!'

'Who are you calling *thing*?'

'Parashurama, Markandeya, stop it please,' said Meera, coming and standing between the two of them, 'Not in front of a mortal!'

'Fine.'

'Maut! Maut! Everything be consumed by Maut!'

'Parashurama! Apologize to each other.'

Parashurama danced, Marty shivered with anger. Without my noticing, Hanuji was standing just on my side, his smile radiant, coming out of his weathered hairy white face. But there was a glint in his eye. A glint of mischievousness. On his shoulder sat Basudi, the immortal crow. Something was going to go wrong, I could just feel it in my bones.

'Now!'

'So. I will leave you guys alone to di—' I began, stepping back. Basudi's eyes, black beads shivered, as his beak opened, it was large, like a whole black universe. I stood transfixed. He hopped from Hanuji's shoulder, his wings opening like an umbrella of black sky, his eyes staring into mine.

'Humans. Such flickers of light. Like fireflies,' said Hanuji. He touched my cheek, his hand like a dried leaf. Basudi's beak reached my left eye and clamped on my eyeball. I didn't feel anything, still, transfixed, frozen, more fascinated than horrified, seeing streams of lights, one after the other, pulled by the black beak, pulled away from my eye, one leading to another, like a web, a series of strings, being pulled. Ashwa, was my last thought, and it too got pulled away, like a mote from the eye.

For the first time in so many days, Neel smiled, his blue eyes lighting up like twin lamps. He rushed forward and took me in his arms. 'Anu, Anu, Anu!' He kissed my forehead, my lips, my wet cheeks.

'You remember?' I asked, not wanting to believe. His blue eyes turned dark like the rainy clouds. 'I will never let you go!' I promised, wounding my arms around his warm body. My hands clutched him tighter and tighter and tighter, clasping him, trying so hard, so hard to keep him, but like a wisp of wind, smoke from a candle, he slipped away, his Neel face crumpling, scattering to the winds like dry leaves. My heart leaped and he noticed, a cruel smile in the scattered face. Maggots started to wriggle out of his eyes and his mouth and ears.

'Neel!' I screamed. 'Stop it!'

'Do you want it?'

'What?' His hand snaked up, sliding between my breasts, my neck and then trailing fingers on the nape, turning to my left breast. 'Immortality.' He squeezed again. I pushed him away, turning, though my feet refused to, forcing myself to turn and walk out. 'Think about it. Think about what it would be like, you and him, together, forever. In eternity. Nothing will tear you apart again. No heartbreak, Anantya. Your heart,' he touched my left breast delicately. 'Will stay intact.'

A dark cloud surrounded me, bubble wrap of claws and pincers and stings.

'Let me go!' I said, scratching and tearing at the bubble wrap, pushing myself forward. 'Awayaaai!' Thump. I thrashed on the cold floor.

'Of all the creepy maggots in the world,' I whispered, turning around, breathing hard, my heart screeching. I heaved, puking my guts out, nothing came except this vague sense of déjà vu. My head felt heavy, my eyes grew dim, and my chest heaved. I sputtered, emptiness and spit and bile, on the floor, looking at a pair of feet. Pulling up, I saw Neel, staring at me, through me with his blue, blue eyes.

My hands flew to him, giving him a hard shove. I jumped, reaching out for my boneblade and putting it on Neel's neck, pressing it before I could see that it had been only a dream.

I was in my home and afternoon light streamed from the broken ceiling above. He didn't say anything, just looked at me with his blue, blue eyes, blank, dead eyes.

'Why don't you talk!' I cried, throwing the blade away, angry. I pushed him them, as a fury took over me, making him tumble from the bed on the ground. I was on top of him immediately. I tore his clothes, ripping his shirt, his trousers with my boneblade, wanting to know what he had been hiding all this while, wanting him, aching for him. Him in real, not him in a dream of wisps of memories. I felt him getting hard.

'Talk!' I cried, taking him in then, trashing on him, clawing on his chest with my blunt nails, hitting him, biting him. Inside me, he was cold and hard, immobile, still, but hard. I rode him, in a frenzy, crying out tears of frustration, the frustration and anger that had been building up in me all these days. 'Fuck you!' I cried again, tears streaming down my face, scratching him, wanting to scratch the calm out of him.

I straddled him, frenzied – a madness taking hold of me, wanting to take, not to give anything to him. Wetness exploded between my legs, lubricating his cold hardness. I tightened my thighs, wanting to take, to make him feel, to take an ounce of his blood, of his semen, into me. I cried and rode and rode till I exploded, wetting myself all over his thighs, flopping onto his chest, exhausted. He lay still, quiet, looking up at me with his blue eyes, naked of all anger, naked of all feeling. Still. I took a deep, ragged breath.

'Shakti's shit,' I cried, shaking and falling by his side. 'Fuck you, Manu Manava!' I cried looking up at the broken ceiling that covered the haveli, wanting to hit something, tears rolling down the corner of my eyes. 'Fuck you!' I went to the kitchen, putting on a pan of tea.

Calling Manu, I told him everything that had happened, how the nishadas were missing. He sounded disappointed, clicking the phone off, even before I'd had a chance to explain. Pissed I threw the phone on the bed, feeling like I was forgetting something. That there was something wrong here. I walked to the rasayana lab, trying to calm myself down by making a potion. I put curdled goat's milk on the boil in a vat, chopping some fish scales, wondering why the word 'fish' felt suddenly strange. The colour of the vat changed to puke-green, becoming a huge bubble. I added the last layer of iron fillings, covering it up with the liver of an ox, recently dead, and powdered bones of a frog and a newly captured yatu shadow. I slit my wrist and added a drop of my own blood. The boiling liquid rose up, turning into the unique colour that was me – a neon purple. I took out a mug, scooped the liquid up and took a sip. It was boiling hot, tasted like horse's crap and I needed to drink it all. That was the most difficult part of the Yaddash potion. Well, I had the whole night. Manu won't stand up to his mother and there was nothing that I could think of doing.

Saranyu. What was it about her and her twin children that I was forgetting? I shook my head, wondering if a soma-on-the-rocks at Bedardi bar would help. My pal, Ashwa, would most probably not be there. Not? Why won't he be there? He had told me something, something about going off for a long, long time. By his own choice. Well, friends came and friends left. As Shukra had. After taking advantage of my trust in him. I took another swig of the potion, turning to look at the other end of the courtyard, where the couch was. The ladle in my hand trembled and fell on the floor with a clatter.

Neel floated in the middle of the room, his back bent, like half a moon, his arms and legs spread, suspended. I ran, blindly clasping my boneblade and running towards him, only hitting myself hard on a wall. An invisible wall. Kriti.

'Harharhar! You silly wart,' Grrhat's voice muffled from inside the kriti, the natural yantra that a rakshasa could make. He became visible, a black skeleton-like all-black body. His hands were clasped around Neel's neck and crotch, pulling him in an umbrella position. I cried from outside the bubble, plunging the boneblade into the invisible wall with force. The wall bounced me back, like a chute exhausting smoke.

'Release him,' I said, my heart hammering in my chest, 'or I will skin your bones.'

'Harharharharhar! You should've thought about that when you played that silly trick, tantrik!' He pulled, a monkey with a stick. Something crunched, my heart lurched.

'Grr, come on,' I begged. 'He has done nothing.'

'And nothing will be done to him. You owe Barbareeka a bounty with interest. He remains with me, till you find her bounty and return it to her. In Lavana.'

'She will roast me alive if I do that,' I said, wondering how I could break his kriti. I had the right mantra, but he could do anything to Neel in that split second.

'Yes, she dreams of that. Tonight. Bring the bounty back.'

'I can't! Someone has taken them away.'

'Not my problem, is it?' Neel glimmered and started to fade, as did Grrhat. I screamed, plunging my boneblade helplessly into the invisible bubble. It went in effortlessly and hit the concrete floor.

16

THE MOON peeked from behind a gang of storm clouds. I dumped the three lamb carcasses a little before the bungalow property that housed Triya Art gallery and parked nearby. I had visited the gallery twice. Once I had the paintbrush to let me in, the other time, it had been during the day. Now it was night and the gallery was shut and for some reason, I anticipated trouble. So I had got some arsenal along.

Usually, such suicidal missions could be enjoyable. Today, a stone of dread lay heavy in my stomach. If that Grrhat did anything to my Neel, I would skin him layer by layer and stitch him together. I angrily brushed away the wetness that formed in my eyes. Maybe Shukra was right, had been right about this all along. Maybe Neel's being here and being like this wasn't really helping too much. It was changing me. It was making me wish that I didn't have to face danger, do stuff that may end up killing me or put him in any danger. Maybe I would finish this, get Neel back and then start my life again – a normal life.

I threw the three carcasses of lamb inside, I reached back to Chhotu and took out the bottle that I'd tied inside. The blood from the lambs I had slaughtered an hour ago, was starting to congeal, but was still fresh enough for my purpose. I stretched my arms on top of my head, holding the bottle, opened its cap and upturned it on myself. It poured, gushed and spread all over my body, till I was drenched in its iron smell. With a bloodied left hand, I plucked a hair from my wet head, tied it around my neck with a piece from the lamb's bones and uttered the Ojhal mantra.

'Shareer jaa, saans jaa, sugandh jaa aur preta
Chhup jaa, so jaa, ojhal ho jaa!'

The main gate lay open, inviting. I walked in, confident in the power of the mantra. There was a reason I had used so much more blood. Blood was the power of a mantra. With nishadas, only a drop of rakta had been enough for the creatures of the second plane, but here, I didn't know what to expect. More blood made the spell more effective. A lamb's blood would not only delete my existence from the physical plane, as in no human could see me, but also block the things about me that could be caught by other senses – the smell of my sweat or greasy skin, the noises that I make while walking, the way the atmosphere changed with my body's warmth and my breathing, not only on this plane but all seven planes, hiding me from all kinds of creatures, including asuras, dasyus, and chandaalis. As much as it was possible.

I was so busy smiling at this cool idea as I sauntered on to the path that led to the main gallery, towards the moat like fountain, that I didn't notice that there was something different about the path today. It seemed too empty and I could look at the sky without the massive yalis, covering up the path with a gigantic canopy above with their stone paws. The yalis were missing and there was a simple reason for that.

One of the reasons was standing just above my head on the left, unseen, its golden eyes shining in the darkness, bright red flexed with black, staring in my general direction. Its tusks trembled as its lion snout sniffed, trying to smell the source of its irritation. Last time I had been here, I had counted the elephant-sized animals that made the ugly canopy to the entrance. There had been ten of them. I stopped, stopped walking, stopped breathing, stopped thinking, my hand inching towards the scabbard.

Another one came behind me and then another, eyes shining like rubies in the darkness. The moon peeped out from the clouds above, spreading its dirty silver on the giant yalis around me. The monster on my left looked at the monster on my right through me, its lips moving to say things.

'Mrrrpphhhhaaw!' said the first one.

'Mrrphahahahaw!' answered the one across from me. Then the one on right, looked straight into my eyes and smiled, sending its paw into my general direction, like a cat playing. I fell back, just in time for its sharpened claws swiping like a credit card just a few inches from my body. Kali's shit, I thought.

I stood still, helpless, under them, a mice trapped in between cats. The monster-lion yali behind me guffawed or at least it sounded like he did as his growl thundered in my face. In a feline motion, it pawed in my general direction, missing by a few inches as I fell back on all fours, staring up at the giant monstrosities. It looked at me and grinned, just like the other one had done. My heart jumped out of the ribcage and started to do a tandav.

As if on cue, the others started to do the same, their red eyes glittering, surrounding me, looking at me and attacking one by one.

Swish, paw, just missed, swish, swish in the cold air, just missed.

I danced, hopping, jumping, crouching, missing the cold, icy claws, glistening like a sharpened boneblade in the moonlight. They guffawed, like a bunch of bullies, laughing as they played with me.

They could see me of course. Or sense me. And if they wanted to, any one of them would've killed me with a single swipe of its paw. But they didn't. Yalis were old creatures, older than anything human, older than even rakshasas and asuras. Who knew what kind of magic they had in them? We parried, like children with wooden swords, parried and danced together, the ten cats circling me, never letting me escape, but not hurting me badly, not yet anyway. They were just enjoying themselves too much. And I decided to take advantage of their amusement.

I ducked and rolled, missing the sword-like claws from all directions and jumped up the thigh of one of them, clinging to its hairy body like my life depended on it. Like a gang of wolves they sniffed, their snouts on the floor, a few maybe younger ones, getting impatient, moving their elephantine tusks towards the thigh of their mate. The monster I was clinging on thumped his foot, my body jerked, flying around, just in time for an impatient claw to dig into my hip. I screamed as pieces of bones and muscle flew off my shattered hip, but kept clinging to his thigh. Holding his fat hairy thigh with my right, swiping my boneblade into my rather leaky hip, I screamed, in desperation, in pain.

'*Ghoom aa phata jaa*!'

The Visphota mantra shot through my boneblade and blasted an edge of the yali's mouth, chipping his glistening tusk. Another claw scraped my back, pawing, playing, tearing off my shirt. I winced, not waiting to see but climbing up, cringing as my right hip protested, climbing up the yali's trunk-like leg, underbelly now, the irritated elephantine legs trying to scratch the itch that was me with his powerful claws, like a dog gets rid of fleas. A claw missed me by inches, slashing a deep wound in the monster I rode on. The monster started to sprint, wildly, blindly, crashing into another monster who stood in his way. My hand slipped, falling, but I dug my boneblade into his thick hide and swung, just as it crashed into another yali. The floor under me vibrated. If I fell, it would be the end of me.

'Oye! You! Fatso mythical beast! Here, I am here! Yoohoo!' The yali turned, his eyes turning a brighter black with malevolence on seeing me. An incensed claw slashed the belly of the beast I clung to, his thick hide ripping just a few inches above me. I lost my grip on the boneblade and dangled, while the wounded beast began to howl and hop around. I swung hard, and just as the other beast tried to claw its way to get to me, I landed into his open wound, sinking into the belly, losing my boneblade. I felt the yali's breath become cumbersome, about to plunge into the black hole of death. Grabbing onto a rib, I bit the throbbing heart.

'Kaala khleem. vasha hreem, damaashh aatma hlin kreem!'

The mantra bubbled up, snaked through the stomach and lungs and brain and nose of the beast to become a leash for the yali, pulling back the breath of life that was oozing out of him. I pulled, hard, with all my might, clinging on to his fast escaping soul, fighting against death. There was only one time before this that I had even tried to use this mantra and the consequences of it had been horrific enough for my whole life to change.

The Mrityansh mantra was one of the few that Dhuma had taught me from the Black book of tantrism with warnings. *Death is natural, never try to control it. If someone dies, let them go,* she'd said and I know she would've hit me with her jhaadu had she found that I was using this mantra, that too on an innocent yali.

The beast got up, its head lolling where it had been broken, trying to pull me out. Claws and tusks pierced its skin, but I had enough cushion of bile, tissue and bones now to protect myself. The only problem was, I couldn't see and it was fast becoming difficult to breathe. Holding on to the reins of his soul, I muttered another Visphota mantra.

The yali sprayed all around me, from inside out, like a pumpkin broken. I fell out, along with the innards of the beast. The other yalis surrounded the beast, staring, looking into it, pawing to test where their mouse was hiding. I didn't give them a chance.

Standing up, covered in blood, bile, tissue and bone, I pulled at the yali's soul, mercilessly like a puppeteer beginning the first act with its puppets. The animal bound by my magic, got together, piece by piece and wobbled. It took a split second for the other yalis to realize that it wasn't awake, that it was a living dead, an undead in my control which was all the time I needed. I recalled the mantra, spitting out the piece of his heart, still in my mouth. A heavy burden lifted from me as his life's breath set loose, sawing off an edge of his tusk.

'Sorry, dude, but it had to be done,' I said, patting the carcass regretfully, trying to not listen to a voice inside me that told me that I had been selfish and abused a helpless beast. I fished for my boneblade, sat on his broken leaking neck and made him jump in the air, jumping straight in the entrance of the art gallery. Somersaulting, I slipped and kept on rolling till I reached the end of the gallery. Outside, the yalis created a ruckus, shrieking in their unearthly voices, clawing through the dead carcass.

I turned and ran in, aiming for the gallery's main entrance, as fast as my legs would carry me. The screams filled the gallery as I ran, going past the first, second and the third—*wait a minute!*

I retraced my steps into the second gallery, the main one where I had stood a few days ago, disguised as a nishada girl and where I had visited just this morning. I stood in front of the painting which had the naked nishada girl in a red boudoir. How could I have missed this? Now there were none. I looked around. The other paintings, all exotic rooms, a room full of dolls, room with a view of a violet sky, room with a clean white bed with a white sheet on top of it. All empty. All without the nishadas. Where were the nishadas who had been, now that I remember, hugging herself in one and lying naked in another. Changing. I walked back to the red boudoir painting, closer, closer enough so that the paints all but blurred, mixing together in their contrasting strokes of red. My eyes watered but I kept moving towards the painting, now just specs, blurs, strokes movements of reds and blues and shades of plum, shades of blood, shades of pomegranate.

'Fuck my ass to Kali's hell!'

Could it be really that simple? I poked the painting. It was squishy, like an overripe mango. I was pissed at myself for having missed this. I poked again, and with a jelly-like resistance, my finger was pushed back. What did it need? I pulled back, and with my whole weight, shouldered myself into the painting, hoping it won't break my head.

It wobbled and pushed me back, resistant. I pushed away and ran towards the painting, ramming into it in with all my might, and just like that, it flung me back, straight into the gallery's centre. I got up, messaging my temple. The yalis had now stopped screaming, the stench of the dead yali beginning to fill the galleries. I took out sifter from my satchel and blowing it on the painting, whispered.

'*Khol khal tod phod samapta shakti banke jod.*'

Nothing happened. I left all subtleties and used the Visphota mantra. A blast later, the painting remained untouched.

'Hmm,' I said, pacing in front of the painting. In the still, dead air came a voice. Two voices, faint, soft giggles, coming from far, far away. A dampness leaked off the wall next to the painting and suddenly, something bubbled and oozed out. I slammed myself flat next to the boudoir painting, not daring to breathe, my boneblade ready.

'Clean her up and wrap her up with oil ...'

A foot, then a lean body formed out of the wall, like a boil bursting on a greasy forehead. The first twin entered the gallery.

'... and then and then we will use the new tools. Oh, oh! wouldn't it be nice to use the *new* tools on her?' called out the second twin, coming out from the leaky boil in the wall, dragging something with him, as a child would pull a cart.

It was a nishada, her black body glistening in the dark, wet and limp. She left streaks of paint, no – blood, they were streaks of black blood. I gulped, sliding my boneblade into the wet dampness of the wall.

'Mother told us not to touch them.'

'Mother will not find out.' The first twin reached the yali.

'Look what happened to Magayali, Das.' The other one followed, dragging the nishada with him.

'Looks like he has been clawed, Nas.'

'You are right, Das. Someone painted him, looks like. We will have to tell Mother, won't we?'

'Yes. Let's tell her about this. But we won't tell her about this one, okay? She just gets so mad about these ones in particular. We won't, would we?'

'Give me a splosh!' cried one of them. They did a choreographed jiggle and then clamped their hands together. I held my breath.

'Let's hide her in the monster room. Mother never goes there. Hates it because it reminds her of that monster.'

'Yes, yes. Let's hide her from Mother in the monster's moor.'

They ran, like two giggly schoolgirls. I slipped through the dampness, trying to get inside the wall. It threw me out onto the gallery floor. The scientist's skin on the wall and the paintbrush.

Paint.

Using my boneblade, I slashed my finger and put a drop of blood on the painting. It shimmered and started to leak. I pulled and pushed into the painting, headlong, plunging into darkness.

A bright rich palette of colours shimmered in the room, a small one, with a table and a chair, a rich woody brown and a cupboard behind. Done up in a canary blue, the room shimmered, like wet paint from a painter's palette. In the far corner of the room, a woman, a shimmer of black and grey scales sat, sobs emerging from her stomach. I moved my hand, slowly. She wiped off her tears, facing me.

It was Baza.

'… I have just sent the girl in for Mister Vaa—' She stared at me. I wasn't sure how I looked, doused in blood and entrails. 'Who …?' she managed to croak.

'And hello to you to, Baza,' I answered, stepping closer, my boneblade a silver streak here, ready. 'Remember me? Anantya

Tantrist? I came by the other day, looking for your sisters. The same ones you've been pimping.' I jumped and plunged towards her, a streak of red, a streak of black. We tussled as I struggled to get my blade against her neck. My boneblade slipped, but I managed to get a hold of her, ready to strangle. 'How do I find them? Quick, before I slice your treacherous throat.'

'I—' she genuinely tried to speak, but maybe I was pressing on her neck too hard, the atmosphere of the room confusing me. I relaxed my grip. 'Where?'

'I … I can't. Just—' Her eyes flickered to the table, to a pen stand that stood on top of it. I dragged her up, grabbing the thin sticks jutting from them. Paint brushes. 'They're in the black room. Golden's the key.'

'Your princes, I will kill them tonight. But before that, the girls.'

'… Can't be killed,' she mumbled. I left her, surprised. She stood up, her face down, straightening her painted skirt. 'Take us too, please.'

'You? You want to come?'

'Yes. We are tired of the Goddess and the princes. Please take us with you. We will wait here and warn you if the princes come. Go!' Her eyes, painted a luminous yellow, flicked to the other end. There was no door.

'How?' I asked. I felt her impatience. 'What do you have?' I looked at the brush in my hand. It was a paintbrush, three of them. One dripping blue, one red and one green.

'Paint?' She nodded. 'You don't fucking expect me to *paint*.' She raised her eyebrows and said. 'I will try to keep them away for as long as I can. You need to start fast.'

I twiddled, holding the paintbrush like it was my boneblade and jabbed into the wall on the other side with its wet edge. It left a blob of blue on the dampened, shimmering wall.

'Faster, you nincompoop,' said Baza.

'Kali's shit,' I muttered, doodling. My aim was to make a rectangle, but it ended up a series of blobs, coloured in to make a blue window of sorts in the wall. It was luminescent and I could see shadows inside. I pushed, it didn't open. Baza didn't say anything but her eyes were focused on my left hand, holding the paintbrushes. I jabbed the golden brush on the blob of a window I had painted and then, with my hand, turned the knobbly excuse of a doorknob. It turned and opened, straight into a room, a dungeon of grey shades. Huddled in the middle were the nishadas. I counted fifteen.

'One of you is missing,' I said. 'Where?'

'Baza just took one of us to the red velvet room.' I took out the red paintbrush and dabbled again, quickly. I was getting better at this already. It was the red boudoir all right, with its overwhelming flower-printed maroon brocade curtains, its brightly lit up carved chandelier and the four poster bed with a red satin sheet which was rumpled. Only, like I had seen in the painting last. It wasn't empty. In the centre of it all, was Vajrin Mahendra, his mortal body naked, facing down upon an equally naked nishada girl under him, squirming. His buttocks clenched in action.

'Ahh, Anantya Tantrist,' he said looking sideways, stopping his thrusts, 'We are like two star-crossed lovers, aren't we? We keep meeting each other at the most unexpected of crossroads.' He took himself off the nishada as I still stood in the painted doorway, shocked. 'Some would think we were destined to be together!'

17

MY BONEBLADE acted on its own accord before I could even stop it. It leaped, taking me with it, lashing out and pouncing on top of the naked Vajrin Mahendra, landing straight on his sleek neck.

'Why?' I asked, my left hand gripping the boneblade, shiny, like a piece of light, piercing his neck just a little. 'Give me a reason why I shouldn't just kill you and send you back to Amravati to rot for a few more centuries.' He shrugged, his bony shoulders flexing beneath me.

'Because I can be of help?' I stared into his warm eyes, my fingers clenched. 'Go to your sisters. They're waiting for you,' I said to the nishada. She got off the four poster and ran across the room, outside to the now leaking painted door. All this while, my boneblade remained on his delicate neck, tempted, oh so sorely tempted, to get inside his skin.

'Why?' I asked again, controlling the urge, the urge my boneblade seemed to have to slash his treacherous body into pieces. 'Force yourself on a teen? You want kinky, come to Bedardi!'

'You think this is for sexual deviation? I like my consorts experienced,' He smiled. I gripped the hilt of the boneblade harder, piercing it into his filthy neck. His smile dropped, his eyes widening in the painted world. 'It's my medicine. This body! It has cancer. Those treacherous Kaulas! They gave me a weak, diseased body to live in. That Narahara, he's the biggest tantrik arsehole. Tantriks! It was *deliberate*. The cancer has started to spread, to propogate like it had no business. This is the only way to stop it.'

'And what's that? Sex with a teen?'

'You still don't know this, do you? Nishadas are the *wombs* of immortality. They're the only medium whose body can withstand raaka, the immortality seed.'

'The virus!' Dr Bodhgaya's opinions came back to me. Which is why they've been melting away.

'Exactly. Believe me, the sex, it's *nothing*. Why would I give away all my gold for sex with an inexperienced creature? It's to keep this body from dying. What choice do I have?'

'You could choose to *die*, you eternal scum.'

'And go back to that *shithole* where nothing ever changes? For *centuries*! No thanks, been there done than. I am quite looking forward to exploring your modern world. And why're you so bothered with cattle? I mean the nishadas are reared for this purpose. Saranyu is an old friend, we were gods together! But my mortal body perished and I had to go back to Amravati. But her, she remained her, her body unchanging, but forgotten by those who used to worship her. When she knew about this treatment, she told me about it. They're just nishadas, cattle you know, expendab—'

'Don't you dare call them anything with your filthy, lying tongue. I should have let you rot when I had had the chance! Should have let you *rot*! You should have told me!'

'And what? Sacrifice my life for your noble work? Look, Anantya. I warned you, but do you ever listen? You shouldn't get involved with these people. They're—' The boneblade pierced the delicate white skin, golden-red blood erupting from the vein. 'Och! You cut me!' he cried.

'The only thing stopping my blade going all the way is because it is hoping that you keep telling me something more about these people, something that I don't know already.'

'Oggh. The … Saranyu has another child, a *diseased* mortal, someone she's ashamed of. She doesn't acknowledge him—'

'Wrong answer, hotboy, already know it!' I pressed the boneblade further in his white neck.

'Saranyu! She has only one weakness. She wants to be worshipped, loved, adored by the mortals again, like a goddess. So she plays this game. She supplies her blood and the wombs to someone in Banaras, who then creates raaka wombs. She feels that if she sells long life to mortals, she will be worshipped again.'

'Who is this someone in Banaras?'

'A … a tantrik. He prepares raaka and injects the wombs, sending it back to Saranyu who sells it here. Saranyu is just the supplier. She could never really perform all those tantrik rituals.'

My boneblade slit the side of his ear. His body quivered.

'Anantya, look. I am desperate. Please don't kill me. I … I can't go back to Amravati, not yet. *Please.* I can tell you one more thing about this. The twins, they—'

A blast in the wall and the twins sauntered in, their smug smile radiant in their painted version. Vajrin pushed me away and bounced up, bolting in their direction. 'There, there!' He said huffing and standing behind the twins. 'She's trying to steal your life-giving wombs!'

'You self-centred scum!' I cried, bringing out my boneblade and started to mutter a mantra. One of the twins jiggled, inched and touched me before I could step away, flicking a dripping black paintbrush on my skin. Cold. The cold spread, freezing like burning fire, freezing my skin. I couldn't move. From across the room, Vajrin wore his clothes, looking at me with an expression which screamed of false regret.

'Sorry, darling,' Vajrin said, 'survival comes first. Just one thing more. This is their world. Their masterpiece painting so to say. Your shakti is powerless before them, the artists.'

Filth of an ass. I should have slashed his wrist and broken his treacherous neck when I had the chance. Now, I couldn't speak, couldn't move.

'But look, Nas, look!' said Das, 'It's her, *her*.'

'Yes, yes. Let's paint her. Now!'

'Yes, now! Let's paint her. Now! Before Mother takes her away from us too!'

They jumped, landing next to my inert body on both sides. One fingered a curl of my hair, curling his finger around it. Another touched me lightly, his fingertips like fire on my cold, cold body. His gleeful eyes stared into my furious ones. 'You know,' he said whispering, his cold breath on my wet body. 'I love the intense ones. They're such a pleasure,' he blew a kiss softly on my lips, using a thin knife to tear off my shirt, 'to paint.' I tried to jerk away, scream, wriggle to try and free myself, whispering my shakti to become alive, to rise up, to destroy these two boy beasts. To no avail. The black dabble on me suffocated me, moist and rubbery, like being inside a stale cake. *Too late to realize that, Anantya Tantrist.* Behind, Vajrin turned, looking at me for a split second with an expression that could be mistaken for regret. But it must have been the paint in my eyes for he was gone the next second.

The room was streaked with splashes of blue, shivering like a distanced grey cloud. Something familiar about it. I stood, frozen, naked paralysed, my hands and legs stretched on both and tied up like with blobs of solidified paint. One of the twins came in front of me, his shoulders at level with my face. Using a glistening putty knife, he gently peeled off the skin from my right breast. It came off in a screaming grey-black layer like a rotten fruit. I muffled my pain and rage, my voice of protest, frozen in the stuffiness of the black moist paint. 'Such delicate skin,' said one, his eyes clouded with focus. He peeled more, pulling the skin from my breast, pulling it up to my neck, bending down and licking the inside of the raw skin with his long, thin, orange tongue, touching my raw wound like salt. I screamed, silently, frozen.

'Tasty! Oh, the freshness of the paint! You know what would

have been grand, bro? If she was a giantess. She would have lasted us *weeks*.'

'What to do, Das. I told Mother I wanted more, but she says no. She says these mortals will notice it now. We are in the public eye, she says. She told us and we promised, remember Das? We promised to be good and keep to the fake paintings only for a few days. Mother said the mortals were after us and they will take away our palette, the cattle that belongs to us by our birthright. They will steal it away, Das, if we're not careful. Only a few days, and then we can go back and get as many as we want.'

'Yes, Nas. But she didn't tell us not to paint this one, did she? I am going to take longer on her. Enjoy it. It has been so long since I have had this colour, this beautiful velveteen red!'

'This one? No, this one we can paint as much as we like, and Mother will be glad for it.' Nas brought out a paintbrush, a sable a foot long and dabbed it on my raw breast. It made a deep sucking sound, pulling my heart out of its ribcage. I cried, silent, frozen. A moment later, he pulled it up, soaked red, in my blood. 'What a shimmying red this is. Now, what shall we create today?'

'Oh, I know, I know!' screamed Das. 'Let's make a starred room with this, with a deep maroon tinge. And flexes of gold and yellow with the daeva paint we still have. A good old rumbling sky, a god, angry at the puny humans, bursting with righteous fire!'

'Oh, yes, Das. This paint,' he showed his brother the brush dipped with my blood, 'is such a luscious velvety colour, perfect for a rumbling cloud. And Mother always loves those.'

'Here! Let's make a biiig one! One that covers this whole space!'

'Hmm. You think this human will last that long? I don't want to do an unfinished thing and then the hue never matches with the next human and you don't ever get the perfect shade, ever. I don't want just the outline! It is quite a small one, this one, not enough colour.' Taking the paintbrush, they moved it around in the air, building a dash of colour in thin air. 'More! Das, I need more of the paint!'

'Yes, wait. Don't use too much! It needs to last for *days*. Not like last time. We'll use it less. We'll feed it too. Meat is what mortals feed on. Then it will give us more paint! You have to know how much we can get. Don't waste!'

Then I remembered, my foggy mind throwing in a wastrel fact, maybe to distract me from what was going on here. This was the dark, an indigo splashed around it, but somehow bare, like a dungeon. I hoped that Baza had been able to sneak them out, as much the fuck away as one could get from these fuckwits. Move, I whispered to my toes, my fingertips, concentrating on my shakti, hoping against hope that I could tap into it. But I was helpless. This was their world and my shakti didn't work here. My body sat still, a palette of red for the stormy clouds, my tongue swollen and stiff, like it had been slapped with a popsicle, constantly being licked by the paintbrush. My heart throbbed as did my breast. But not so much. Whatever they had used on me, had paralysed my body, which meant paralyzing half of the pain too.

'Das, where's that paintbrush I gave you in the morning for the cobalt?'

'Somewhere here.' Das shuffled, going to the end of the vast room and coming back in front of me a moment later. 'Here. I will use this one,' he said. 'Much thinner, will make the paint last for longer.'

'Yes, let's make it last for longer. Let's use this paint slowly, slowly.' They turned away from me, moving their paintbrushes in the air, using expert, confident, noiseless strokes. 'It's too silent,' said Nas after some time had passed.

'Nas, let's loosen it up a bit. You so like it when they scream. I see bolder strokes from you then!'

'Ooh, Das,' Nas slapped his twin on his back. 'Why didn't I think of it before? Quick, get a paintbrush, let's do it!' Like an excited child, he stretched his arm and his brother softly sliced his forearm with the same knife he had used for me. Moonlight spread on his forearm, silvering everything. 'Dip, quickly!'

Das dipped his paintbrush in the moon-lit blood and soaked it in. 'Should be enough,' he said. He moved towards my frozen body. My eyes flickered, in panic, as adrenalin rushed into my head, alerting me of danger. He pointed the paintbrush on my chest. 'Not on the paint,' cried Nas. He took the paintbrush upwards, trailing its almost dripping paint from my chest to neck to chin, nose and then like a snake he dabbed the silver, on my eye. Then the other. It burnt. The burning spread from my eyes to my nose, my face, my hair, by chest. Oh, my chest exploded in a million bonfires, bursting from my heart. I grunted, controlling the scream that welled up in the back of my throat. 'Aaarhg!' The stripped skin flapped as I shuddered controlling myself, keeping my vocals from venting what my body felt. A thousand thousand needles pierced my heart. *Don't scream, Anantya Tantrist. Not for them. Don't.* I screamed, shuddering as I throttled it and shut it up.

'Ahh now,' said Nas, as I screamed expletives, in furious pain and helplessness. 'You can paint in peace.' The other dabbed his paintbrush on my chest. I writhed, pressing my lips from keeping me from screaming.

'It doesn't sing,' Das said as he turned to the painting. 'Make her sing, na.' The other twin walked to me, looked in my eyes, smiling charmingly, putting the edge of a knife on my cheek. 'Why do you stop?' he asked softly. 'Maybe more.' He took his knife and made an incision near my eye. A flickering silver blood spread on his forearm

'When …' I licked my lips, to keep the tremble out, the pain out of my voice. 'I … will *chop* you to pieces is when …' I bit my lower lip to keep from screaming. 'I will scream. Oh, how I will scream then, in *joy*.'

Nas put his head back and laughed. 'What an absolute *delight* you are! And humour too. Das, we have to keep this one longer, please? It will try to kill us.' He turned and slapped me with the knife. My head rang halleluiah!

'You know, Nas, I just remembered. There was a time, long back when we tried to murder each other, do you remember that? It gave us such a screaming time for centuries! We tried *so* hard. But no, nothing kills us.' He turned, moving his brush with an expert stroke as if he had forgotten I was there, that I existed.

'Why … do … this?' I asked, my voice weak, exhausted, tired.

'Oh, but what to do? We've tried *all* kinds of paints, they fade away. Only blood stays, powerful, shimmering blood. It's the true paint,' replied Das, or maybe it was Nas.

'Yes, it's the only truth,' nodded Nas. I squirmed, trying to break free from the blob of paints that held me, to no avail. The twins were silent for a few moments, dabbing my bleeding heart once in a while for the stormy cloud they created. I could feel both time and life ebb away from me in this closed, shimmering cobalt room made with tears and blood. I closed my eyes in exhaustion, trying to remember through my foggy mind what Dhuma used to say. What to do if all your tools, all your tantrik weapons are taken from you. I focused my foggy mind to the pit, to my buttocks, to the base of my spine, the sleeping power where the shakti resided. Come on, I whispered to it. The twins worked silently, sponging off my heart, making it beat a little bit slower with every stroke, taking the blood out. So I bled, focusing my remaining energy into the base of my spine. My head fell, drowsy, tired, exhausted so I didn't notice it when one of their heads cocked up.

'Oops,' they said together. 'It's Mother.'

Saranyu entered from a room on my right. I turned, bleary eyed, too exhausted to look at her, as she glided in like a white swan swimming in a spring lake, swollen with monsoon. Except that this was all wrong.

'How did this filth get in?'

'We don't know, Mother. We found her in the red velvet.'

'Where are the nishadas?'

They exchanged a glance. 'I told you it was important that the cattle should stay safe. They're important for our plan to make thankless humanity worship us again. The tantrik from Banaras is trying to control our supplies. Why can't you be of more help, children?' They stood with their heads hung down.

'See how these mortals affect me so? I even talk like them now, hurried, *desperate*.' Saranyu walked to each of them and kissed them on the forehead. 'Oh, if only you monsters could be ... help your mother once in a while, can you?'

'They're in the black room, Mother,' said the twin demurely. 'And we are not the monsters, mother. It's him, your other son.'

'Of course you are not, Nas and Das, you are my beautiful, divine children. Your blood is pure and immortal. Nothing like that deformed monster. *Nothing*. I am sorry I called you monsters, even in jest. You are perfect! Oh I hate his face so much! He's here now with his army of mortals, demanding that he have our cattle. He wants to steal our cattle away, leave us without power. And you know how that leaves your mother in such anger. To see him, a mere mortal son, demanding things from his divine mother, a goddess! Now come with me, my gorgeous boys. We have to make sure they never find our cattle and try and steal them!'

'But, our paint. Our painting,' one said, showing her the dribbles of the story clouds made with my blood.

'It's not going anywhere. You can keep the mortal to do whatever it is you do with it after they've gone.' Their voices faded, my head buzzed with a sleepiness that fed itself on the pain. The muscles in my left breast throbbed, feeding my brain with sleepiness, to black out, to end consciousness, to die. 'Just for a few hours, babies. The accursed monster won't go away before he sees you both and tries to find the cattle. In vain. He won't find a thing. Come.' They left silence behind them.

Such a final thing, such a peaceful thing, death. Yes. I wanted to slip off the precipice of pain, into darkness, into nothingness, into him. *Come to me, Anantya Tantrist, join me.* 'And change. Your clothes reek of filthy mortal blood. It reminds me of *him.*

'... *from the Pashu Department—*' The voice turned to a whisper, and then to the merest hint of sound, falling into silence. My head lolled, free of my will.

'... *according to this warrant, issued in compliance with the Pashu Law by the esteem Judge Tantrik Tvasta of the Pashu Department, the nishada cattle in your ownership belong to honorable Mr Manu Manava* ...

'... *have none of these nishadas. If someone's cattle goes missing, it's not our fault* ...'

The voice drifted in like wisps of wind, in and out. I forced my eyes to open and looked at the unfinished suggestion, the stroke of a stormy red cloud.

'... *we will take your leave* ...'

My eyes flew open. '*No* ...' I whispered, realizing that they would leave, that I would be left alone, helpless, in this painted prison. 'No!' I shook my head, shook it out of its haziness. I took a deep, staggering breath, and collected all the pain my body throbbed with. It shot, through my spine, up to my shoulders, spreading, no not spreading, sent, directed, being taken to both my hands. My hands swelled with blood, with shakti, with pain, beginning to throb like a hungry cat, pound, pulsate, till they swelled and swelled and exploded, blasting my veins, spraying blood all over the painted chains holding me. Red on black. The paint melted, leaked.

I stretched my wounded, throbbing hand, touched the unfinished storm clouds—

'... *if you hear about the location of the cattle* ...'

—and cried:

'*Ghoom aa phat jaa*!'

The outline of the storm cloud burst, splashing blood and paint. I fell forward, into an open space, the cool marble touching my wet cheek.

'That's the tantrik!' someone cried. Faces swam, hazy faces, shadows, together, in commotion.

'*They* …' I gulped hard, ordering my tongue to speak, 'they are inside.' I lay back as an army of people entered the gaping, leaking hole I'd made in the wall to escape. My hands – why were they so wet – crawled towards my yugma locket, the beautiful snake-intertwined locked my mother had given to me, but it wasn't there. Oh, shit, deep trouble that is, I thought. The pain poured like fire, throbbed in my hands, in my chest, like burning lava. They returned a few minutes later, with the nishadas, the girls huddled together. My heart slowed, wanting to stop. Wanting to just lie, delve into the darkness, sink, just die. I could now. I had managed to save them from the real monsters.

'… She needs our help!' Ice ran over my wounds, I cried in pain. How could a single mortal body feel so much pain? Can immortals feel pain? I wondered. But I didn't know any. I cried as ice froze on me, burning it all up. 'Stop … pain,' I whispered.

'Be patient, sister. We will help us.' My eyes flew open to Baza's rigid face, her human eyes swimming with tears. 'The … girls …' I managed to croak.

'We are okay, we are all here, together.' Baza helped me up. I sat with my back to the wall, cringing as a muscle on my breast which I didn't know existed, moved. Someone had put a bandage on it. People ran from one corner of the hall to another. Curious, disgusted, excited faces. 'A … Away,' I whispered, shutting my eyes. '*Water*.'

I drank, seeing the people in front like a tableau, a movie I wasn't too interested in. There was Tvasta from the Pashu Department I'd met a few days ago. He was reading from a booklet. He had a few Tazaak soldiers about him.

'Miss Saranyu, you are charged with incompliance with Pashu Law, illegal abetting and hiding another's cattle and abusing it. We arrest you—'

'They're mine!' cried Saranyu, as hands flew in to grab her. She screamed, a wail of anger and frustration, piercing the head. I winced, hoping she would stop.

'You can't take our cattle,' said one of the twins. 'They're ours. They belong to us. This is stealing.'

'No, Das,' said Manu Maharaj, his face red with anger, 'stealing is what *you* monsters did. You have abused the nishadas for far too long!'

'This is a non-bailable offence and the verdict lies with the owner. I will let Mr Manu Maharaj decide your fate.'

'Here,' said a male voice, gently, pushing a glass to my lips. I gulped. 'Miss Anantya, you've done great service to your kind.' Stratejee sat, his spindly legs folded to show buttocks jutted out. He gave me my satchel. I opened it up and drank rakta straight from my yugma locket. The rawness of it sent an adrenaline kick to my system. Using the rakpiss vial, I poured it on my hands, which still throbbed, raw and painful, and on my chest. Someone had given me a shirt, which seemed kind of familiar. I gulped and said, in a bare whisper. 'The … they …'

'Don't worry. We've got Neel released from Lavana. He's safe. Here.' Mr Stratejee came forward, holding a silent Neel by his shoulders. Blue, blue eyes.

'The … the Banaras tantrik …' I said gulping the rawness I felt in my throat. 'Someone else, someone from Banaras was doing this to the girls. Making raaka of immortal blood and injecting it into wombs,' I pointed to Saranyu, 'Their blood. They're … *immortals* …' My head swam, heavy.

'We will take care of everything,' said Stratejee.

'Thank you for all your help, Tvasta,' said Manu, 'I would like to keep them as volunteers at 6M for a few months. And my mother, I will guard with my heart. Guards, please escort my cattle to the hospice.'

'You filth!' cried Saranyu, her eyes blazing like the sun. 'You'll burn in hell for this. Working for a mere mortal and betraying your mother.'

'You stopped being my mother, *Mother*, when you started to use those girls for your nefarious plans.'

'And what will you do? Cuddle them? They're my pashus! Mr Tvasta, if you let these monsters take me, he will kill us and sell our blood,' said Saranyu.

'Oh, don't be dramatic as always, Mother. If there's any monster, it's your own children. We are just going to ask you to do a little house work around the hospital, clean bedpans and some such.'

The guards arrested Saranyu and the twins and took them away. Manu Maharaj hunched before me, patting me on my head awkwardly.

'Anantya,' He smiled, his lips unmoving. 'Thank you. For keeping my tribe safe from my mother and her mad sons. I have dealt with Barbareeka and paid all her dues. Your friend, Neel, is here. Take him back. Back home.'

'Immortals,' I whispered to myself, holding Neel's hand. What was it that I needed to remember?

'Don't worry. Rest.' He gave me a potion, a drop of it on my tongue. 'It doesn't matter now. Everything is okay. You need to get home, start a new life Anantya, with Neel. Go.' Rough hands on my shoulders. There was something bothering me, something about what Saranyu had said, about the twins when they'd been using my blood to paint, but my mind was too fuzzy to know what that was. So I let them guide me, drop me back home. Someone put me on a bed, and I was lost to the world of darkness. For the first time, I wished I could be like Neel, blank, emptied of everything.

18

THE SECRET room tumbled out of the dungeon, sudden, unexpected. Anantya couldn't help but laugh when Neel got startled, as he stumbled into the passage hidden from everyone in the ritual hall, right in the middle of a thick column of the dungeon, unseen, stealthy, hidden to all except those who knew what to look for. True tantrik magic. She remembered how she had cried with delight when Kaka had shown it to her the first time. She had almost not believed her eyes. Kaka had told her about this place, this secret cell. 'There is a curse on it,' he had said, 'no one can see it unless they're told. And if you tell, you get cursed too. The secret rite takes its toll.'

'Will you be cursed because you told me about this?' she had asked. That made her Kaka bellow with laughter. 'But I am already cursed to have a niece like you,' he teased. She had frowned at that and he had laughed louder as they walked down the passageway.

Now she giggled, her heart trilling, fluttering as she pulled Neel with her, him whispering again and again how this didn't seem like a grand idea.

'Shh,' she said. 'Just trust me. Just come, na.' She wheedled him onwards, through the long passage and down the crooked stairs, up the shaft, and out into the small dark, damp hall with a low ceiling. They crawled like ants one after the other. Crawled till Neel gasped as she knew he would.

The blue lotus room did that to first timers. It was a grand citadel of curved walls, shaped in the style of a lotus just opening its petals. There was no ceiling, but the sky and the stars. The room, a secret in the secret ashram, was created in the shape of the lotus tantra, one of the most powerful tantras for couples, used in high magic. Though Kaka knew about the place, it was only the council who knew the rituals for it. Them and Anantya, who'd learnt it on the sly, much like a tantrik is supposed to learn all his crafts.

The moon glimmered at them making the lotus walls shine. The walls were always damp and shimmering, cool to the touch, even though it was high summer.

Water from the Ganga blesses this place, her Kaka had told her. Anantya knelt on one side of the lotus, at the curve of the petal-shaped wall and lit the matchstick, its yellow wick shivering as an unseen draft touched it and then her hair, caressing them from above. The oil in the hidden shaft caught fire travelling through, like a shooting star all across the room's wall, burning a streak of blue and light blue and sky blue and stormy dark blue all around them. The lotus was luminescent.

'Welcome to the blue lotus,' she said as Neel's face lit up, his blue eyes shining in the icy blue of the light around them. 'Does it have a television?' asked Neel, his brows furrowed.

She laughed taking his hands in hers and kissing them. 'No, something more thrilling than that,' she whispered, taking him by the shoulders and gently putting him in the centre of the lotus, a crater of sorts, big enough for a double bed, big enough for a ritual between a tantrik and his shakti. Power coursed through her, prickling her pores, making her damp between her legs with desire. She ached, oh how she ached to give him, to pour herself into him, as he would pore himself into her, to become one with him. She took off his clothes, touching his moonlit shoulders, his wondrous chest hair tickling her palms, her hands lightly running on his buttocks.

'Anantya ... the tele ...' He sighed, unbridled desire rushing down like a monsoon waterfall through his lips. His eyes, that's what she remembered the most, dark, almost like discs of moonstones, dark with desire. She let her clothes slip off from her, laying him softly on the damp, cold floor, softened by mud. 'Anantya ...' he sighed

again, giving in, to her, to his desire. She made him lie and started to whisper the words. The words of Vajroli, the ritual to feed her shakti to her consort, the tantrik she chose.

'Come to me,' he said, his voice shivering with his naked body, his eyes stormy with desire. 'I can't wait anymore. Come, now, please.' He begged helplessly and like a puppet on a string, love took her, took her towards him, took her into his warmth, his arms that clasped around her. She knew what to do. She had done it before, let others take shakti from her, her father's cronies, old men their backs crooked with age, their eyes full of lust, not for her but for the power she carried. She had seen them change, after the ritual, become younger, stand straighter, filled with her power, their eyes confident and arrogant. Her own eyes clouded, desiring to see that in Neel, her love. She wanted to give him the whole world, the whole of herself, of her shakti. So badly that she ached, throbbed—

'The dead love no one,' said Shukra. He sat outside the crater, his long legs dangling. It was the Shukra she had first met, the arrogant forensics smartmouth she had hated. Thin and unapproachable like an eighty year old. And naked.

'Why are you here and naked?' she cried, pushing away strands of her wet hair. When had they become so short? She remembered them longer. When she was seventeen (wasn't she seventeen now?), her hair had been a mass of curls running down her back, kissing her buttocks. Tantriks had sighed each time she walked by, leaving behind a fragrant trail of jasmine and honey.

'How do I know?' said Shukra. 'You should ask your subconscious, Miss Anantya. I would say it's time you had a discussion about this with your own deep desires.' He looked around. 'Stark place, really. Does it have a teapot? I do feel like taking a cup of tea, it's—'

'Go away!' she cried, trembling, looking around frantically for her clothes. The moment had passed. She didn't understand how Shukra had found her secret place, but he had. She turned to rebuke him again when something pulled her and she fell on her back, her face up towards the dark, stormy, clouded sky. The moon had vanished.

Where did it go? Neel, his face a dark black moon, swam in front of her face, his eyes black as desire, looked at her, handsome, mute.

'I can't wait anymore. Now!' He looked at her, smiling, his teeth glistening, shiny too shiny, his eyes dark and shadowed. 'Will you say no to me again? I have crossed the desert of death for you, my love. Give me yourself. Give me your shakti!' He was the same, the Neel she had loved. She grabbed him by the hair forgetting all about Shukra, the hair matted with dust and filth and kissed him on his warm, plush lips.

'Yes,' she whispered, 'Yes. I will never say no to you, my love. I was created for you, to feed you!'

'Then take me in, suck me, feed me!' He pushed me on my back, 'Seep your powers into mine. Let's become one. Oh we will become so powerful! No one will be able to stop us! It's the time of tantriks!' He hit me, on the face, grabbed my breasts, hungrily, pinching, twisting, all the time muttering. 'You escaped me once! Now I will have you!' I cried out as the ache built up in me. In the darkness, I felt his form, coming on top of me, entering me with such force that it tore my inner walls. 'Yes,' I whispered weakening, under a spell, throbbing, throbbing for him to pull me, pull me into him, take my shakti, own it. His eyes blackened with desire, like black holes. He entered and we started to sway, drunk in desire. He pushed wild and hard, like a hungered lion. I ached and put my hands over his back wanting to scratch him till blood would seep out of his broken skin. But my right hand was bound, cuffed with something. I turned to look what was holding it back. Shukra held my hand with his left one, sipping tea with his right. I cried, frustrated.

'Take this off!' she cried.

'You are the one holding me,' he said sipping his tea.

'Balls of bulls!' she swore, turning. 'Give me a second, darling,' she said, pushing Neel away, taking his swollen penis out of her. 'Let me deal with him first.'

'No!' Neel grabbed her by her hair, pulling hard, his hands like rock and sharp like claws, pushing her into the ground. 'Not again!'

he screamed, his voice echoing in the lotus walls. She cried as her hand, cuffed with Shukra's, pulled too, yanking at her shoulder blade. The walls swam, wavering, melting.

'I will take you!' he said, morphing into something else. He hit her, slapping her on the face, biting her chest with his sharp rotting teeth, his hands rough and hard and frozen and cold like a crocodile's hide, tearing her naked skin. He raised a clawlike hand, leaking into black wisps and pushed it towards her chest, her heart. She screamed, as his hand tore her skin, bones and flesh and muscle flying around. Krrichh. A wet noise as he tore out her heart, her beating heart, red and bloodied.

'I will consume you!' His black-hole like sockets glittered dark, miniature hands and spider legs crawling out like thick black tears. They crawled on her arms and chest and legs and face, biting, nibbling on her flesh till they consumed everything. His shadow bloated, spreading like a wraith of miasma and screeches, all around me. 'Give me!'

Her right hand still bound to Shukra, who seemed unaffected, sipping tea while she struggled single-handed with the monster, she made a naga mudra of her left hand and pierced his empty eye socket, clutching and grabbing hold of a few insects. They melted, scattering into wisps of black.

'No one fucks me without my consent,' She said, hitting him on his chin with a good, solid kick and somersaulting in the air, turning Shukra with her. 'Go!' She screamed to him.

'But my tea!' he answered, looking at the cup. 'Fuck your tea!' She screamed, pushing him. Shukra fell, pulling her with him. They turned and tumbled and fell, up the sky. 'NO!' screamed the monstrous mist, clutching, crawling, and turning into wisps of desperation and screams.

'No!' I cried aloud, my eyes flying open, my body throbbing. My left hand was icy and writhing like an extended worm. Neel was on top of me, his expression blank. I pushed him back hard, sprang up from the bed and rushed, running to the rasayana lab. The throbbing in my left arm and the way my whole body protested when I had sprung up from the bed told me that this wasn't a dream. I had escaped from the tantrik.

Who was he? Somehow I had a feeling I remembered him from before. Shukra, now that was a curious addition to the dream. Almost like he'd come to warn me. I opened my satchel and took out the rakpiss vial, taking a long swig. Tired but alert, I walked to the rasayana lab, deciding to make a charm for my sleep like I'd decided some days ago. For some reason, this had given me a déjà vu feeling. I lit up the fire in a yantra nearby, preparing the requirements on my table. Something hit me from behind.

'Not now Neel!' I shrugged, irritated. *Crunch!* The vial fell from my hands as a sickening pain spread on the side of my neck. I touched my nape, wet, oh so wet. I swirled, turning, as Neel pushed me down, falling hard on my back, the boneblade slipping from my other hand and falling with a dull thud on the floor alongside. He pushed me hard, away from the yagna fire, and pounced on me as I fell, climbing on top of me, a little too much like the nightmare. He opened his mouth, his teeth yellowed, broken and crooked. His mouth a gaping black hole. Too real, too much like the dream. He lurched, his mouth yawning, like a feral animal, his teeth glistening a sickening yellow, and before I could stop him, bit me on the chest, taking a chunk off my flesh. I screamed in pain, as he smiled, the flesh dangling from his lips, the lips I had wanted to kiss.

The smile came then, for the first time in many days, his blue eyes, not blue anymore but dark, matte black. He stopped, distracted for a second and pinched his forehead, plucking something from it. A maggot, I realized in horror, my eyes doubling. I pushed him with the remainder of my strength, repulsed by the sickeningly sweet smell of rottenness that came from him, turning my body. But he was heavy, sitting on top of me. We struggled, throwing and rolled. My hands crawled, for something, anything, to use against him. He opened his jaws wide, now bloodied, with my blood.

I squirmed, helpless, trying to move my body but his dead weight kept me pinned. My hands spread, needles of pain shooting through them as they crawled like the maggots coming out of Neel's ears. Plop, one of them dropped on my breast, crawling upwards. I gagged at the sickeningly sweet smell from his rotting flesh. Why hadn't I smelled it before? I wondered helplessly as Neel's yellowed teeth yawned, sharp and glistening rotten, ready to bite. My fingertips touched something sleek and cold, a piece of a broken vase, under the table. I gripped it and swung hard, hitting him on the side of his head. With a sickening crunch it hit him square on the side of his head, cracking his skull. He snatched it as if it were a toy and threw it away, grinning, his tongueless mouth yawning again, the crooked teeth peeking through.

As he lurched forward, I grabbed his hair and yanked, managing to squeeze out from under him. I rolled, his hands grabbing me, and crawled up. He pulled me, making me fall on the burning fire bricks, the heat searing my back. Black flames rose as he plunged back on top of me. I squirmed, my hands desperately reaching out behind, cringing as the heat from the burning fire became too strong. My fingertips touched the rough texture of a burning log. I pulled it out from the yagna fire and pierced it right through his eye, his black eye which was blue no more. He pulled away, falling on his back, convulsing on the floor. Not waiting, I pulled another log from the black fire and pierced it in his shoulder, and again in his thigh. He squirmed, his mouth opening up in pain, it's tongue-less cavity sending a shiver through me. I ran to my satchel and took out a piece of mayan rope. He crawled on all fours, wounded on the shoulder and flesh falling from his eye – rotten flesh – I noticed with a gasp. Rotten without blood. Ignoring how my heart was beating with the sound of fuck, fuck, fuck, I picked up my boneblade, slashed both his wrists, binding them together with mayan ropes, till he had become a tied up mummy, a caterpillar without wings. He moved, and silently stared at me with his expressionless black hole of an eye. The flesh had fallen from the other one and bone jutted out from there.

'Bloody hell, Neel!' I said, my hands shaking. 'You finally decide to communicate and all you want to do is bite? And not in an I-appreciate-it sort of a way either!' I kicked him in frustration, trying hard, trying hard to be angry and not to flop down and cry out in pain as my heart continued to beat, to beat in the rhythm of fuck, fuck, fuck. I got up, opened up my yugma locket and sipped on rakpiss, drinking more than I should have, desperate for a beedi. I slashed one of his veins, taking out the blood into a bone cup. Shukra had told me something about his blood and I'd ignored him. Now it was coming back to bite me in the ass, literally. I fished out Lala, my skull cup, from my satchel. Opening the cap of a ceramic vat, cupping the skull into the vat of viscous liquid, minced entrails of a deer, pouring it into the pot that burnt over the fire. It flamed up, licking hungrily as I fed it a few corpse wood logs. Time was running short. I whirled around the lab, picking up the things I required for the new ritual—two tongues of a chameleon, the anguished cry of a rudaali dipped in honey, clippings from a dasyu's deadened wings, powdered bones of a brattoad and eyes of a blotloris. The fire burnt, consuming it all, its tongues becoming black. The fumes of truth rose. All I had to do was inhale them to know who the tantrik was that controlled Neel. Just one more ingredient left before that, I thought. Asura's blood. I opened the bottle of the blood I had saved. It was empty! Cracked in our struggle.

'Fuck the fishes!' I cried out aloud. I put the fire out, black smoke sprouting out of it. Now where could I get fresh supply of asura blood? I grabbed a vial and turned it upside down, trapping the smoke erupting from the black fire, into the emptiness of it. It crystallized and became a silvery white liquid. Dragging the squirming Neel, I went out of my house, spreading his body vertically across Chhotu's seat, his legs dangling, and tying him squarely with mayan ropes.

'Umm … Miss Anantya?' I turned to see the owner of the sing-song voice, frowning the hell away. She was a petite lady, weirdly dressed, wearing a human skin around her like a gown, her hair plaited neatly with pieces of bones. On her shoulder sat a raven, double the size of a normal one.

'*Craw! Craw!*'

'You don't remember me but—'

'I am in a hurry, lady!' I cut her off, feeling a weird sense of déjà vu. 'Wait for it.'

'Its … rather urgent,' she said. Her voice didn't convey any urgency. Neel squirmed. 'Even by immortal standards.'

'Shakti's ass, I am so going to regret this. Come, sit behind me, tell me on the way,' I said. I sat on his neck, gripping it with my legs, keeping those very sharp teeth of his facing down and started my bike, zooming in the afternoon sun.

'You know me,' said the mysterious lady as we chugged on Chhotu, me wishing I had a mantra to speed up Chhotu. I honked at a seriously suicidal driver and screamed to the woman, 'No, I don't!'

'Yes you do and that's why I've come to you. I … I miss them … all the silly boys. I would want your help to get them back.'

'Who?'

'You'll have to remember first.' We reached Defence Colony. I got off, dolefully looking at the squirming body that Neel had become. Shukra's cuboid shaped home stood in front of us.

'Remember what?'

'Rather weird hut to live in,' said the raven.

'Wait till you meet the person who lives here,' I said walking to the backdoor and ringing the bell. 'Remember what, lady?'

'My name. Basudi, please.'

'Hanuji didn't want them to be with her,' said Basudi, the raven.

'Well, Hanuji isn't here and I would rather that he's here to order both of us around.' She put her hand in her plait.

'You deal with him later then,' said Basudi. He opened his beak and out came tendrils, spidery web, gnarled and strangely alluring.

'What's that?' I asked.

'Identify yourself,' asked a metallic voice from the speaker.

'It's me, Anantya. Open up, Shuks!'

'I won't!'

'Open it or I will blow it away!' I said, pissed off.

'Don't nursery-rhyme me, Anantya. I have had it with you and your irrational emotions.'

'Shukra ...' I gulped, looking at the writhing mass that was my boyfriend, and gulped again staring at the intercom. 'Look, I am sorry I screamed at you. I need your help, *please.* You were right about Neel.' A hand grabbed me by my curls, pulled my head back forcibly, and I saw the raven's beak looming above. He dunked down and pecked me on my eye, hard. 'Ow!' I cried, eyes widening, as something cold spread from my eye to my brain, causing brain freeze. I grabbed onto my skull.

'What in fuckness!'

'Just gave you what Hanumanji took from you,' she said, smiling gently. 'Don't worry, you will remember soon.' My head reeled and I tried to grab something. The door behind creaked open a few inches and Shukra's familiar recently-shaved face peeped through, his eyes shining with suspicion behind the glasses too small for his rugged face. His eyes flicked from me, frowning from the girl to the crow and to Neel.

'Who's them?' he asked.

'Meera and Basudi,' I answered, surprised that I knew her name. 'Sorry, Shuks, but I have to do this. No time to explain.'

Using my boneblade, I slashed the plump vein on his hairy arm, pumping blood faster. 'Ow!' he screamed as blood spurted out, deep red, rich with the smell of earth and its hidden womb of metals, into my skull cup. I breathed deeply. 'Rich. Just perfect.'

'May I ask why your boyfriend is tied up?' asked Shukra pointing at Neel's body, still firmly bound by mayan ropes, wriggling as his tongue-less mouth opened to bite on invisible flesh.

'I can see you need answers. You were right about testing Neel. It was,' words fell, tumbling from my brain to my lips, uncontrollable. 'I needed your blood to find out who is controlling him. I don't even know hi—Shakti's arse!' I stopped and turned, eyeing Meera.

'Matsya Curse! The preta tantrik attacked didn't he? Took all the immortals?'

'Yes he did,' Meera said.

'And you?'

'I am not part of the Matsya Curse ten. But I do miss the boys. Can you try to do something about it? Like bring them back?'

'Why did you take my memories away? I was trying to solve a fucking case.' Basudi the raven shook his little black beaded head.

'You'll have to ask him.'

'Fuck, fuck fuck!' I cried out loud as the tendrils of my memories made themselves known. 'I was there! I knew that Saranyu and the twins were immortals. I could've warned them, even though they're the scummiest of scums! But no, I let them go and now they're with Manu who surely doesn't love them much. If the preta tantrik who is after them finds Manu! He just came from Banaras! He told me about the thirteen people he had found, including Neel. And Neel's under the vashita spell. And he has the nishadas too. What if he is … Oh, there's definitely a rotten smell here!'

'Where? I think you might be mistaken. I had a bath, though this Neel does smell a little,' said Shukra.

'... But if he's the tantrik, why hand me Neel? Unless, he, my Neel, was a way to keep—Oh, if he's the tantrik, he's true evil. And we'll find out soon, won't we? Meera, Basundi, you both go back to the Matsya cemetery and wait for me there. Shukra, I need you man.'

'You're not making any sense, Anantya. Need what?'

'More of your blood,' I said taking out the skull cup. Once it was filled with Shukra's blood, I took out the carefully packed glass vial, with its shimmering silver smoke, and immersed it in, opening it inside. It bubbled and out came a scream of horror. Shukra clamped his hands on his ears. I put the skull on my face, blood dribbling all over, and inhaled the freezing white smoke, gasping like a fish out of water as its coldness hit the lungs. Like a cold, cringing stone, it came in my stomach, sudden and heavy. The realization was freezing and hard, stone hard, and heady.

'Fuck my ass to eternity,' I exclaimed, shivering as the cold chill from the smoke escaped, leaving behind wet hair and a smear of grease. 'Such a powerful spell!'

Someone was controlling Neel's prana, just like I had done with the yali. Drinking from his soul, killing him bit by bit. It was a dark spell indeed, the work of a black tantrik. The Vashita mantra. No wonder he had looked like he'd seen a ghost. I wiped my face with the back of my hand. Shukra stared at me with horror in his eyes.

'Let's go.'

19

THE EVENING sun slanted, cutting us into half. We zoomed. I laughed, hysterical for no good reason really, for reason had gone off to pee somewhere in one of those ornamental bushes on Delhi's roads. Shaking my head, I remembered a song that Dhuma used to sing when she had had too much charak.

'Come here, you lout
Take a bout,
Grab my boobies and scream aloud
For the night is young
And my moon shivers
Come take a bite
And rest my mad fevers!'

I sang aloud. Neel's head lolled and hit mine from behind, trying to kiss it.

'Look out,' screamed Shukra. He shivered, making Chhotu shiver. I giggled. 'Anantya, are you drunk?'

'Nooooo! But the moon is …' I said, giggling. And so was the mobike. Chhotu seemed hell bent on going zigzag rather than straight, as much as I shouted at it. My stomach tickled from inside. I giggled and sang Dhuma's song again.

'Come here, you lout
Take a bout,
Grab my boobies and scream aloud …'

'Your boyfriend stinks!' cried the ape-man from behind. I laughed. Neel, my boyfriend, who was possessed.

'He wants to bite,' I screamed back, biting the wind, my mouth opening as his had opened, and teeth crashing together in an avalanche. I giggled and fell off the bike, running.

'Where are you *going*? Stop!'

'... *Grab my boobies and scream aloud* ...' I sang, giggling some more, crawling and bawling. It was here, here, I'd reached it! I flapped around. Something cold splashed on top of me, my body throbbing, itching, my lips moving. Above a face, clean gelled hair, something familiar about it.

Crash and scream.

Singing and ringing in my ears. A cold gush of water. I shivered as a cold wind hit my wet body.

'I am wet!' I swiped damp hair out of my eyes.

'Yeah, real perceptive ...'

'You, you threw water at me.'

'And you cut my wrist, which is much ruder than splashes of H_2O.' Shukra stood with his arms folded across his chest, his lips pursed. 'And almost killed me in that crash. And then scared the living hell out of me by having an epileptic attack.'

'Fine,' I said clutching my stomach. It felt curiously empty. 'We'll call it quits then.' We were in a parking lot of sorts and there was something eerily familiar about it, but my head throbbed still. I needed a beedi.

'So? Why did you get us here of all places?'

We were in the forest behind Qutub Institutional Area. In front of us was an old stonebrick warehouse, with a tin roof.

'To meet Manu Manava. You stay here—'

'Of course not. I am coming with you.'

The door creaked open, protesting. The warehouse inside had changed. The long platform was filled with just a few low-lying beds, otherwise empty as were the ledges halfway up the ceiling. A robust diya lit up the shrine of Lord Dhanwantari across from the hall. Manu sat there, crouched on top of a patient's body, working on something on his chest, muttering to himself, his paralysed left hand by his side.

'Manu,' I called out. Shukra put the unconscious Neel on one of the beds.

'A … Anantya,' said Manu, looking up. His eyes were wild, roving and shiny. His hair awry. A tick worked on his non-paralysed cheek. My boneblade slipped out of my scabbard, my left hand making a fist around its carved handle. 'What are you doing here?'

'I just remembered something I had to ask you,' I said, slashing my wrist. Manu frowned. I pointed the boneblade, dipped in my blood, and shouted.

'*Aim hreem bhuta aa, kar de kreem, Jaalikah*!'

'No!' he cried as Jaalika's silky dark threads shot like a web of arrows towards him, hitting him straight into the chest, making his stagger. He fell back, like a stone, rolling as the threads wrapped themselves around him. They were translucent and breathing, sighing from my boneblade's tip to Manu's body.

'Wait!'

'Now. Explain to me why you decided it would be a good idea to have my boyfriend under a Vashita mantra?' I asked, keeping the boneblade pointed to him while going around him and moving so that Jaalika's fine threads moved with me, building a web all around him.

'Ex,' muttered Shukra from behind. The patient who had been lying got up, straggling away as Manu rolled in Jaalika's web.

'You don't understand, Anantya!'

The patient got up, rubbing his hands on his face, as if confused. 'My apprentice has been causing trouble again I see,' he muttered. His hair was spread out like a cuckoo's nest and he had a vapid, confused smile on his face.

'Dr Bodhgaya?' said Shukra.

'Of course, it's not apt. One minute I was working and the next, my apprentice comes in and destroys everything that I'm working on. And then I wake up here, and I don't,' he looked around. 'Most … most inconvenient.'

'Don't take him!' screamed Manu. 'You're making a mistake!'

I opened the vial of rakta in my yugma locket and put a drop of it on Jaalika's web. She sizzled with pleasure, the red passing in the dark smoky tendrils like a pulse all across the web.

'Your apprentice?' asked Shukra.

'Fees? No. I refuse to charge any. I did it for the pleasure of science, only my apprentice interrupted rather rudely. Most inconvenient.'

'You're one evil jealous thing aren't you, Manu Manava? Where are your mother and brothers?'

'I can't tell you!'

'Come with me, doctor,' said Shukra, taking Dr Bodhgaya away from me and Manu. I pulled Jaalika, making Manu squirm.

'And the nishadas?'

'The nishadas are safe, away from him,' he said, pointing to Dr Bodhgaya.

'The immortals?'

'What immortals?'

With a snap, I tightened the web of Jaalika around Manu.

'Agrh—' From the darkness, I could feel several pairs of eyes on me, of the few patients I'd seen in the hall. His deformed body hunched up, so that he lay crouched on his stomach, his huge, bulging eyes staring at me.

'The ones, you've been kidnapping from all over Delhi. The once with the Matsya blood.'

'I don't know anything about Matsya!'

'Don't lie, you leech!' I twisted my boneblade, he spasmed painfully. His breathing became effortful. Behind me, a scuffle. I turned to see a patient, who had tried to attack, being deftly stopped by Shukra's bouncer avatar. He'd just thrust a palm on his face. 'Tell the truth, or I'll make you!'

'I won't tell you about my mother! I won't tell you or Stratejee. Do whatever you want to with me.'

'Stratejee? What has he got to do—'

'He's after Mother too. It was our deal that I will get Mother to do as I desire,' he screamed. 'After years and years of abuse, I deserve it! She was horrible to me, you know? She made me a plaything for her perfect sons. They kept me in a pen with their other animals, the tortoises and the monkeys and the jackals. I was made to race with monkeys and if I lost, oh if I lost, they would … they would … It was a hobby for them, making things race with each other. I ran away from them, as far away as I could. I didn't want to see her face again.' His head hung and his body shook as a sob travelled through it. 'You won't understand. When your whole family is immortal and physically perfect and you're the only one who is a … a nothing. I've planned this for months! When he gave me a chance—'

There was a malicious, mad glitter in Manu's eyes.

'Who he?'

'You're not stupid enough to think I am the powerful tantrik who can control pretas and create the immortality seed? I am just playing a part. A very small part!'

'If you're not the preta tantrik, who—'

There was a scuffle somewhere behind us and I knew, as suddenly as lightening strikes. I twisted, just in time to see two creatures pouncing in my direction. I tumbled, rolling and escaping as their limbs fell where I was with a silent thud, getting up again, their eyes dull and black like Neel's had been.

'I can tell you …'

I turned. Standing behind was the short figure of Dr Bodhgaya, his eyes staring at me with something like regret in his face. He held a long dark blade dipped in blood in his one hand.

A shadowsword. His other hand held Shukra by his hair, who whimpered like a wounded dog, on his knees. His face was bloodied, his clothes torn. Behind him stood the patients, their mouths wounded and dripping blood, their eyes shining black, like the shadowsword. I gripped my boneblade, Jaalika slipping away and whooshing around madly.

'… but I'm afraid you might not like the answer,' said Dr Bodhgaya, frowning in a lost way.

'But you wanted to save them.' I said, recalling Jaalika back into my boneblade.

'Yes, I did,' said Bodhgaya. 'But my apprentice, he has other plans.' A head popped out from his left shoulder, rising up vertically. A thin, long head I knew really well. Stratejee smiled politely.

'What can I say? It's a hostile takeover.' He casually flicked his thin wrist, his black blade shining as it moved in an arc and three bodies flew in between us, like puppets on a string. I recognized one of them as a patient I had seen when I'd first come to this place. Something wet and hard smashed the side of my head. The boneblade fell with a dull clatter, making me fall. Above me, stood Neel or rather, I forced myself to think it, his body, his eyes black holes of nothingness, holding a chopped human arm in his hand with which he had just hit me. He smiled, his lips making a mockery of the loving smile I had seen all those years ago, and snatched my satchel away. I hesitated, not wanting to attack him as two other corpses pounced on me from either direction, their mouth wide open, their teeth twisted and monstrous ready to bite. I twisted and smashed my elbow into one's face, hard enough to hear the crunching of bones and twisted my foot so that I hit the other's teeth shin, shattering them. I waved my boneblade, slashing one's face, another's arm and another's neck. Stratejee waved his hands like a conductor of classical music. Neel snarled like a hungry dog, as the three pounced again, their eyes empty, their mouths open, their teeth blackened and crooked, their bodies leaking the blood that I'd split. They were unaffected and came back, attacking me, pushing me down on the floor. I squirmed, struggling against them. A glint showed me my boneblade being used by one undead to cut off fingers of another, who sat beside him. Both guffawed as the boneblade chopped another finger. My bag was nowhere to be seen. Shit of a dasyu.

'Give up, Anantya. You've lost,' said Stratejee. 'Give up or I'll make a dead man out of your lover.' He held a long blackened, rusted sword, thin on both sides, one of them touching Shukra's throat, its edge dripping blood.

'No!' I cried before I could stop myself.

'Like this one here, don't you? Forgetting your older lover? You want to know where we found Neel? In a pit, tongueless, left to *die*. We *saved* him. So you could do jiggle-jaggle with him. Was he good? Did you like it? Please describe the event.'

Bile rose up my throat. *Neel, what had you made me do?*

'Come here little boy. Little monkey.' Stratejee waved his blade and Neel pounced towards him, like a pet. 'He is loyal, feeds me his prana.'

Neel smiled, his tongueless mouth opening up. Stratejee touched his fingertips on Neel's head, petting him. 'I need some of that energy Neel. I feel so tired.' With a flick of his sword, like a conductor of music, he bound me and Manu together with tendrils of smoke. I struggled, only for the smoke tightening around us a bit more.

With another swing of the sword, he brought all the people around him. Thirteen, I counted. The ones that Manu had told me they'd found in Banaras. They came together, their left hand stretched, like spokes of a wheel, with Stratejee's hand on top. With his right hand, Stratejee heaved the rusted sword into his left wrist. The sword glided like melted butter from his wrist to the thirteen other wrists below him. I watched horrified as Stratejee started to speak the Mrityansh mantra.

'*Kaala khleem, vasha hreem, damaashh aatma hlin kreem*!'

The thirteen screamed, in ecstasy and pain, as black tendrils of blood leaked from their veins, floating, rising, leavening and entering Stratejee's pores. Like shadows of blood drops, they came all together, consumed by Stratejee. He smiled.

'What did you do to them?' I asked.

'A slight but rather effective modification to the Mrityansh,' said Stratejee. 'It not only keep their souls locked into their bodies, but also splits it so their living soul can constantly feed us, making us live.'

'Praniks. You've turned them into praniks!' I whispered.

'Immortality is quite a marvel, isn't it? They live and feed their prana to us!' said Stratejee. 'Just wait for a few minutes more, Anantya Tantrist. When I send you and your ape back to hell, that's what you'd be pleading for too.'

'I am quite apologetic,' said Dr Bodhgaya, his head bobbing on Stratejee's chest. 'Shushrut has always been quite an ambitious and impolite creature.'

'You're the one who Ashwa gave the nagamani to.'

'Yes. He trusted me to give him death,' said Dr Bodhgaya.

'And we did grant him death. Ahh, these immortals. Don't value what's been given to them by nature!'

'I can understand their need to rest,' said Bodhgaya.

'Oh, stop snivelling, Guru*ji*,' cried Stratejee. 'If you didn't want to come back from death, you could've just said no to us. No one forced you to create that raaka—'

'I wanted to, but the price of it,' he shook his head. 'I … I didn't know what he would use it for. I didn't know it would create praniks of these innocent people. We are wrong, Shushrut, we are. We are healers, not this,' he said. I squirmed, trying to find a way out of the smokey tendrils that held me. My hand felt freer only to hear a gasp from behind. Manu was being choked. I stopped.

'You were always so *weak*. That's what killed you, all those centuries ago. Never prepared to do what it takes to achieve the end.'

'Why did you create raaka?' I asked Bodhgaya. He nodded. Shushrut smiled, his teeth gleaming in the darkness.

'I didn't think this through. My quest consumed me,' said Bodhgaya, 'I was a powerful tantrik, I made miraculous medicines for diseases, wrote shastras on plants that could cure the yellow fever, cure birth abnormalities, thinning blood, flushing out fevers. I knew everything about healing, leaves that could cure malaria overnight, seeds that could save one from Black Death, and piss that could heal sores and constipation. I had the power and the ability to strike at the heart of death, to take people from its very clutches back to life. But it wasn't enough. I wanted to *conquer* death, to overcome it, to take it in my very mortal hands and throttle it. So I started to experiment, research, test, finger, find ways to evolve life, evolve the human body so that it would never have to die. But it took years of my time, this research, this finding and without my realising, my hair turned white, my face wrinkled, my body started to behave irrationally, not agreeing to my commands. I had grown old in my quest, closer to death, but still not understanding it. Which is when I made the terrible, terrible mistake of taking Shushrut on as an apprentice. I taught him everything I knew and had learnt.'

'And wasn't I a brave scientist?' asked Shushrut, 'Didn't I take your rather rudimentary teachings to a whole new level? It was I who discovered that the raaka can be used for rejuvenating cells. I who figured the way dead could be revived, so we could be brought back, so our teachings wouldn't go to waste. You had the knowledge but not the daring to use it! If I hadn't tried to bring you back, for the love of you my teacher, the treacherous Matsya Curse wouldn't have hit me and I would still be alive, immortal. I was smart enough to leave my teachings in Banaras, and start the Bhairavanas, a group of tantriks who didn't hesitate, who were ready to go all the way to achieve the ultimate, power and immortality! Unlike the soppy, manava-pandering tantriks of today. It was the apprentice of my clan who brought us back, revived us so we could continue our research. And this is how you repay me? For a second life?' The weirdass transfusion stopped and Stratejee shook his head.

'Wooie!' he said. All thirteen, including Neel had blackened holes for eyes. 'Have you ever seen such a vashita spell, Anantya Tantrist? One which is able to not only rule another, but split the soul to feed dead ones? For that's what we've been able to achieve!'

'Who?' I asked. A pranik behind Stratejee moved and I saw a flash of my khaki bag.

'My apprentice with my teachings! See Charaka, unlike you, I am not jealous of my apprentice's powers. I am proud of him! We share the same desire, him and I. We've been waiting all these centuries for immortality and finally, we have it in our grasp! Once we're this powerful, we can achieve anything. Use this power for greater good.'

I scoffed. 'And world domination?'

'If the world cannot think for itself, yes! We can take it to a whole new level.'

'That's just so banal,' I said. 'The usual pedestrian villainous thinking. I would've expected better ideas from you, Stratejee.' His eyes flared with anger. He flicked his black blade and a bunch of the undead attacked, like ferocious wolves, eyes gleaming with dark malice.

'Tantriks will rule, will lead humanity to a better world.'

I spat. 'Tantriks are fucking selfish toads and will lead anyone to the bottom of Naraka, which is where you're going.'

The angry wolves fell on us, biting, taking off chunks of flesh and blood. I squirmed trying to kick but the tendrils tightened around us, making it quite hard to do anything really.

'You are right,' said Bodhgaya. 'He's just a twisted thing with a massive ego.' Maddened, Stratejee growled and butted the scientist on his head, making it loll.

'Shut up you traitor! Stop!' The praniks stopped, stilling in their action, waiting for their master's next command. Shukra fell onto the floor as Stratejee walked towards us, rotating his sword like a baton. He walked around me, pulling me by the hair and throwing me with Shukra. Raising both his hands, he held something in them.

'Rise, my dead friends, Gupta, Kamal, Rajesh, Amar, Asim …'

The names went on.

Crunch! Ghhatch! The dead rose from all round us, from the ground, heaving up and surrounding us all. He touched his shadowsword to his neck, opening his jacket with a stroke. A bright light like a million stars pierced the sky.

'Aim hreem pretayeh astubhyam namastubhya.'

The pretas swam in through the darkness of their planes, attracted by the undead standing around us. 'Now, my friend,' He said it in a way to send maggots running down my spine. 'We do need your mother you know?' His fingertip crawled from Manu's nose to his chest. 'The one you were silly enough to put in your bleeding heart.' His hands became like claws. I looked around. 'You all must be hungry after the transfusion,' he said looking back at the undead and pointing to me and Shukra. 'That's your dinner.'

'But …' Manu cried, clutching his heart with fisted fingers, 'you promised. Please!'

'Ah, a mother's love. So pure.' His hand moved with a smooth slash, cutting through Manu's upper chest. Blood sprouted out, like a fountain, falling on the incoming traffic of the undead who attacked me and Shukra from all directions.

20

MANY THINGS happened at once. Someone grabbed my leg, piercing nails dragging from my thigh to ankle as I dived. Shukra woke up. Stratejee pushed his hand into Manu's ribcage. Bodhgaya screamed in horror. Undeads walked towards us, their fingernails filled with dirt and filth. I rolled, pouncing on the undead who was playing with my boneblade, smashing the face of another undead with its hilt. 'Not for kids,' I said, grabbing it and slashing his neck. He yawned, his tongueless cavity of a mouth, showing dagger-like canines. I kicked, tumbling and scrounging towards my satchel, which lay further up. Taking out the matchbox, and lighting one stick, I screamed.

'*Jal bhun bhasm ho ja*!'

The Agni mantra blasted in the undead's face. He stopped, considered, and then attacked, his mouth opening chasm-like.

'Shiiit!' I cried, scrambing backwards. I needed lala, my skull cup. I kicked him in his burning mouth, slinging the satchel on me. It didn't have the skull cup. Where was it? The undead chased me. I ran, seeing Shukra, up and struggling with a bunch of life-eating undead too. Three others pounced on me, one pulling my leg and biting the calf before I could stop him, the other pulling on my shoulder, swooping like an eagle on its prey. This wasn't going to work out as I had imagined it. Then I saw it, the skull cup, right next to Stratejee's feet. He crouched, his arm halfway inside Manu's chest. Shit.

'Bodhgaya!' I shouted, 'The skull cup!' I screamed. Bodhgaya thankfully heard me, took control of the body and kicked the skull cup my way.

'Nooo!' screamed Stratejee. I flung myself, struggling, kicking, swerving, pulling myself on an undead's shoulder and grabbed lala with both my hands, rolling away as a couple of undead pounced, heading towards Shukra.

'You traitor!' screamed Stratejee, swiping his sword angrily, cutting off Bodhgaya's head from his body and smashing it with his foot.

Shukra nodded as he fought with two undeads, slamming his elbow into one and his knee into another. I ducked between their legs, crawling upwards, into the circle, with my back to Shukra's back. Manu started to squeal in a thin, eerie voice. Distracted, I looked at him.

An undead got his teeth into my right leg's calf. I cringed, using my other leg to hit him straight on the face. With the skull cup in one hand and the boneblade in another, I slashed Shukra on his shoulder, cutting his vein in a neat gash.

'Arugh!' he said, as blood gushed out, straight into the skull cup. 'What the fuck, Anantya!'

'You're learning to say "fuck"? That's a start!' I said, elbowing another undead as my skull cup filled with his asura blood. Three more lurched towards us. 'Hold me tight and swirl me, babe,' I whispered in his ear, grazing his stubble with my lips. Shukra didn't argue, bringing his thick arms around my waist, he picked me up like a doll and rotated. Holding the boneblade in my lips, I firmly held the skull cup in both of my palms and screamed.

'*Aim Hreem rakta varaharim*!'

Powered and maddened by Shukra's powerful blood, the bloodboar poured out of the skullcup, their snouts sniffing for vashita blood, their mouths open wide and large, their smoky teeth sharp and glistening. They floated and wove in all directions, rushing out of the skull cup, like an army of maddened hungry pigs, desperate for a bite of blood.

'Drink from their filthy veins!' I screamed, spilling more bloodboars around me, from the skull cup straight into the oncoming undeads' faces. The undead fell back, screaming, writhing, in pain as the smoky bloodboars drank the darkness in them.

The undead were on the floor, withering in a kind of panic, as if they didn't want to change. Black wraiths rose from the undead burning in a translucent black. I kicked an undead and ran towards Stratejee and Manu. They had a sort of a wall around them, a haze of form, like jelly.

'No no no!' said Stratejee, staggering away, Manu's beating heart in his hand. He muttered something and a portal opened behind him, the black hole of Naraka yawned. Pretas emerged, hungry, smelling the undead and attacking them. If he went in, he would be safe, something I didn't want to happen.

'Oh no you don't!' I screamed, lunging in his direction. I grabbed his wrist, which held Manu's beating heart, still connected to an unconscious Manu's chest. Bringing my right hand forward, I spilled the last dregs of smoke in the skullcup, straight into Stratejee's face. He screamed in madness, his hand dropping the beating heart as it went up to defend his face from the bloodboars. He muttered a mantra and kalafire yawned in my direction, consuming, licking, desperate for flesh. My back started to burn, but I ignored it, grabbing hold of Stratejee's ankle. 'You are not going anywhere, you sicko!'

In a desperate flick of his sword, he caught hold of an undead, slashed his neck and pushed him towards me. The man screamed silently, his blue, blue eyes full of terror. My hand fell away. Stratejee hit the side of my face, making me bleed.

'You laugh at immortality? Here, I give you death. See its finality, feel its pain. Let it eat you up. See him die. Come to me, if you want him alive.' He jumped into the open portal of Naraka. With a quiet zip, the portal closed. Stratejee's laugh remained, a dark aura behind, Neel who fell, face forward, blood gushing out from his slashed neck.

'No!' His eyes were blue so blue that they reflected the purple, darkening like they did with desire. My Neel, with his blue, blue eyes full of pain. I clung to him, wailing in a high-pitched tone, to let me be. 'No!'

Blood poured out of my eye, which was swollen, spreading wetness on my cheek. *Tears of blood are the best remedy for a broken heart*, Dhuma had told me once, making me drink from a skull cup. I clutched him, blocking the gushing blood with my bare hands. Bloodbloars gorged everything around me, their hunger not satiated. 'No!' I cried.

His eyes stared, blank, vacant of life, the blue eyes, marble like in a body of nothingness. I clutched him, hugging him. 'No! Don't die again don't die …'

Someone peeled him away from me.

'*No*!' I protested, hitting him, slapping his arms, his face, raging like the fire, wanting to consume everything.

'How do we stop these hounds?'

'No, *no*!' Iron hands around my face. A face swam through the red tears. It was someone I once recognized, but not anymore. 'Would—you—please—stop—the—hound before they drink off all the nishadas?' I shook my head which was hard to do considering it was helmeted. 'Stop being so irrational. He was already dead.'

'No!' I pulled out my boneblade and put it against Shukra's neck. He didn't flinch as much as I wanted him to.

'Killing me won't bring him back,' he said it gently. I sank to the floor, a sob bursting out. Shukra's heavy hand lay softly on the small of my back. 'You can't do anything for him, Anantya,' he said. 'But you still have work to do. Save him.' He pulled me up and pointed at someone on the other side of the wall. Manu lay with his hand clutching his heart, which had been pulled out by Stratejee. Grief tore at my veins. I nodded, picking up the boneblade and skull cup.

'Find the nishadas and bring them here. And find something to burn this place down with.' The praniks who had been attacking us were heaps of flesh now, their souls ripped from them, drunken by a greedy tantrik. Like Neel, said something inside me. I walked, an undead amongst the undeads, distracted, automated, calling back all the bloodboars and sending them to Naraka.

'Stop …' Manu said weakly waving his hand. I wore my septifocals and saw a preta, biting his flesh. Opening my vial of rakta, I spilled it and drew a circle around me and Manu. Fire rose from the blood, black like vacuum. The strong smell of rakta distracted the preta who looked up, finding me, its long snout sniffing. I cocked the almost empty rakta bottle and said:

'*Um hum dhum pretam narakam!*'

There was a swish of shakti and the preta was pulled into the vial. Manu lay on his back now, clutching his heart, which poked out from his ribcage like a tumour. 'Keep it together, dude,' I said.

'… *can't* …'

'Put it back in your chest or I will sew it to your frozen nose!' I screamed.

'… *beyond* … please … kill … *him* …' said Manu, his voice mere whispers, his palm clutching his still beating heart in his hand.

'You know I will have to kill you, don't you?' I said, gently, crouching towards him. 'Let me sew this for you.' He held my hand. 'No.' He pointed a shaking finger to the side of his neck where Stratejee had severed it. '… I … *dead* … stop …' he swallowed, '*him*.' His eyes went out of focus. With shaking fingers, he lifted his beating heart up, giving it to me. 'Please … take her … out … *please* …'

I nodded, emotionless, for emotion had gone out for the night. Manu lay back, his breathing erratic. I took his beating heart gently into my palms, touching it with my fingertips. I whispered to it, like a mother to a child.

When Dhuma had taught me Prathakik, the mantra of separating a possessing spirit from a body, she had made me do it to a rakshasa, who had drunk a bhuta as a dare and it was now stuck in her throat and filling her blood with nightmares. I whispered to Manu's heart, black now after being possened. Blackened like the blood that flew out of his tired veins. I opened my mouth and touching my tongue to his beating heart, suckled on it. Taking in a mouthful of blood, I closed my eyes and rotated it in my mouth, its dark taste staining the walls of my inner cheeks and gums. In the blood, I saw her, like a drip of oil in water. I spat it in my hand where I held an eye gorged from a corpse.

'Jal se machhali, baal se ujala, judaa kar, prithak kar, shareer se bhavana!'

I whispered it, a mere breath, my hands feeling his throbbing heart, my tongue rolling in his blood. I squeezed the heart, squeezing it tighter and tighter and tighter till it burst into my hands.

Saranyu emerged from inside Manu, bloodied and angry, her body broken into pieces, liquidated, joined all wrong – arms on under the chin, head looking upwards, legs growing from the back of her head and ankles stuck to her palms. 'I will kill that deformed monster! I don't care if it was born out of my womb!' the mouth, stuck to her breast, spoke.

'You already did,' I answered softly. Manu's crumpled body lay at her feet, like a loyal puppy, his expression calm, something that he seemed to have finally found in death if not in life.

'Good riddance. Now who will put me back together?'

'Oh, I like you like this,' I said, taking her hair in my hand and dragging her out. 'Kind of shows what you really are. Twisted.' Her right eye from her left cheek, eyed me suspiciously.

'Where is that tantrik who's been kidnapping the Matsya blood immortals?'

'So you knew about it?'

'Yes.' She turned around. 'Silly things, tantriks are. Try it every few centuries and die in the process. Ever since I signed that stupid piece of covenant. Do humans never learn?'

'And you didn't care to stop it?' Her shoulder, stuck to her right leg, shrugged. 'I don't care what any humans do. They pop off before I blink my eye.' She blinked her eye perched on top of her nose.

'But you still worked with them.'

'I like them to worship me,' she answered simply.

'Umm ... Anantya ...' Shukra's voice echoed in the hall, 'there might be a kind of a prob—what the hell is *that*?'

'Our little bundle of joy,' I answered not taking my eyes off Saranyu. 'Would it make a difference to your indifference if I tell you that your sicko twins are with him? The preta tantrik?'

'Aswins? They're not here.' It wasn't a question. Her eyes widened, her hand went up to her open mouth. 'My babies.'

'So,' I said, touching her eyelashes gently and then her nose, on top of which the eye perched. 'Want to save the rotten apples of your eye?'

She blinked. 'Good, then you need to set the nishadas free.'

'What? They're my cattle. *Never*!'

'Fine,' I dusted my hands and got up. 'I will just put you in this birdcage then and invite the preta tantrik to take you to his personal hell. Happy knowing you!'

'You can't do that!'

'Watch me,' I said.

The nishadas huddled, their arms around each other, looking at Saranyu, their amber eyes wide. Shukra started to burn the warehouse.

'Fine,' she said, the lips on top of her breast pouting.

21

'THIS IS a stupid idea, with the probability of death as high as one to minus three hundred thousand,' cried Shukra, who stood in front of me, his beefy arms crossed. 'Let me remind you that your immortality hasn't been proven.'

Do you have any other solution except masturbating your brain out? I have no nagamani, so I can't go there in flesh!' I cried. Shukra helped me pull Neel's body onto the grass.

'Why go if you have to kill yourself?'

'It's not death-death, just in the process of releasing your prana. It's a proven—'

'It's hogwash is what it is,' Shukra's lips thinned as he frowned. 'He's dead, Anantya! *Dead!* You can't do anything—'

'Yes I can and I *will*. I will save him. If I go there, there's a chance—'

'You can't kill yourself to save a dead, you ancient 286! Stratejee's gone. He's not coming back. The nishadas are safe, *free*. Anantya, the case is *over*!'

'Just give me the fucking cage, Shukra,' I said, taking a deep, precarious breath. He didn't. I snatched it from his still hands and threw it on the ground. My eyes blurred. I wiped off the saltiness with the back of my hand, tying pieces of bones and flesh to the cage, to convert it into a defence yantra.

'Why do you want to save immortals?' asked Saranyu, a black blob on the dew-filled grass. 'It's not like we *die*.'

'You should be thankful, cactus,' I said, opening the cage and splashing it with blood.

'In my experience, your kind are usually survivalists and not suicidal,' said the wise Saranyu. I grabbed her mass of flesh and plonked her into the cage with a wham.

She howled satisfactorily. I pushed my septifocals over my eyes, and poured the preta from the vial I'd trapped it in, right on to her. With a splosh of black mist, the preta fell. It sniffed, sniffed again and opened his thin mouth with sharp claw-like teeth and bit her breast. Saranyu yelped. The preta bit her again.

'Just your fat luck I'm different,' I said. 'Let's go.'

'Anantya, I won't let you do it either,' said Shukra, jumping on top of me, wrestling. I struggled, as he tried to keep me down, trying to hold both of my wrists. I kneed him in the groin, he doubled up. Shukra didn't know how to fight and hadn't learnt to use his sheer size yet. I was on top of him in under a minute, cupping his balls. 'If you move, I will crush them,' I said.

'Anantya, please! Listen to—' There were times I heard him and he was right. Tonight wasn't one of them. It was this or go back home, sit on the empty couch and think of the colour blue. No. This. Blue no more. I had to find Neel again. My hands reached out for a bottle of water he'd got for me. I threw water on his hair, slashed my wrist and cried:

'Ghani bhavati!'

Shukra's body froze in foetal position, his eyebrows raised in surprise.

'You'll unfreeze in half an hour,' I said. 'Protect Neel's body till I come back. And Shukra?' I got up, looking at his inert body, wanting to hug him one last time. My friend. 'If I'm not back, call Narahara. Tell him about the Matsya Curse, the immortals, the nishadas and raaka. *Everything.* He might be interested if there's money involved.' I felt his eyes boring my back, as I walked away. 'Take this slippery creep off me!' cried Saranyu, as we reached my bike.

'Don't worry,' I said, getting up and snatching the cage. 'It's not going to kill you.' With the boneblade, wet with my blood, I pulled out the preta from the cage. The boneblade shivered in my hand, I took the tip of the blackened edge of the preta's formless body and put it on the tip of my tongue, dabbing on it, just a bit. The darkness bled onto my tongue, possessing my spit and blood, making it rush. My head swam, my eyes watered, and I knew where the tantrik's entrance to Naraka was. Why wasn't I surprised?

The cage rattled furiously. I sniffed, my eyes high, the road weaving and whining. The preta ran in my blood, loose, feeding.

The International Russian Circus lay shrouded in darkness. Chhotu's engine sputtered and died. I tottered off, checking my satchel, boneblade and septifocals, more out of habit than need. The path, last time covered with flickering fairylights was dark and silent. And not empty.

It was covered with four houses. They were all different. One tall and thin tower with a torret and small windows. One with a glass front and elegant angles, one small and squat like a hurriedly made hut and the last one with stilt legs and a square, frog-like hut.

'Hello there,' I said, aloud.

'Why're you talking to a hou—' Saranyu's voice died as the houses all rose up, with a deafening crunch, liquidating and turning into huge forms leading up to the sky, becoming daityas

'We are here to surrender,' I cried out aloud.

'We are sorry but our customer care is all busy right now,' said the one with the windows. 'We will attend to your very important query in a moment. Please bear with us.'

The daitya turned, thundered to the tall, thin daitya and said, 'Kanchi, what does surrender mean?'

'Attack!' cried Kanchi. The houses thundered towards us. I flattened myself to the ground.

'Aaaayi!' The small and squat daitya hammered on me, making me tumble. Saranyu's cage rattled and fell.

'Wait!' I cried, jumping just in time to save myself from a boulder that flew in my direction from another, landing inches away from me. Saranyu wailed, the birdcage turning over and over and going towards one of the daityas.

'Can we talk?' I screamed, standing, raising my hands to show them they were empty. They thundered and rumbled and crashed and roared all around me, like a really angry storm. I lunged towards the cage and grabbed it.

'Here!' I said, showing it to them. 'A gift for Stratejee. Your master.' I held up the cage, to show them in the darkness. Shukra stood close behind me. From what I remembered, daityas had a sharp vision. Which meant they will see it even though it was dark. Except—

'Gift?' asked the one who was a monster made of glassware.

'Yeah. Like a present?' I answered, carefully placing the cage in between me and them. The glass monster crouched, her eye, which was the size of a door, staring at the puny cage. She put on a soft jingle of being on hold. '... Please bear with us.' The glass monster rose up and whispered.

'Kanchi, did Mr Stratejee say something about a gift?'

'Attack!' said Kanchi.

'Wait!' I cried again. 'Can't we *talk* about this?'

'Talk?'

'Yes. You know, speaking words instead of throwing rocks?' Their bodies were like rocks, unbreakable by any magic. There was no tantrik trick I could use for them which could defend me or affect them in any way. Nothing, except for *one*. They had to know the daityas who'd met me outside Bedardi Bar.

'We do that?'

'Of course, only the other day, I met one of your kinds,

Indumati was her name? The one who wore that frilly *skirt*?' I opened up my yugma locket, the side which kept the rakta and carefully dipped my boneblade's tip into it.

'She talks about Bhoosa's seester,' rumbled the window monster.

'Oh, good,' I said, pouring a little bit more of chandaali rakta on the boneblade. 'You her brother?'

'Bhoosa!' he cried back. 'Att—'

'You have problem with her?' asked the stilt house daitya. He had really thin legs.

'Attack!' said Kanchi from the other side, but they didn't heed.

'No, no! I was just telling you about talking. You see, what we do is, see each other eye to eye,' I said, looking up at Bhoosa. 'To talk, you have to see in my eye, like your sister did.'

'Bhoosa?' he asked, crouching before me, so that his eye, the size of a door, was just above me.

'Lower. You have to see into my *eye*.'

'Bhoosa?' he asked, crouching so that his chin touched the ground.

'Here,' I answered pointing to my eye. Bhoosa crouched, his massive face, he was the biggest of them all, coming really close to my body. 'We are best of friends. See,' I showed the top of my palm, to Bhoosa. 'See?'

'I don't like *talk*,' said Kanchi spitting each word out so that I was covered with his glue-like spit from head to toe. 'Attack!' I heard him swing his long hand, the size of a multi-apartment building, towards me. I pounced at the same instant, aiming for Bhoosa's eye, piercing it with the rakta-dipped boneblade and screaming.

'Tunde maha gotti kunde!'

It was a simple prick in his stone-eyes but the rakta spread as the vein caught the drop of blood, spreading like a virus through his eye into his body. He rose up in surprise, stopped midway and turned. He became the squat hut again and his eye became the door. I opened it, pulled the cage inside and ran in. The room, with its mirrors and broken bulbs around it, looked very familiar.

'Bhooosaaaa,' the house shook, itching to turn back to his daitya self.

'It's okay, Bhoosa. I will deal with her,' said Kaka, the clown. The gandhara lay on a lounge seat, in blue pyjamas with stars prints, smoking a cigar.

'Ahh,' I said. 'You're part of Stratejee's gang, I take it?'

'That was a good performance,' he said looking at the smoke he blew from the cigar. 'You're two things that work well for the circus, entertaining and suicidal. Ever think of joining?'

'Looks like I am trying to.' I checked on Saranyu, who seemed unnaturally quiet. She looked dead. Except I bet she would be just unconscious for she couldn't die now, could she? 'Never thought surrendering would be such a bitch,' I said.

'Let me help you on that,' said Kaka, sitting at the window and whispering. 'Bhoosa, House of Horrors, please.'

Bhoosa hummed, shook, shivered, like it was trying to get rid of fleas. Staring out of a window behind the gandharva I wondered which one of his orifices was the window. Daityas were like rocks with holes in them, which is why they made brilliant houses for tantriks. No tantra could pierce them. The only sensitive part of a daitya was the eye, and that was usually way too high for anything to reach. I sat alongside him, taking out a beedi. 'Mind if I smoke?'

'Would prefer something classier myself,' he answered, puffing out smoke made in the shape of a voluptuous woman. I took a long, long drag from the lit beedi, eyeing him from the haze my lungs produced. 'So when did Stratejee recruit you?'

'He hasn't. Bhoosa was kind enough to let me inside him, when Stratejee showed up with his rather dour group of grumps earlier in the evening, looking like someone ate his whole birthday cake. I guess you have something to do with that?'

'Yeah,' I grinned, taking another long drag. 'Hogged at it while he got his tongue cut.'

'Hmm. People get crazy on birthdays. Always did.'

'You plan to keep inside Bhoosa for long?'

'Oh, yes. Very much so. For this one, I will be in the audience, crying, laughing and clapping while people cut themselves on stage. No performance anxiety that way. Unlike you,' he said looked at me with his lidded eyes. I looked back at him, tightening up my scabbard.

'What makes you think I'm going to make trouble? I could be joining Stratejee.'

'Nah. Somehow you don't seem like a team player. You work alone.'

We smoked, eyeing each other. Bhoosa stopped and turned into a house again.

'Break a leg!' cried the gandharva from behind. I stopped, turned and smiled. 'I thought you had decided not to take sides,' I said, stepping out into the dark misty night.

The House of Horrors stared at me from a dangling, flickering signage. It was a garishly made building, in the shape of a monster's face, a sharabha by the looks of it, a powerful sup which had become extinct now. His sharp jagged teeth were crooked and yellowed with age, opening and closing slowing with a loud mechanical crunch. His eyes bulged out, successively with the opening of the mouth, massive white eggs with red veins popping in them. His mouth open and inviting, his tongue, dusty, a rusted red, spread like red carpet. A deep rumble came from inside as if the sharabha was burping, digesting the people who dared to go inside. I clutched my boneblade and walked in, stepping onto the tongue first, telling myself it was all mechanical. Nothing magic here. All mechanical. Problem was, I never really understood mechanical.

Moist and rubbery to my instep, the tongue trembled slightly. Inside the monster's gullet, lay nothing. I muttered the Dhumra mantra and the gullet lit up. I put on my septifocals. The world came alive in multi-coloured nothingness. I walked into the sheer wall, clutching the cage, my one lifeline to make sure I got out of this alive.

From somewhere far ahead, an inhuman scream echoed on the walls. The mouth had become a cave of sinuous walls whispering screams of pain. My footsteps made loud squelching sounds on the floor, sounds which seemed similar to walking in the innards of an animal. Maybe they were, it certainly smelled so. My human senses were alert, but insufficient. Humans can sense the spirits, but not really see them, so you see I was blind like a bat in daylight.

Something jumped at me from the left, a dark shadow with red eyes and a loud cackle. I twisted and put my boneblade into its gullet. The skeleton crumbled, the red lightbulbs in its eyes flickering out, its jaw still frozen in a devious grin. I stopped, took a deep breath and continued.

The walkway turned, lighting up with electric blue. As I stepped in, a bharunda flew into my face, screeching like a hurricane, her voice piercing. A real bharunda's cry would've cut holes in my skull. I stood still, seeing her mechanical antics, her owl face flat, her eyes garishly painted, her mouth open. A moment later, she retreated back into the mechanical hole she emerged from.

The snake-like corridor ended at a room with a door hanging in the middle of it. It was an old kind of a door, the kinds you find in the rubble of Chandni Chowk's dilapidated antique shops. The door hung from the low ceiling, its end trailing, dragging so that it hung on an incline, like an attic's door. Inside the room, in the middle was a tub like depression in the floor. On top of it, at the dais, sat a nishada's severed head, bobbing like those irritating bobble-head dolls. Bob bob bob it went, constantly, hanging from something above. I smelled a peculiar smell, a dark velvety perfume, heady and hypnotic at the same time. It came from an agarbatti lit up on top of the nishada's head. I took out a clip and put it on my nose, to stop breathing from my nose. I walked inside, not touching anything, walking around the depression, checking the floors for any markings to alert me of tantrism at play. There was nothing.

I took out a darzit and put a drop of it on the door, to check for tantrik magic. Nothing. My septifocals showed nothing.

You can't come with anything, Tantrist. It was a merest of whispers, not to my ears but to my blood which curdled with each word.

You. Can't. Material. A soft velvety quality, like golden sleep. As if in a trance, I removed my clothes, satchel, locket and septifocals. Naked, a helpless, powerless human and nothing more.

'Now, let's get over with this,' I said aloud, picking up the cage, opening the door, and raising my hands as high as I could and with all my strength, I dashed it into the middle of the empty depression inside. The birdcage crashed and the immortal ex-goddess's scream echoed in the small room and elsewhere.

'Ahh, you're awake.' I picked up her mulched body, scattering it on me as if it was a mud pack. Leaning on the door, I slashed both of my wrists, the blood leaking into the depression I sat in. I grabbed Saranyu's hair and closed my fist tightly around it, the blood gushing over her head. I whispered the Prana mantra: '*Aum hreem kreem aatma jaa prana jaa shareer ra!*'

'Stratejee. I am here. Open the doors to your fucking hell!' I cried.

22

IN THE darkness, the nishada's lips moved, starting to sing. Light emerged, so strong and powerful it pierced my soul, making me cry. The nagamani. Stratejee was here. Thin hands and wisps of craving, little mouths with hooks of hunger.

A black river, undammed, like a whirlpool surrounded us, swarming like a hive of bees around the broken pieces of Saranyu.

'I will kill you, Tantrist!' Saranyu screamed. I got up, saw Saranyu's dried skin on my inert body, lying in a pool of blood. Someone familiar lay by its side, desolation haunting his face, wringing his hands, looking at his watch. Time had stopped. Or maybe not. The nishada's lips opened up.

'I beat you to it, cactus,' I said, grabbing her by her hair and dragging her towards the head, which grew in size, bigger and bigger, it's mouth yawning open. My voice sounded alien. A feather, a dried leaf, floating in nothingness, like I was there but not completely, or that I wasn't me. A sea of pretas snaked around, like a tornado gathering force, gathering darkness. I stood there unflinchingly, as they became one smooth swirling tower around me. 'A present for your master.'

I walked into the direction of the light. I flew and swam and fell through a glistening fluid dark hole. Images rushed past me, horror flashes of hidden memories, helpless screams from stifled pasts. They all became real, in technicolour, like flashes of screens on both sides. An arid landscape of pain and suffering came alive. The desert floor was scorching hot. A sea of panic and pain rose up around me. I walked. *Water, a drop of water, please,* screamed a lost soul. My daughter, please, save her, said another. The sun shone bright and pierced like daggers eating away bits of the flesh. I walked.

The tantrik's magic held the lost souls of the arid land away, but couldn't sieve their pain. Anguished screams of the dead rose together, tattering my self, scattering it to the dry winds. I gasped, trying to keep it together, to not be lost, for if I stopped, I would be lost forever. I walked, my fist curled around Saranyu's hair.

The river of misery and death, Vaitarni, moved sluggishly, meandering through this arid land of the dead. Filled with pus and blood and screams and mulch. Next to the river, on the banks of bones, rose the womb.

Made of skulls and bones of the human dead, it lay like a carcass in the middle of a hungry coven, its walls throbbing, pulsing with life. Spirits that lived in Naraka, of all kinds, sizes and shapes swam to it, attracted by its lifeblood in the land of the dead. Betalas, pretas, bhutas and human dead surrounded it, crawling on its surface, their mouths agape, their claws out, emitting screams of frustration at being unable to get in.

My preta escorts took me in through a door made of skulls, where a line-up of hungry spirits had already gathered, their screeches and screams piercing the velvety darkness. I was sucked inside the womb, my fingertips clutching Saranyu's tresses. The hive I had been dreaming of crawled as one, same as the nightmare, but more real. It smelled here, smelled of lavender and velvet and everything soft. Squishy. I float-walked in a corridor, the floor squelchy to every step and the walls made of pretas formless or formed in their past human lives, their faces twisted and frozen in pain, frustration and anger. The corridor finished off at a wall, an endless wall of human skulls piled up on top of each other, each of them glistening and glowing blue, like multiple countless blue eyes staring at me. 'Neel,' screamed my soul, but I didn't heed. Through a chink in the skull wall, I was taken inside, my hands clutching on Saranyu's hair.

'Tantrist,' said Stratejee, standing tall and gaunt, wearing a shroud of dark sinewy shreds. His forehead gleamed with the nagamani stone. In his one hand he held the shadowsword. The scientist's head lay inert, fallen on his chest, blackened blood oozing out of it, a parasitic extension. 'Welcome to the Womb, our manufacturing plant!' He spread his arms like a virus, a presenter in the middle of a stage. I shivered. The vast empty cavern screamed, made of billowing walls of layer upon layer of formless pretas and spirits, stretched and glazed over. Their eyeless bodies and liquidated arms brought texture to the walls. It was lit up in a soft blue like the eyes and felt like being inside an ice bucket with millions of frozen bodies. They all blinked and screamed and waded, through the watery layer that bound them, forever trapped, turned into a wall. A sweet, curdling smell clung to the womb – something lavender-like, soft and velvety to hide the dourness.

'The skulls. You've trapped all these souls?' I whispered, to myself. Stratejee smiled, his weaving dark shroud flapping around his lean body excitedly.

'Yes. Division of work. Employee empowerment. Shows you the possibility of collective tantrism. It took my team *years* to collect these skulls and call their spirits and weave the womb out of them. It's a marvel of forced compliance.' He whispered, fascinated, a mad gleam in his eyes. 'It's here that we pivot tantrism to a new direction, perform actions which our ancients were too scared to try.' The scientist's dead head nodded on his chest, like a sleeping boy.

Saranyu screamed with rage.

'Like the *décor*?'

'Umm, I don't know,' I replied, walking around the cavern. 'It's too … *bright* … you know?' I said. 'You should've gone for black.'

'Lavender is the new black,' said Stratejee.

I snorted.

'Enough of games. Give me the immortal if you want Neel back.'

'Yeah, except I am waiting for your master to arrive,' I said, holding up Saranyu's body.

'My master?'

'The tantrik who created this womb thingy,' I said waving my hand.

'*I* am the master of the womb!' cried Stratejee. Pretas wove around him, sinewy, black wisps.

'Clearly you're not.'

'I so am! This is my clan's work,' he said.

'Yeah … but you died and your apprentice. I mean he's the one who brings you and Shushrut back. Of course, he's more powerful than you both put together. I wouldn't want to take a chance with my Neel's life. So he's the one I'll negotiate with.'

'Oh, no Tantrist. You'll negotiate with no one but *me*.' Stratejee swiped his black sword and the cavern was layered with a mist. Pretas whirled around me, angry and hungry, sniffing, licking, snapping, snatching Saranyu's body. I pulled back. Saranyu screamed.

'I also have the nishadas, Stratejee,' I said calmly. 'If you betray me, you're so never going to find them.'

Angered, Stratejee screamed, the womb pulsated with fury, turning and rotating all at once, as if we were inside a creature, creating a stage of bodies under his feet. Something whooshed under me, like a magic carpet and I rose, tumbling and turned. 'See what I'm capable of?' He spread out both his hands, spirits dripping from his arms and bellowing behind him like a cape. 'See my power?' he said, grabbing me and bringing me forcefully to face him, his eyes shining with madness. I pulled my hand back and poked him in his empty socket of an eye.

'You're all bark. I want to talk to the dog who bites,' I said. He increased in size, like a massive thlen, which lunged at me, grabbing me and playing with me. I stood still, watching, waiting.

'I am here, Anantya,' whispered a soft voice, in my brain. As if badly in sync in a jazz concert, Saranyu began to screech in pain, writhe and twist, her many body parts still jumbled together as a badly assembled crossword puzzle. The tantrik stood in a shadow behind Stratejee, a mere shadow of a person, like a badly tuned, garbled screen. 'I am the Bhairava of our clan. Hand her over to Stratejee and I will make Neel live again.'

'How do I know you're not bluffing?' I said, opening and clutching my empty fingers.

'You have no choice in my womb, Anantya,' whispered the tantrik's voice. A whisper of a wind. As if in a trance, my hand rose at its own accord, and handed over Saranyu. Stratejee grabbed her, hungrily, his eyes shining brighter with greed. He headed to a clump of egg-like embryos, hanging away from us. I followed him, furious, helpless, my hand clasping and unclasping, missing my boneblade. The clump had the nine immortals, their bodies bound by amber-like substance, shiny and translucent, so I could just see their faces and body and legs and hands ripped off, jumbled up together in a giant washing machine. Raw and bleeding. Their blood dripped, drop by drop into a little skull bowl at the bottom. I walked to it, sitting on my hunches to see the blood, red and inky, with a heady smell.

'Lovely artwork,' I said, touching a lump of amber that oozed from the embryo. Even though it was bloody, I could see it was Ashwa's face, his worm-filled forehead, raw and bloodied. 'Who will keep on eye on them when you're gone?'

'I will,' said Stratejee, putting Saranyu into the embryo. 'I will sacrifice the rest of my eternity protecting my kind from the Matsya Curse so that we can achieve, without hindrance, true power, true science, true tantrism! The age of tantriks!'

'What a noble thought. But what if someone attacks this

'Goodbye, Neel.'

The courtyard with the empty graves shone. I knew the immortals were doing a huge thing for Neel, preparing this funeral for him, as a way to thank me, but I had no gratitude left. My thoughts were focused on one thing: the Banaras tantrik. Who was Bhairava and what was his connection to my mother? There were more than a few unanswered questions left about him and it irked me that he'd gotten away so easily. But at least his plans had been thwarted. For now.

'Here!' cried Marty handing me a khullar, a claypot. 'The best amrita we have. It's time to celebrate!'

'Be careful with that Anantya,' said Meera breezing through the other side of the courtyard, 'these boys can make a strong thing. Get drunk at every party, we do.'

'That,' I said, draining the thing, 'sounds like a fabulous idea.'

'Sky burns, skin burns. Maut makes everything burn, burn, burn.'

'Maut take my life,' cried Marty, 'his poetry is killing me.' He picked up a guitar and handed it to Manasa, who'd also come to the funeral. She sat across from me, eyeing me over the firelight and laughing. From here, her skin shimmered gold and her half-snake skin blue-black, itching to be touched. Her hair flowed around her shoulders.

The immortals had decided to move to the Himalayas, taking Vasuki, Saranyu and the twins with them. Having gained their freedom, the nishadas had returned to their tribe. Baza had stayed back. She was too much of a city woman not to. Now she worked as an art curator for a gallery in South Delhi. CAT had quietly closed the Ministry of Miracles after Narahara had found Manu Manava murdered in the burnt down hospice. Tazaak was now investigating the case, looking for the assistant Chhoti Stratejee who had been last seen with him. This was one of the reasons Saranyu and her twins had decided to leave Delhi with the others. That, and the fact that the twins couldn't stand their mother in her new monstrous avatar. It was too much for them. Grrhat had dropped by to tell me that Barbareeka hadn't forgiven me and had declared a bounty on my head. Expected, I guess.

'With all due respect, madam,' said Shukra aloud, who was sitting next to me. 'I do not dance.'

'When we celebrate Maut, everyone dances,' said Meera, dragging him up and swinging her braided hair around him. Shukra started to dance with them, like sticks rattling in a box, even though he wasn't thin anymore. I took the last drag of the beedi. It didn't taste so bad after all, I thought. Shaking my hair free, I took another drink of amrita and started to dance, my feet tottering, my head heady and light.

My heart might be heavy, but my feet would celebrate, for we celebrated death tonight. Manasa glided to my side, starting to dance with me, her skin gleaming in the firelight. She sang an old naga song, full of longing for her mate. I itched, to scratch her like I'd done all these years when she'd been Zaazee. But now it could never be. My eyes closed as moonlight streamed towards me, bright and wintery and alive. I felt guilty.

'You were right,' said Manasa, her webbed hand on a strand of my hair. Her breath rich with the amrita-brandy Marty had been handing out. 'About saving them. You were right.'

Parashurama screamed, swinging from the banyan tree. Manasa touched my cheek. 'I have to leave now, to rebuild Bhogawati.'

'Yes, I know,' I took a last drag from the beedi, crushing it under my chappal.

'I've always wondered,' she said. I felt her come close to me, touch my chin with her soft webbed hand. 'What it would be like.' She took my head in both her hands and kissed me on my cheeks and then, with a moment's hesitation, on my lower lip, waiting. 'About this.'

My lip lowered, welcoming her flickering, curious fang. She took me by the hand and away from the courtyard, and into the jungle, to celebrate life until Maut took it away.

Acknowledgements

ANANTYA TANTRIST first visited my head while I was napping in an office, hugging a book. I still remember her – insistent, furious, impatient as today's generation – demanding that I drop sleep, food and drinking till I'd fleshed her out and written her story. It's been five years since and though there are times when I curse that day because of all kinds of flotsams it brought into the sea of my mind, I'm secretly in awe of the creative powers of the Goddess that she chose me.

This tantrik rollercoaster would have been hard to survive without many friends who have brought stillness into my world. Life partner Ashwani Sharma who silently suffered the ghosts. Mum, Dad and Delhi family who are like monsoon to the soul. Fairy godmother Samit Basu who shows me paths to tread through the confounding world that is the publishing industry. George Mathen (Appupen) for witty comebacks and fantastical covers. Kanishka Gupta, lightening quick agent and friend who said yes to Anantya in a day. For initial feedback I'm in gratitude to Achala Upendran, Kanchan Rajanna and Varun Taneja. To my Vague friends for Kurseong tea and offices for free. I couldn't have survived without the constant support, encouragement and kindness shown by authors Ashwin Sanghi, Zac O'Yeah, Anand Neelkanthan, Sharath Komarraju, and my Bangalore Whatsapp group of fantastic writers.

HarperCollins India took a chance on this series when it was an untested being. For this, my gratitude to Ajitha G.S.

and Karthika V.K. who nurtured Anantya and taught me many things. Prerna Gill and Shantanu Ray Chaudhuri for combing through the manuscript with care. Amrita Talwar for rooting for this series and making marketing plans that wowed me. Sameer Mahale and team for plucking out torrent links from the chaotic online world, responding to midnight requests and giving me constant updates on sales.

Finally, to the readers who've messaged me online asking for the second Anantya adventure and all others who've waited patiently as I write more of Anantya's stories. Without you, she wouldn't be.